CAREER
Criminal

The First of a Trilogy
By: D. Henderson

Life Changing Books
Published by Life Changing Books
P.O. Box 423
Brandywine, MD 20613

Library of Congress Cataloging-in-Publication Data;

www.lifechangingbooks.net

13 Digit: 9781943174126

Follow Us:

Twitter: www.twitter.com/lcbooks

Facebook: Life Changing Books/lcbooks

Instagram: Lcbooks

Pinterest: Life Changing Books

Dedication

First and foremost, I must pay homage to my Lord and Savior, The Almighty, One and Only, The All Knowing, Purest of the Pure, King of Kings, GOD. Had it not been for his Love, Forgiveness and Mercy I would have perished many years ago. I would also like to salute the most important person in my life, an Angel on Earth, my Rock, the One person I could count on, in spite of my flaws, imperfections has never forsaken me. Mere words cannot truly express my love for this woman. If I had to Die today for Her to see another day I would go gracefully. I love you, Mama.

Writing has always been a passion of mine; in my darkest times I've used writing as a mechanism to escape the madness that surrounded me. After serving 15 years for Bank Robbery, and vowing I would never return to captivity, I realized the first thing I had to change was the way I thought. Regardless how hard life became, committing a crime was no longer an option. Unable to find gainful employment upon my release, I found myself working at Labor Ready for $7.25 an hour. Frustrated and discouraged, feet to concrete, I pressed forward, relying on the inspirational words from the Steve Harvey's Morning Show to humble me and get me through the day; and for that I'd like to thank the Man of the Year, Mr. Steve Harvey. Keep doing what you're doing.

D. Henderson

@d.henderson3488

With This Ring
– Chapter 1 –

The sound of heavy rain bouncing off the bedroom window played like a musical drum inside my mind. I opened my eyes slowly and adjusted them to the lovely figure standing before the mirror. Barefoot, naked, and a little over five months pregnant Nicole never looked more beautiful as she did at that very moment. I paused for a moment to savor her beauty, half black, half Japanese she was a sight to behold.

"Why are you looking at me like that?" she asked, blushing by my apparent affection.

"Because you're so beautiful," I answered. Rising from the bed I came up behind her, and took her inside my arms. "How are you feeling?" I asked and gently caressed her stomach.

"I feel fine." She softly answered and surrendered to my warm embrace. The softness of her body instantly reminded me of everything that was pure and righteous in my life. After nearly a year of courtship I could no longer ignore this strong sensation stirring inside my chest. A smile here, a laugh there was all it took to ignite the most intense feelings I ever felt. It was a joy so profound, so complete, for the first time in my life I understood the true definition of love.

"Close your eyes," I whispered.

"Why?" she asked.

"I got a surprise for you."

"You do! What is it?" she asked growing more excited by the second.

"If I tell you it won't be a surprise. Now close your eyes before I change my mind."

I swirled her around and slid out of the room. A few seconds later I reappeared with a two carat diamond ring. It was most definitely the biggest and most beautiful diamond I had ever laid eyes on.

"You can open your eyes now," I said and studied her reaction.

From the moment I laid eyes on her I knew she was the one. Nicole was a beautiful, highly intelligent young woman with a heart of gold and a billion dollar smile. I kissed her on the lips and studied her closely as she opened her eyes and was immediately drawn to the huge sparkling diamond. It was a magical moment, one I would remember for the rest of my life.

"Miss Nicole Marie Winters, will you marry me?" I asked and took one knee.

"Marry you," she repeated with a glow that seemed to light up the entire room. "Yes, I'll marry you Mr. Floyd Eugene Anderson."

I took her hand and felt a slight tremble run through her fingers. I held my breath and slowly placed the ring on her finger praying it fit.

"Baby, it's so beautiful, where did you get it? It must have cost a fortune."

"You like it?" I asked, staring into her beautiful hazel eyes.

"Like it, I love it. It's so beautiful."

Stunned by the size and beauty of her ring Nicole stood there and studied every small detail with growing affection. Suddenly I felt a deep sense of guilt. For a brief moment I wondered how she would feel if she knew I acquired the ring during a home invasion where I damn near pistol whipped a man to death and manhandled his wife to gain access to his safe.

At the naive age of eighteen Nicole had lived a quiet, sheltered life in the suburbs of Temecula, a secluded area on the outskirts of San Diego. Innocent to the ways of street life, little did she know she had fallen in love with a stone cold gangster that made a living packing a pistol and robbing people.

"Baby, can we invite my parents to dinner? I want my mother to be the first to receive the news. I know she's going to be so happy."

"What about dear old dad?" I said already knowing the answer.

"He will come around, you'll see. He loves me, and he knows how much I love you. Once the baby is born I promise he'll start looking at you differently."

"You know if it wasn't for you I wouldn't give a damn. But I know how much you love and care about him. And to be honest I can't fault a man for wanting the best for his daughter, even if he thinks that best is not me. If that's what you want, that's what you got. Today is your day; your wish is my every command."

I didn't dislike her father. To the contrary I understood exactly where he was coming from. His main concern was how could a young man with no job afford a 2- bedroom condo in one of San Diego's most exclusive downtown high rise?

"You said today, do you mean the entire day, like from right now until tomorrow?"

"That's exactly what I mean. I'm yours for the rest of the day." No sooner than the words left my lips the phone rang.

"Hello!" I whispered into the receiver wondering who could be calling this early in the morning.

"Pretty Boy," the familiar voice of Lil Bull came over the line.

"What's up Cuz?" I asked, somewhat startled to find Lil Bull up so early. Cuz most definitely was not a morning person.

"Doc called an emergency meeting," he said in a tone that suggested something serious was in the midst.

"When and where?" I asked wondering what was so important.

"At the shop as soon as you can get here!"

"I'm on my way. I hung up the phone and turned towards Nicole who was standing quietly behind me. I reached for her hand and she pulled away. As much as I wanted to comfort her I couldn't. When Doc called you had to go, there was no ifs, ands or buts about it.

3

Nicole was sitting on the balcony with her eyes fixated on her ring. I didn't want to disturb her, nor did I want to leave things the way they were. In the crime game it was considered bad luck to argue with your girl before going on a mission. With Doc there was no telling what he wanted, and the only thing certain, whatever it was it was illegal.

"Come here Baby and give me a kiss before I leave," I stated in a desperate attempt to break the ice.

"No, you come here," she said, determined not to give an inch.

I looked at my watch and realized I was running late. My immediate thought was to keep moving. Regardless how much I loved Nicole, Eastside Rollin 40's Crips came first in my life. Everything started and stop with the homies. If she ever put me in a position to choose she'd lose.

"You know I love you, baby. I love you more than the air I breathe. But you've been with me long enough to know when duty calls I got to go. Baby, every move I make, I make with you and our baby in mind." I leaned over and kissed her on the side of her face.

As I turned to walk away she grabbed my hand. I stopped, looked into her eyes and felt the weight of the world lift from my shoulders. It was at that moment I realized things had to change. As my future wife and the mother of my unborn child, it was time I started putting her wants and needs before all others.

Doc was a small man, barely five feet four inches tall, weighing a hundred and forty pounds soaking wet. But it wasn't his height or weight that caught your immediate attention, it was the huge coke bottle glasses that did. At first glance one would assume they were dealing with a straight nerd, when in actuality they were dealing with one of the shrewdest gangsters that ever played the game.

As Doc would say; "Success in the Underworld was dependent on perception in the Real World." It wasn't what you did, but how you did it. In these times the problem with most players, they wanted to be recognized for the wrong shit. The gangster with the biggest score, the dope dealer with the biggest sack, the pimp with the most hoes, the gang banger with the most bodies. He on the other hand wanted to be recognized as a legitimate business man. Like EF Hudson, when Doc spoke you paid attention, and 99 percent of the time you walked away with valuable knowledge.

As a first generation of Mexican Americans, Doc enjoyed all the benefits of being a U.S citizen, while maintaining strong family ties in Mexico. Unlike most Mexicans, Doc dealt with blacks. On the surface blacks appeared to be the only race he dealt with, but being in his inner circle I had firsthand knowledge of the moves he was making, and who he was making them with.

Doc had his hand in everything and everybody. The primary supplier of weapons and drugs in the Southeast, Doc had a strong connection in every hood. Just as quick as he flipped it, he turned it into something legit with a hood twist, legal money with no taxes.

I was getting the game from a top notch player with a gangster's hand. Doc was a teacher of the game, a master trap setter; such was the case with his bootlegged detail shop that catered to the biggest pimps, players and hustlers in the city. Little did they know while their cars were getting the deluxe treatment, Doc was duplicating their keys, and retrieving their residential information off registration cards, insurance policies, bills, and any other paper work that contain vital information.

I pulled up at the rear of the shop and entered through the back door. Belinda was at the cashier counter busy as ever. No sooner than the door closed behind me she turned to see who came in. Sharper than a Homicide Detective not much escaped her beautiful cat eyes. Belinda was a stone cold beauty, caramel complexion with a body straight off the sandy beaches of Venezuela. Doc met her when she was sixteen, married her at eighteen, she was now twenty-seven. Overly friendly with an infectious personality, players and square Johns arrived daily and showered her with gifts and conversation. Doc encouraged the advancements from the average Joe, but took special offense when one of his associates or understudies tried to get at his wife behind his back. To Doc that was considered disrespect and an act punishable by death.

Doc and Lil Bull were sharing a laugh when I entered the

room. Doc was a hard man to read, even under the most extreme circumstances his demeanor never changed. One of his strongest suits was his ability to conceal his motives. The same mannerism he displayed when planning a party, he displayed when planning a robbery or a murder.

"Pretty Boy, one thing I like about you, you be on top of your business. A young man, eighteen years old and living the family life. That's the first sign of future success. A family keeps a man grounded and out of traffic. The more you got to lose, the more cautious you become. Get you something to eat and grab a seat." He said and waved towards a platter of fresh fruits and Danish pastries. I took a seat and shot a glance at Lil Bull who appeared laid back. Best friends since the seventh grade I could detect trouble by a mere glance.

Never one to beat around the bush Doc got right to the point. "We got a situation. On the last heist you took a ring and I need it back." He said to no one in particular.

"I got the ring Doc," I said without delay.

"I would have guessed Lil Bull, can't be right every time." He said and turned his attention towards me. "Pretty Boy you disappointed me, you know better. When you take a job on consignment, you take what's instructed. The woman you manhandled was my wife's cousin, and she wants it back"

"I can go get it right now," I said in hopes of bringing this awkward situation to an end.

"No! That won't be necessary. I need you to give it to her personally and apologize. Y'all can meet her at this address at 11 pm tonight," he said and handed me a piece of paper.

I accepted the paper and stuck it in my pocket. I couldn't afford to display any emotions. The situation had deteriorated rapidly. I could feel Doc's eyes scrutinizing my every move, searching for the slightest clue that would give him a better reading on my thinking. Taught by the best I kept my emotions in check.

"I got a dentist appointment at ten-thirty; make sure you lock the door before you leave." Doc rose from his seat shook Lil Bull's hand and patted him on the arm.

"Pretty Boy, Pretty Boy," he repeated and shook his head

6

slightly. "You know if you were anybody else I would kill you."
Not knowing how to respond I remained silent and met his stare.
After a brief silence, Doc reached out and gave me a hug, which I
found odd. Doc wasn't the type of man that displayed affection. In
the six years I've known him I could count on one hand how many
times I had seen him laugh.

No sooner than Doc left the room I removed the paper from
my pocket. I read the address and handed it to Lil Bull. Doc
wanted us to take the ring to an address in Tijuana, an area we had
frequented before, but under different circumstances. The writing
was on the wall, and it was evident Doc had every intentions on
killing us. Doc was emotionless, incapable of forgiveness, and
would kill you quicker than a stranger on the streets. I fucked up,
not only did I put my life in jeopardy; I also risked the life of my
road-dog. Doc knew he couldn't kill me and let Lil Bull live. Just
like he knew he couldn't kill Lil Bull and let me live.

"Damn Cuz what are we going to do?" Lil Bull asked as he
contemplated our present situation.

"Cuz it's only one thing we could do, we got to kill Doc before he kills us."

"That's more easily said then done. Cuz we don't even
know where Doc lives."

"We don't, but Salt-Rock do," I said as my mind instantly
focused on the best way to retrieve this information from Cuz.

"You think Cuz will tell us?"

"Nah I think we got to trick Cuz out for the information. I
had much love and respect for Salt-Rock, but I been in the game
long enough to know a man's loyalty lies with the motherfuckers
that paid him. Salt-Rock was Doc's main man; he would be a fool
to cross him. We can't ask him, we got to trick him into showing
us. Call Cuz and tell him we got three bitches lined up tonight, and
we'll be over there around nine to pick him up. In the meantime we
need to snatch a car."

Lil Bull and I went way back, not only was he my homie,
he was also my best friend, and the closest thing I had to a family
within twenty-five miles. Although similar in many ways we were
opposite as night and day. Where he was short and of a lighter

complexion, I was tall and dark complected. Where he was loud and aggressive I was quiet and laid back. Where he loved to be the center of attention, I liked to lay in the cut, the one you didn't see until it was too late. Friends since the 5th grade, I trusted Lil Bull with my life, and I loved him like a brother. It was because of this love our friendship preceded everything, even our alliance to Doc and the Eastside Rollin 40's Crip Gang. Everyone that knew us; knew if you had a problem with one, you had a problem with the other. That's how we were coming, in two's, with force more deadly than the average gangster could withstand. But Doc wasn't your average gangster. Everything we knew about the game he taught us; but the one thing he didn't know, unlike everyone else we didn't fear him. He was a man like us, bled like us, and could die like us.

Killing Doc was more easily said than done. Although my eyes or mannerism didn't reflect, for the first time in my life I was worried. I'd been in the game long enough to realize the consequences that came with failure. We needed time to figure this out, and time was something we most definitely didn't have.

I couldn't remember the last time I spent a quiet afternoon at home. To my surprise it had a soothing effect. It provided the time I so desperately needed to figure this shit out. Unlike the majority of my homies I had a safe haven I could retreat to when the pressure associated with a life of crime became to intense to bear. And right now was one of those occasions. In preparation for war Doc taught us to first; make a fair assessment of your enemy's strengths, and second search for his weakness. I held no illusion; Doc was by far the most powerful man I knew in the crime game. Throughout the years he had recruited a network of street killers from almost every Hood.

Even with the whole Hood riding behind us, we were still no match for him; he absolutely had too many resources. His only weakness was his arrogance, his belief that he was too powerful to get faded. It was this belief, along with the element of surprise that I felt confident in our ability to end his life.

At the age of eighteen, in the eyes of society I was considered a career criminal. A three-time graduate of the California

Youth Authority and a ward of the courts since the age of ten, I had been in the midst of gangster shit since I learned the difference between a twenty and a hundred. Growing up in a system where survival was dependent on wit and courage, I learned early in life that the winner of most conflicts was determined by who struck first, and a man's courage was measured not behind the gun but in front of it. A stone cold coward could pull the trigger, but only a true gangster could face death without fear.

Nicole was sound asleep, resting peacefully, with a smile on her face that glowed brighter than the ring on her finger. After gathering my clothes I placed a light kiss on her lips and tiptoed out of the room. Lately she had become extremely emotional every time I had to leave, especially at night. The last thing I needed was to open a floodgate of tears and not be able to stick around and console her.

Lil Bull was waiting in the cab when I arrived downstairs. I noticed the look in the cab driver's eyes when I got in the backseat.

"Meadowbrook's apartment complex," I said then handed him a twenty dollar bill to erase any concerns he may have had.

The money seemed to instantly relax him. He thanked me, changed the radio station to an R&B station and fell back in his seat.

"You guys from San Diego?" he asked in a meager attempt to strike up small conversation.

"Check game player, we're not in the mood to chit chat." I made eye contact with him through the rear view mirror. He got the message.

The Meadowbrook's apartment complex was located in Skyline, the territory of the Eastside Piru gang, our archenemy. I knew from past experience it was a tricky situation being dropped off behind enemy lines. There was a magnitude of things that could go wrong, including the distinct possibility one of our enemies spotting us before we had a chance to jack a car. In an effort to give the police elsewhere to investigate it was a risk worth taking.

We arrived at our destination in full combat mode ready and prepared to deal with anything that came our way. It was close to eight o'clock and all appeared quiet, which was a good sign. No sooner than we exited the cab we spotted a yellow Z28 Camaro entering the parking lot. Like a well-rehearsed play we converged on the car without the driver having the slightest clue. Lil Bull fell back while I maneuvered my way in front of him. Crouched down between two parked cars I waited patiently for the driver to exit his vehicle.

"Excuse me Sir," I said, approaching him from the front.

"Yes, how can I help you?" he replied, wondering where the hell I came from.

"You could start off by dropping to your mother fucking knees!" Lil Bull shouted from behind.

The driver looked over his shoulder and observed Lil Bull with a 45 leveled at his head. He did as he was instructed. I relieved him of his wallet, watch, and car keys. Just that fast we were back on the road, pushing a brand new Z28 Camaro with less than a thousand miles on it. I hit Paradise Valley Road and aired it out. The Z28 accelerated like it was built to race. It was by far the fastest car I ever drove. Topping speeds greater than 100 I eased off the gas and felt pure adrenaline rushing through my veins.

"Damn, Cuz this mother fucker is fast!" I said with a smile on my face.

"Why did you stop?" Lil Bull asked, obviously disappointed I didn't max it out.

"Shit Cuz that wasn't fast enough for you?"

"Hell nah I want to see what it can do."

"You want to drive?" I asked already knowing the answer.

"You fucking right, let me push this bitch!" He said with a gleam in his eyes. Lil Bull was a speed fiend, and perhaps the best driver in our hood. He wasted no time putting the pedal to the metal as the Z28 took off like a rocket. I glanced at the speedometer and noticed we had hit speeds greater than 120 and steady climbing. Familiar with the area, as we passed Paradise Hills Recreation Center I told Cuz to slow down. Shortly ahead was a set of traffic lights that lead directly into National City, a part of San Diego County that most gangsters avoided at all cost.

We had our fun, now it was time to get back to business. Analyzing the situation from a criminal perspective we had the perfect car but the wrong color. A canary yellow Camaro wasn't the ideal car to commit a crime. The car stuck out like a campfire in the middle of the desert. It was too late now, there simply wasn't enough time to snatch another car and pick up Salt-Rock and make it to Doc's house by eleven.

Salt-Rock was standing outside his apartment when we pulled up. I could tell by the expression on his face something was up. His demeanor was too serious, and he didn't look like a man that was dressed to entertain. As we pulled to a stop I reached under my seat and retrieved my 9mm and placed it between my legs.

"Cuz!" Salt-Rock shouted. "Doc been trying to get in contact with y'all. He said to cancel the move and call him in the morning. Damn Cuz! Wait, where did you snatch this?" he asked and took a few steps back to admire the car.

"Snatched it right off the Showroom floor; you know how we do it," I said jokingly.

"Knowing you Niggas I wouldn't put it pass you. Yeah Cuz I can't make it tonight, my girl had to work and I got to babysit. What's up Lil Bull?" Salt-Rock asked and stuck his hand through the passenger window.

Reluctantly Lil Bull shook it. Unbeknownst to Salt-Rock, Lil Bull really didn't care for him. Whatever beef Lil Bull had with Salt-Rock he never spoke on it, nor did it affect my relationship with Salt-Rock. Cuz was the homie, and I was fond of him.

"Alright Salt we're about to make a move, we'll talk to you tomorrow." I shook Cuz' hand before we departed. "Lets get off these streets Cuz; this car is probably hot as a mother fucker right now!"

"Where you want to go?"

"Let's shoot by Tanya's; we can park the car in the back of her apartment complex."

"That sounds like a winner to me. I sure hope they don't have anyone over there."

Although I still had a key to Tanya's apartment it had been months since I last used it. We stood at the door for a brief minute and put our ears to the door to see if we could hear any strange voices. Tanya and Rhonda were known to fraternize with enemy factions. Satisfied everything was straight I rang the doorbell.

"Who is it?" Tanya hollered through the door.

"Pretty Boy," I shot back.

Tanya opened the door in a most revealing outfit. Dressed in a loose fitting blouse and a pair of silk panties with her nipples and pussy imprint so vivid it left little for the imagination. She made no attempts to cover herself as we stepped inside the apartment.

"Where is Rhonda?" Lil Bull asked as he took in a full frontal view of her most prized possessions.

"She's in her room," Tanya replied and made a meager attempt to cover herself.

"So, what do I owe the pleasure of your company?"

"I was in the neighborhood and decided to check on you. It's been awhile since I last seen you. How have you been?"

"Pretty Boy you got your nerve. I haven't seen or heard from you in months. Where have you been, and please don't lie and say you been in jail, because I know that isn't true."

"Check it out Baby, I don't have to lie to you; and besides it's not like you have been sitting by the phone waiting for me to call."

"What do you mean by that?"

"Don't act like you're Miss innocent, every time I turn around one of these lames ass cats got your name in their mouth."

"Like who?" she shouted, obviously looking for a argument.

"Don't worry about it, it's not that serious. We both know this shit been over for quite some time, there's no sense in faking with it any longer. Here is your key, tell Lil Bull I'll catch up with him in the morning."

"Pretty Boy why are you tripping, what did I do wrong? Please baby don't go, talk to me."

"I'm ma keep it real with you, the reason I stepped back is because I got a kid on the way and I'm about to get married."

"You mean to tell me you got some bitch pregnant? Who's the bitch, do I know her?"

"You got to miss me with all these bitches; I'm not going to stand here and let you disrespect my girl. As a matter of fact let me get the fuck out of here before I trip." I said and started walking towards the door.

"I'm sorry, baby I didn't mean any disrespect. Please baby don't go, let's go in the bedroom and talk." She wiped away her fake ass tears and started walking towards the bedroom.

Unable to resist the urge I glanced back. Damn Tanya was fine, a professional dick teaser with the type of body that'll make a preacher cheat on his wife. Sexy in every way imaginable, Tanya had the most seductive walk a woman could ever possess. Stopping in the doorway she slowly turned around.

"Are you coming?" she asked.

"Nah, baby I'm cool," I replied and met her stare.

Much to my surprise I felt nothing, not the slightest desire, or any form of physical lust. Whatever we had was gone. I called a cab and waited outside for it to arrive. I looked up and found Tanya standing at the window staring down at me. She was baffled, desperately trying to understand how any man in his right mind could refuse the pleasure of her company. As my cab arrived she turned from the window and closed the curtains. Had I known it would be years before I saw her again I might have ended things on a much better note. But one thing about life, the future wasn't promised, and only God knew what tomorrow had in store.

A Man Without a Plan
– Chapter 2 –

I stepped out of the shower feeling a cloud of uncertainty hovering over my head. Unlike Lil Bull I didn't feel Doc had a change of heart. I had been around him long enough to know he wasn't the type of man to forgive and forget. Doc took extreme pleasure in writing all wrongs. It was like he lived for the opportunity to hurt those he was closest to. To Doc killing a close associate served as a message that no one was above capital punishment. I paused in front of the mirror and felt like I was staring at a complete stranger. The cheerful glow of a carefree teenager was now replaced by the image of a more serious young man. I was at a defining period in my life, and it was time to make some cold hard decisions concerning my future. With the addition of Nicole, and a child on the way I had a lot more to consider. I was no longer living for one, I was living for three.

"Floyd your food is getting cold!" Nicole yelled from the kitchen.

Nicole was very meticulous when it came to preparing meals; I guess it was understandable being that her family was in the restaurant business. Breakfast was served with the eggs and sausage on one plate, and the pancakes on another, with the syrup set to the side. The orange juice was chilled and served in a glass while the milk was served in a cup.

Nicole was sitting at the dining room table nibbling on a piece of grapefruit when I entered the room. Breakfast was my favorite meal, and depending on my day sometimes my only meal.

After saying my blessing I took the plate with the eggs and sausage and dumped them on the plate with the pancakes before I applied the syrup. I knew this upset Nicole because she was dead set on grooming me on the finer points of fine dining. After shooting me an evil look, all of a sudden her eyes became tender with affection.

"Baby, I talked to my parents yesterday and told them we were getting married," she said and studied my reaction.

"How did they take it?" I asked between bites.

"My mother was happy; you know she always liked you."

"How about dear old dad; I bet he wasn't too happy?" I said and shot her a quick glance.

"My father doesn't dislike you; he's just concerned with how you're going to provide for me and our child when you don't have a job."

"If he's so concerned about me not having a job, why doesn't he give me one?" I asked trying to see where she was going with all this.

"If he offers you a job would you take it?" she asked and looked up once again to study my reaction.

"I don't know. I guess it would depend on what type of job he's talking about. If he thinks for a minute I'ma wash dishes or wait on tables he got me fucked up. He could save that sucker shit for the next lame. As a matter of fact you can tell him I'll take a corner office, and you can be my secretary."

"Stop kidding."

"Who's kidding, I'm dead serious." We both started laughing.

"Okay if you're serious you can tell him yourself, they invited us to dinner tonight."

"No way, say it isn't so. You mean to tell me daddy dearest invited me to dinner. The same man that said I would never be welcome inside his house as long as I lived. Make sure you bring the camera this is most certainly a Kodak moment."

"So, that means you're coming?"

"I wouldn't miss it for anything in the world."

I sat at the table long after Nicole cleared the dishes. I often wondered what would have become of my life had my father not died when I was two, or my mother had not remarried and moved to California. I couldn't deny it, I missed New Orleans, my mother, brothers, and so many cousins I didn't need any outside friends. It was funny how troubled situations made us reflect on the past, and contemplate events that altered the course of life. The prospect of squaring up and working was a frightening thought.

I'd been doing wrong so long I didn't know if I was capable of doing right. With things being the way they were I knew it was foolish to look ahead when I had so much shit to deal with from behind.

We were scheduled to meet Doc at 3:00 p.m., but I decided to show up thirty minutes earlier and was surprised to find him standing in the back parking lot talking to a woman that closely resembled the woman I jacked for her diamond ring. I studied her carefully and quickly determined it wasn't her. One thing I never forgot was a face, especially one that I violated. Upon seeing me, Doc dismissed the woman and she disappeared inside the shop. I quickly turned my attention towards Doc, searching for the slightest clue of ill intentions. I saw none.

"Pretty Boy you never fail to amaze me, I like your style. Every time I turn around I see a 280ZX. You're the first I seen with the Mazda RX7. It fits you well. Bring it in next week and I'll have Troy hit you with the Super Deluxe treatment. It'll have you glowing for a month. Come on let's go inside."

I followed Doc to his office trailing a short distance behind him. I was baffled, either Doc was the best actor in the world, or I was reading the situation all wrong. Whatever it was, it didn't erase the uneasiness in the pit of my stomach.

"Pretty Boy I hear you're about to be a father soon," he said.

"Four months and two weeks to be exact."

"I know from past experience sometimes a child can change a man's perspective. I got a couple of business ventures in the works, so if you're looking to go legit I could use someone I can trust to run this place. You already know the ins and outs of this operation. If you like the job it's yours."

"I appreciate that Doc, and I might take you up on it." I

said as I silently wondered how Doc could possibly know I was about to be a father or even considering going legit.

"Think about it, when you bring your car in next week we'll sit down and talk about it. I wonder what's taking Lil Bull so long; it's not like him to be late."

"I talked to him a few hours ago; his girl had stomach cramps and had to be rushed to the hospital. I think she got food poisoning. He said he was going to shoot to the hospital check on her and be here as soon as possible." I lied, knowing Lil Bull had no intentions of showing up.

"Oh, that explains it; food poisoning is nothing to play with, I hope she's okay, she's a pretty little thing but I wonder why he didn't call."

"He probably did while you were outside talking to that lady." I shot back without missing a beat.

"Yeah, perhaps he did," Doc said and glanced at his Rolex. "Oh well, you can fill him in later. The reason for this meeting, well you know, it's the ring. After thinking about the situation I realized there was no bad intent on your behalf. How could you possibly know that was my wife's cousin? Don't get me wrong, you were dead wrong by taking it. When I pay you to do a job, you do it to the letter. The ring was not on the list of things to take; therefore you shouldn't have taken it. I'm ma overlook it this time, but I still need you to return it, however, there's no need to apologize to her. For all she knows you're just returning it, she don't need to know you're the one that took it. She wanted your heads, and I was obliged to give it to her. You've been with me too long, and you're far too valuable to lose over something that I see was simply a lapse in judgment. But be mindful, this cannot happen again. I don't make it a practice giving out passes, it's bad for business. You give an inch, next time they'll take a yard; you give a yard, next time they'll take the whole house. You understand what I'm saying?"

"I know exactly what you're saying, and to be straight up with you I recognized the error immediately. Rest assured it will never happen again, I give you my word."

"I'm confident it won't. I got to run up front, get on the

phone and see if you can locate Lil Bull. I'd like to wrap this up today."

I waited for Doc to exit the room before I picked up the phone and called home. After the second ring I hung up, sat back and closed my eyes. Doc taught me to never give a motherfucker the benefit of doubt. When in doubt always assume and prepare for the worst. Unlike the court of law where you were presumed innocent until proven guilty, in street justice you were presumed guilty until proven innocent. So far he had yet to convince me of his sincerity. Doc was a master at deception, a snake in the grass, and a cold-blooded killer. In all the years I've known him; I've never known him to forgive anyone that he felt crossed or disrespected him in any form. Would we be the first, I wouldn't bet my life on it.

Doc returned a few moments later, he appeared agitated, preoccupied with something that was weighing heavy on his mind. "Did you locate him?" He asked and he took a seat.

"His father said he was still at the hospital, it sounded like his girl is in pretty bad shape. But check, I could shoot home and snatch the ring and run it where it needs to go. I really don't need Lil Bull to accompany me."

"No! What I need you to do is go to the hospital, find Lil Bull and call me."

Hands up. That was it, I had my instructions, and the meeting was over. I rose from my seat and quietly exited his office. I paused in the hallway for a brief second and pondered over what just happened. I felt a slight sensation at the realization I played chess with the best and won. In a moment of frustration Doc exposed his hand. I knew his next move, but he didn't know mines.

As I proceeded to the rear exit I came face to face with the woman I spotted Doc talking to. Her striking resemblance to the woman who we jacked meant only one thing, they were related. I nodded and smiled, and in return she shot me a glance that was so vicious, if looks could kill I would have been dead. It was obvious by her reaction I was the topic of their conversation when I pulled up. Typical of most women, baby girl wore her emotions on her sleeves, and was incapable of concealing her disdain. Unfazed by her response, I walked away and made a mental note if I ever saw her again I would deal with her worse than I dealt with her relative.

I called Lil Bull and told him to snatch up Salt-Rock and meet me at my place. I had a few errands to run. In the event something went wrong, and I didn't make it I had to make sure Nicole was provided for. I had seventy-five thousand dollars saved, which was more than enough for Nicole to care for our child. Seventy-five thousand dollars in 1981 was probably equivalent to a quarter of a million dollars in modern times. Back then you could buy a pack of cigarettes for fifty cents, or buy a soda and a bag of chips for less than a quarter.

Nicole was playing the perfect hostess when I arrived home. Lil Bull and Salt-Rock were sitting at the dining room table, while Nicole was rambling on about our wedding. I gave her a slight nod and she rose from the table and followed me to the bedroom. With everything going on there was no way possible I could attend a family dinner. I prayed Nicole didn't make a fuss about it. Right now was a critical period, one that required my full and immediate attention. I had to figure this shit out, and I didn't have a lot of time to do it.

"Here, put this in a safe place," I said, handing her a brown paper bag.

"What is it?" she asked.

"It's seventy-five thousand." I answered, and placed my finger to her lips. Sensing something was troubling me she did as I asked. After placing the bag inside the closet she returned and took my face inside the palms of her hands. All of a sudden I felt tired and wore down. It felt like a lifetime of doing wrong had finally caught up with me. The mere thought of going after Doc was overwhelming. We were out of our league, and for the first time in my young life I had serious doubts. Doubts I'd never see my child born, or hold this beautiful young lady inside my arms again was too much to bear.

"What's wrong, baby?" Nicole asked, and lifted my head. I looked up and felt like I feel in love all over again.

"Baby, I got some bad news, something came up, and I can't make it to dinner tonight."

"Is that what's bothering you, because if it is, don't worry about it. I wasn't being fair; I should have spoken to you first before I made plans. We can do it another time," she stated with a tenderness that sent a warm and soothing sensation throughout my body.

"Are you sure?" I asked knowing dinner plans were the least of my troubles.

"Yes, I'm sure," she answered and held my head against her stomach. Suddenly I felt a light kick against my face and for a brief second nothing else in the entire world seemed to matter.

Like most successful gangsters, Doc resided in a secluded suburb far away from the madness he dispensed on a daily basis. Sun City was well over an hour drive from San Diego, but on this particular night it felt much longer. We were three deep, with one in the blind, and on a cold campaign to murder one of the most dangerous figures in the city, and the cold part about it was we didn't have a plan. On all accounts this was a recipe for disaster. The only thing we had in our favor was the element of surprise, which was the biggest advantage one could possibly hope for in times of conflict.

I looked in the rearview mirror and observed Salt-Rock bobbing his head to the latest tunes coming from the radio. He didn't have the slightest clue what was materializing around him. In all due respect, we had no right to involve him in a crime that we knew if he had a choice he would surely decline. But in the hood there was nothing fair about the game we played, and sometimes you didn't get to choose. Hanging with the wrong homies at the wrong time could get you a life sentence. I had much love and respect for Salt-Rock, but there was nothing he could do to stop what was about to go down.

As we approached the I-15 check-point, I turned down the radio and motioned for Lil Bull to buckle his seatbelt. It was understood, pulling over was not an option. I sat upright in my seat and started smiling and laughing as if we were having a wonderful time. As we came to a stop the agent smiled and glanced inside the vehicle. Without a second thought he gave us the signal to proceed. The Interstate-15 checkpoint was the last obstacle between us and our intended target. A confrontation with Doc was inevitable, and there was no turning back now.

Doc resided in an upper class neighborhood where the average home was tipping the scale at a half million dollars or better. Salt-Rock scooted to the edge of his seat and directed us straight to it. Lil Bull pulled up at a four way stop sign, and there it was third house from the corner with the garage door open. Sitting behind dark tinted windows, we drove past the house and spotted Doc wiping down his most prized possession, his 1955 Cherry Red Chevy truck.

"Cuz where are you going, you just past the house?" Salt-Rock asked.

"Yeah Cuz we can see that," I said then turned my attention towards Lil Bull.

Salt tried to interrupt again but I whispered to Bull, even though Salt could still hear me, "Check it out Cuz, pull over at the end the block and let me out. I'll double back and post up on the side of his garage. I want you to bend the block, and as soon as you hit the corner I'mma rush him. When I make my move I want you to pull inside the garage and go straight to the garage door opener and shut the door."

"I got you!" Lil Bull shot back, grimacing in Salt's direction.

"Hold up Cuz, what the fuck is going on?" Salt-Rock shouted, searching for answers.

"Check game Cuz, I don't have time to explain, you got to trust me on this one." I huffed in exasperation, ready to make my move.

"Cuz it's not about trust, whatever you Niggas are up to I don't want no parts of it, you could let me out right here."

"Fuck that Nigga Cuz, let him out!" Lil Bull injected, growing more agitated by the second.

"Can't do that, if someone spots Cuz wandering around this neighborhood they'll call the police." I spoke through gritted teeth.

As a member of the Eastside Rollin 40's Crips Gang Salt-Rock was obligated to ride with us, against his own family if the situation demanded it. I didn't know what the fuck Cuz was tripping about, as much as I wanted to resolve this issue with Salt-Rock there simply wasn't enough time. As fate would have it we couldn't have asked for a better situation than the one we found, Doc was straight slipping. Determined not to miss the opportunity, I stormed from the car and slammed the door behind me locking Salt-Rock inside.

Like a thief in the night, I covered the huge block in less than a minute. I scanned the surrounding homes, satisfied no one was aware of my presence. I crept along the side of the house and noticed Doc's shadow emanating from inside the garage. I removed the 38 from my pocket and waited for the Camaro to hit the corner. At the sight of approaching headlights I became excited; my immediate thought was to run inside the garage and gun him down. But that wasn't the plan; we couldn't just kill Doc we had to dispose of his body. Without hesitation, I stormed inside the garage and caught Doc squatting down applying Amoral to his tires. Before he had a chance to react I was standing directly over him.

"What's up, you bitch ass Nigga?" I shouted with a smile on face.

Never in my life had I ever felt so excited about drawing my gun on a motherfucker. All a sudden Doc wasn't the big bad wolf that everybody and their mama feared. He was a regular Nigga in a shit load of trouble.

"Pretty Boy what the fuck is wrong with you, get that fucking gun out my face," He ordered as though he was still in charge.

"Nigga shut the fuck up, I'm the boss now." I took a few steps to the side to allow Lil Bull enough room to maneuver the Camaro inside the garage. He jumped from the car and rushed to shut the garage door.

"After all I've done for you, this is how you repay me by coming inside my home and pointing a gun at me?"

"Nigga, I told you to shut your bitch ass up! You know what the deal is. What did you think, I was going to lie down and let you turn my lights out. You got to be one of the dumbest motherfuckers I ever met." Doc cringed at the realization that two of his most trusted soldiers had not only turned on him, but also had the ups on him. There was no mistaking our intentions, we came to kill him, and that he was certain of.

"What you want, some money? Is that what it is? You came to rob me. I got five hundred thousand in the house, take the money and leave. I swear to god I won't retaliate, I give you my word," he pleaded.

"Nigga, I'm not going to tell you again shut the fuck up!"

"Hold up Cuz!" Lil Bull intervened. "Cuz let's get the money," he said, not recognizing the ploy.

Doc was simply trying to buy time. The lure of a half million dollars was enough to stop any street Nigga dead in his tracks. Doc was a highly intelligent criminal, he understood the implications. He knew we came to kill him, and every second he could buy was a second longer to think of a way to survive.

"Cuz this Nigga don't keep money in the house; I'm telling you he's playing games," I said in an attempt to get Lil Bull back on the right page.

"Cuz how do you know," Lil Bull asked. "It's not going to hurt to look?"

"Cuz, if Doc say he got a half of million in the house I believe him," Salt-Rock said as he emerged from the car with his palms up, acknowledging Doc. "Cuz Doc is a man of his word, if he said he won't retaliate, he won't. Cuz I don't know what's going on, but I'm sure we can figure a way to work this out without anyone dying."

"Cuz is you fucking serious?" I asked. "If we let this Nigga live all three of us will be dead within a week." I shot back; mad as a motherfucker I was even entertaining this shit.

"Pretty Boy I swear I won't, that's on my life."

My first blow caught Doc right above his temple, his glasses flew off, and blood quickly poured from his wound. At the sight of his own blood he became hysterical and tried to rush me. My second blow came with the butt of the gun, which broke him to his knees knocking the fight out of him. Defenseless and bleeding profusely I continued to pistol whip him until he was unconscious.

"Damn, Cuz I think you killed him," Lil Bull said and knelt down to see if he was still breathing.

"Pretty Boy you tripping, Cuz you didn't have to do that,"

Salt-Rock said, obviously upset.

"Cuz I'm not trying to hear that shit. It's not a fucking thing you could say or do that's going to stop me from killing this Nigga. Instead of you trying to save his ass you need to be helping us."

Salt-Rock was gradually venturing into a gray area. Tensions were high and tolerance was at its lowest. The last thing I wanted to do was flip the script on Cuz. Sometimes all it took was a simple suggestion to get a Nigga killed.

"Cuz I know this Nigga got some shovels around here somewhere," I said out loud as I scanned every inch of the garage.

"They're inside the garden shack in the backyard," Salt-Rock offered. "The keys are on that hook right there."

It was amazing how quick one went from an unwilling participant to an actual conspirator in a murder. It took a trained ear to recognize danger in a man's overtones. Cuz peeped game and got his mind right.

While Salt-Rock went to retrieve the shovels, Lil Bull and I searched the garage for something to wrap Doc's body in. Finding nothing, I decided to enter the house. Just as I reached for the door handle I was startled by a loud humming sound. I quickly turned towards the garage door and observed it slowly ascending. Lil Bull quickly moved to the front of the garage, while I shot to the driver side of the Camaro hoping he left the keys in the ignition, he did.

Just as the door reached the halfway mark Lil Bull ducked under the door and rushed the driver side of Belinda's Continental, catching her completely by surprise. A look of sheer fear ran across her face as Lil Bull confronted her. He reached for the door handle, it was locked.

"Unlock the door bitch!" he yelled.

Belinda quickly regained her composure, instead of unlocking the door she threw the car in reverse and slammed on the gas. The Continental shot backward. "Forget her Cuz!" I yelled at Lil Bull in an attempt to freeze any thoughts he had of shooting. The last thing we needed was a gang of cops converging on the area before we had chance to get away.

"Where is Doc?" Salt-Rock asked when he returned to the garage holding two shovels.

In the heat of the moment we lost focus. I looked at the door leading into the house and noticed it was slightly ajar.

"Come on Cuz let's get the fuck out of here!" I yelled.

"What about Doc?" Lil Bull asked as he contemplated rushing inside the house.

"Fuck Doc Cuz. Let's get out of here while we still can." Storming the house was not smart at all, the possibility Doc was armed and laying in the cut was more than likely. As I punched it out of the garage I regretted not killing him when I had the chance, it was a decision that would haunt us years later.

The Chase Is On
– Chapter 3 –

There was an eerie silence drifting inside the car. By the expression on everyone's face it was evident we were all thinking the same thing. Failure to kill Doc would have devastating consequences. Doc was the shrewdest, most ruthless individual I ever met. A cold calculating killer, Doc received enormous pleasure from the pain he inflicted on his enemies. As he would say; killing was always personal, it was never business.

"Cuz, that punk bitch played me for a straight joke; I should have blasted her ass," Lil Bull said.

"Cuz, you played it right. If you would've blasted her, the police would have been on the scene quick as shit. How far you think we would have gotten in this loud ass car?" I asked.

"That bitch was staring death right in the eyes and went for broke. Doc always said don't let the pretty face fool you, baby girl got heart."

"Yeah, I know," I quietly whispered.

"Cuz I think we should shake this car, just in case someone called the police," Salt-Rock said from the back seat.

"I was thinking the same thing," I said, taking the next exit.

Unfamiliar with the area we drove around until we found a small Mexican restaurant, with several cars in the parking lot that appeared to be on the verge of closing. I circled the parking lot several times looking for a car worth taking, seeing none I turned towards the exit.

"Stop the car!" Lil Bull shouted.

I hit the brakes and quickly scanned the area to see what Lil Bull had seen. Before I had a chance to ask him, he flew out of the passenger door with Salt-Rock right on his heels. I hit the lights, and was about to exit the car when I spotted the mark strolling across the parking lot holding what appeared to be a money bag. The take down was quick, quiet and violent. Salt-Rock was extremely aggressive for no apparent reason, which was one of several reasons I didn't like robbing with Cuz.

As long as a mark did as he was instructed I felt no need to inflict unnecessary pain. Robbing wasn't personal it was business; it was all about moving money from one hand to the other. After relieving the mark of his valuables, they raced back to the car like two kids returning from the playground.

"Cuz you Niggas are tripping, I bet you didn't get over a thousand dollars."

"Pretty Boy I wouldn't bet if I was you, this bag feels kind of heavy," Salt-Rock said.

"What's that smell Cuz?" I asked.

"Cuz had a few burritos, you want one?"

"You fucking right, I'm hungry as a mother fucker."

"What about you Lil Bull?"

"Nah Cuz I'm cool. What's the count?"

"Hold up a second, eighteen hundred and forty-five dollars." He said after a quick calculation. "That's six-fifteen a piece."

"Shit all we need now is to find a mark carrying a six pack and we'll be set," Salt-Rock continued to joke.

It was funny how a vicious act of malice could bring temporary joy to three trouble souls. We needed a good laugh, a distraction, something to take our minds off Doc, and a bleak future.

"You know what Cuz I was thinking it might be a good idea if we shake the town for a minute, at least until we get a better handle on the situation," I said, trying to get a feel on how the homies were thinking.

"I'm not feeling that Cuz. I got a lot of shit going on right now. Fuck Doc, Cuz can bring his ass around the hood if he wants, I got something for him, this thing I call a 44."

"I feel the same way," Salt-Rock replied, switching up his

tune. "Fuck that Nigga!"

I wish it was that simple, but I knew it was far from it. The odds of us catching Doc off guard again was highly unlikely. How can you kill a ghost, a motherfucker you can't see, with more muscles than the mob? Unlike the homies, I wasn't about to trick myself into believing I couldn't get faded. Only a fool overestimated his strengths. Lil Bull and Salt-Rock weren't being realistic, what they shared was a false sense of bravado that one usually felt right before he got killed. Fuck what they were talking about I was about to bust a move, at least long enough to figure this shit out.

"Don't look back, we got company," I said as I spotted a police car traveling at a safe distance behind us.

Lil Bull sunk down in his seat and adjusted the side view mirror to get a better look.

"Cuz I don't like the way this look," he said after a quick glimpse.

"Me neither," I replied, maintaining the speed limit.

In the crime game when shit didn't look right and didn't feel right more times than not it wasn't right. The police wasted no time exposing their hand, less than a half of mile up the highway two more police vehicles were laying in the cut on the onramp. They quickly fell in formation, with one car behind us and one on the passenger and driver side, any doubts we may have had concerning their intentions were quickly put to rest.

As a showing of force they activated their police sirens simultaneously. I answered by applying pressure on the gas pedal. Like a world class thoroughbred the Z28 quickly displayed its dominance by leaving California's finest in the wake of our tail lights. It was obvious from the gate they were no match for the high performance 350 engine. Unable to compete, they quickly became a faint image of flashing lights. I couldn't believe we shook them that easy. I'd never known Five-O to give up without a fight, The Boys in Blue were known to be vigorous in times of pursuit. Determined to push the full extent, they captured 90 percent of the occupants in high-speed chases. We were forty-minutes from our hood, and I was determined to get us there.

It was fair to assume by now they were privy to the details

surrounding the yellow Camaro carjacking. That was nothing new to us, we snatched a new car every other day. If that was the case, more than likely they figured we were heading back to San Diego.

A slight drizzle began to fall as we entered San Diego county limits. The sky was dark and the highway was empty. It was entirely too quiet, nevertheless I kept the pedal to the metal and pushed the Camaro to its limits. Eddie Rabbit's "How I Love the Rainy Nights" filled the air and we sang along, savoring another brief moment of enjoyment. It wasn't until the song went off we heard a light buzzing sound coming from above us.

"Cuz I think we got company," Lil Bull said and rolled down his window. "Yeah, Cuz they're right on top of us."

With the addition of an eye in the sky the police quickly tipped the scale back in their favor. Although the advantage was clearly on their side it was still too early to panic. Fearing they were setting up a road block ahead I took the Central City Parkway exit which was a two lane highway leading directly to the city of Escondido.

As we raced towards the city we could see flashing police lights heading in our direction. It wasn't until we hit a straight-away that I noticed the police vehicle was traveling in the same lane as we were. Instead of slowing down I pressed on the gas knowing a head on collision at these speeds would result in the immediate death of all parties involved. I didn't know what kind of bullshit this cop was on, but he most definitely picked the right motherfucker to play chicken with. As the distance between us swiftly closed, I experienced a calmness like never felt before.

Everyone was quiet, stunned at the events taking place before them. Everything appeared to be moving in slow motion, like an unforeseen force was guiding my every move. As the end grew near, and a crash seemed inevitable the police vehicle attempted to swerve right but he was a fraction of a second too late. I slammed on the brakes and tried to avoid hitting him but the road was too narrow. The Z28 clipped the rear of his vehicle and sent it into an uncontrollable tail-spin. As I finally regained control of the Camaro I looked in the rearview mirror and saw no signs of him.

"Where did he go?" I asked.

"He went over the embankment," Salt-Rock responded still looking out the rearview window.

Operating off sheer adrenaline I hit the city of Escondido pushing speeds greater than 120. I sped through every red light with total disregard for our safety or anyone else. In an effort to throw the ground forces off our trail I killed the lights and made a quick right turn heading back towards the freeway. The rain continued to pour making it extremely difficult to see. I reduced the speed and adjusted my eyes to guide us through the darkness when suddenly the vast light from the helicopter beamed down on a huge brick wall directly in our path. I slammed on the brakes and braced myself to soften the impact.

Thinking about my unborn child and lady at home, I felt like I was dreaming but felt pain at the same time. I was the first to regain consciousness, I snapped back feeling daze and disoriented. As I struggled to clear my head, I could hear distant police sirens closing in. I reached over and shook Lil Bull until he regained consciousness. I looked back and found Salt-Rock struggling to clear his head. Satisfied that everyone was in full use of their faculties I fled out of the driver side window and hit the ground in full flight. The massive searchlight covered every inch of our surroundings making it nearly impossible to find somewhere to hide. Using the trees as my shelter I maneuvered my way from one backyard to the next desperately searching for an escape. Finding none, I fled inside a vacant house that was in the beginning stages of construction. No sooner than I entered the house the police converged on the area in full force.

Trapped inside a house with no walls, I could hear the police issuing orders for the residents to stay inside their homes and lock their doors and windows.

"One of them ran inside there!" I heard a lady shout.

For a brief second I thought about surrendering, trapped with no place to hide, and the last thing I wanted was to confront the police in an enclosed area. San Diego Police were notorious for killing blacks. As I made my way towards the exit I noticed several stacks of tar paper rolled up in a corner. Using every bit of strength I could muster I managed to move a roll far enough away from the wall to squeeze my small frame inside the crevice. Just as I inched the paper back in place the police moved in, flashlights in one hand, guns in the other.

I closed my eyes and tried to control my breathing, seconds felt like minutes, and minutes felt like hours. I could sense their presence; they were so close I could smell them. Tension had an aroma of its own, a mixture of fear and excitement all in one. After a quick sweep of the house they left, leaving me stunned in disbelief. I couldn't believe my fortune. How I managed to evade capture only the skies above could really say.

Lil Bull and Salt-Rock were apprehended quickly. I felt for the homies, but we all knew the risk that came with living the life of a gangster. Death and imprisonment was as certain as a straight A. student going to college. Most homies welcomed imprisonment with open arms, it was just one of many forms of paying your dues.

The rain stopped, and the loud chatter from a chaotic evening eventually became a quiet whisper. After what seemed like eternity I finally emerged from my hiding place. It was 3:00 a.m., and I had no recollection of how long I'd been in hiding. I reached inside my coat pocket and retrieved the 38 revolver. As long as I had a gun the odds of me making it back to the hood greatly increase, like a thousand folds over.

I exited the house and took off in a slight jog, fast enough to put distance between myself and the crash scene, but slow enough to scan every house in my path. By the time I reached the main Boulevard I was mentally prepared for anything that might come my way. Traffic was relatively light which allowed me to move more quickly. The closer I got to the red light district the more exposed I became. Two blocks away I spotted a cab parked in front of a Dunkin Donuts.

It wasn't until I was a block away I noticed the driver was still sitting inside. I took off in a full sprint praying that I reached him before he left. Just as I made my move I spotted a police vehicle three blocks away heading from the opposite direction. By the time I reached the cab the police vehicle was less than a block and a half away and steadily approaching. I reached for the door handle expecting to jump inside the cab, pull my gun on the driver and force him to take me to my hood. The door was locked.

"How can I help you?" the driver asked through a small crack in the window.

"Sir, I need a ride to downtown San Diego," I said as I removed my hand from my coat pocket.

"Sorry, I clocked off ten minutes ago. If you like I can call dispatch and send another cab."

"No, that won't be necessary. I'm really in a hurry. I'll give you a hundred dollars and you can keep the change."

"Give it here!"

I handed him five twenties through the window. After a quick visual count he hit the power lock. I slid in the backseat and bent over as if I was tying my shoe. When I rose up, the police vehicle had already passed.

Home sweet home, I thought as the cabbie cranked his engine and headed towards the freeway. A slight smile played across my face, I still couldn't believe I got away. I sunk in my seat and closed my eyes and felt the weight of a troubled day lift from my shoulders. Never in my life had I felt more alive than I did at that very moment. I opened my eyes and felt a renewed sense of joy. Although I had traveled up and down Interstate 15 many times this was the first time I actually paid attention to the scenery.

The closer I got home the more excited I became. I couldn't wait to see Nicole, take her in my arms and tell her how much I loved her. It was funny how a close call brought out the sentimental side in a gangster, and made him want to straighten out his life. The only problem with that, the urge to do right never lasted long.

A warm sensation traveled throughout my body as the downtown skyscrapers came into view. I turned towards the driver to instruct him to take the next exit and noticed his eyes were fixated on the rearview mirror. He wasn't looking at me, he was looking beyond me. It was clear by the reflection in his eye something was terribly wrong.

Reluctantly I turned around, and much to my dismay I was confronted by a caravan of police cars trailing behind us. The cabbie took the next exit and came to a complete stop in the middle of the street. In the haze of blinding lights I removed the 38 from my pocket and stuffed it in between the seat. I was ordered from the cab with my hands up and instructed to lay face down on the ground. The chase was over.

Back Against The Wall
– Chapter 4 –

I was transported to the Escondido Police Department where I was paraded through the police station like I was a serial killer. I could feel the stares and hear their chatter.

"How old is he, he doesn't look a day over fifteen?" one inquired.

"Sgt. said they're certain he's the driver," another one added.

Their comment went in one ear and came out the other. I was escorted to a holding cage where I found Lil Bull and Salt-Rock huddled in a corner engaged in a deep conversation. They turned towards the doors with instant familiarity in their eyes. I shot them a hard look, a silent communication indicating we didn't know each other. I took a seat on the opposite side of the room without acknowledging them.

With his back to the camera, Lil Bull shot me a series of hand signals to interpret. Although I didn't have the slightest clue what he was trying to tell me, nevertheless I made up some signals of my own and shot them back at him. Salt-Rock looked on in amazement, actually believing we had a secret communication going on. Regardless of how grim our situation appeared the homies always found humor in our most trying times.

"Banks, Hodges, let's go!" a deputy shouted from the grill gate. The homies rose from their seat and exited the room without looking in my direction.

I looked around the holding cage and bowed my head in

disgust. I went through too much shit for the story to end like this. Physically drained and emotionally exhausted I closed my eyes and tried to figure out where I went wrong. If I would have, could have, should have was a thought that most criminals entertain immediately after being apprehended. In actuality, it did very little to console the pain one felt the first day in jail. Unable to think straight, or shake this bizarre nightmare that was consuming my every waking moment, I lied on the hard steel bench and drifted into a quiet peaceful sleep.

"Anderson! Anderson!"

My name penetrated my sleep like a dagger going inside my chest. I opened my eyes and found a tall black gentlemen standing over me. "Sorry to wake you, I need to speak to you. Could you please follow me?" I rose to my feet and followed him down a short hallway to an interview room.

"Please have a seat. Would you like something to drink, a snack or something?"

"I'll take soda and a cigarette if you got one."

"What kind do you smoke?"

"Kool's Filter Kings if you find one, if not any cigarette would do."

Detective Brooks returned a few minutes later with a fresh pack of Kool's and a book of matches. I wasted no time firing one up. The cigarette immediately hit the spot, I took one long hit, held it for a minute, blew a couple of smoke rings and released the rest out my nostrils.

Without making eye contact I could sense Detective Brooks sizing me up, trying to figure out the best way to approach me. I was young but far from naïve, I knew the way the game went, saw it a hundred times.

"Floyd, what's your date of birth?" Brooks got right down to business with a #2 pencil, freshly sharpened.

"August 17, 1962." Sitting straight up just like I was taught, I planned to answer securely and firmly.

"So, that makes you eighteen, correct?"

"Yes."

"To be so young, where did you learn how to drive like

that?"

"Drive like what? I was in a cab."

"Kenneth and Eric said you were the driver."

"Kenneth and Eric, I'm not familiar with those names, am I supposed to know them?"

"You can cut the act. You know exactly who Kenneth and Eric are. And we know you were the driver, several of my officers identified you as being the driver. I would rather you sit there and not say a word than to sit there and lie to my face."

Visibly defeated by my words, the officer grew red.

Putting on the act of my life, "Lie, Sir I would never lie to a police officer, and I swear I don't have a clue what you're talking about. I don't know anyone by the names of Kenneth or Eric, and I wasn't driving, I was in a cab. You can ask your officers."

"So, that's your story and you're sticking to it?"

"Yes! I don't know what else you want me to say," I responded, throwing my hands up and making a face that said 'next question'.

"You can start off by telling the truth." Brooks slammed a Manila folder on the table.

"I'm telling you the truth."

Detective Brooks shook his head from side to side and commence to gather his papers. As he turned to leave he paused at the door, turned around and retrieved the pack of Kool's from the table.

"Mr. Anderson, you have a good day. I'll be seeing you in court."

It was a trip how the police got upset and acted like it was unsportsmanlike when a suspect didn't admit guilt or show any signs of remorse after being captured. Shortly after my encounter with Detective Brooks, I was transferred to the Vista County Jail and booked on Carjacking and Assault with a Deadly Weapon on a Police Officer.

Unlike the San Diego County Jail, which was predominately black and governed by Crips and Bloods, Vista County Jail had an overwhelming number of Whites and Mexicans, with a strong presence of the Aryan Brotherhood. Every Crip and Blood in the city had heard of the brutality the AB's inflicted on blacks in San Diego Northern County Jail. I wasn't tripping, I'd been going against the odds my entire life.

One of the perks of being arrested on a violent felony, jail officials expedited the booking process and secured you behind steel bars as quickly as possible. Without delay I was strip searched, dressed out in county blues, and given a booking slip. I was than instructed to follow the yellow line, which lead to a huge control booth that oversaw four glass enclosed units. One of three deputies exited the booth and met me at the entrance.

"Let me have your booking slip," he requested then eyed me suspiciously.

"This can't be correct," he said and reached for his radio. "Section C to control."

"Section C go head."

"Fran, I have an inmate named Anderson, his bed slip has him assigned to Unit 8. Can you confirm the correct housing unit?" Detective Ward was puzzled, scrunching his face up.

"Unit 8 is the correct unit," the voice responded.

"May I ask on whose authority?" he asked, obviously not satisfied with the answers he just received.

"Captain Willis," Fran answered with sass, annoyed at Ward's worrisome questioning.

"Thank you."

"I don't know what you did to piss off the Captain, but someone up high is awfully hot at you. You're assigned to room 232; it's the third room up the stairs to your left. Now listen, each room is equipped with an emergency button, and there are several located throughout the unit, if you have any problems push the button, that's what they're there for."

In so many words Deputy Ward was warning me of impending dangers lurking inside Unit 8. I approached the glass door leading inside the unit and did a quick visual inspection before the door opened. I entered the unit and became the focus of every inmate there. Without a simple nod I climbed the stairs leading to my room. I was happy to find the room empty. Most inmates enjoyed the company of a cellmate; I on the other hand enjoyed the solitude of a single cell. After making my bunk I emerged from my room in time for lunch.

I retrieved a tray and stepped to the food cart. I took notice that the white boy serving the French Fries gave me far less than he gave the prisoner in front of me. I paid little attention to the stare and small chatter that was going on around me. Stopping at the first available table I sat down, said a quick grace and commenced to devour the hamburger and fries.

"Say boy!" I heard a voice travel from the other end of the table. I ignored it.

"Nigger I know you hear me talking to you!" I looked up and was confronted by a white boy with pure hatred in his eyes.

"Yeah Nigger I'm talking to you!" he taunted me.

"Fuck you, you white motherfucker!" I shot back, furious that this cracker was trying to play me like I was a chump or something.

"Nigger, I see I'm ma have to teach your black ass some manners." He stood up, displaying his six foot five, two hundred and fifty pound frame. As he approached me I jumped up, dumped the remainder of my food on the table and held the metal tray as a weapon.

"Roger! Front and center!" Deputy Ward shouted over the intercom.

"Nigger you can bet your black ass this shit is not over." He threatened and proceeded towards the control booth. Never one to talk shit I placed my tray on the table and proceeded to my room where I remained the rest of the afternoon.

Too agitated to sleep, I sat on the edge of my bed and tried to figure out a way to conquer this monster looking white boy. My first order of business was to secure a weapon, something I could attach to the braided end of a sheet, and strike and move from a distance. Although a knife was the most effective weapon one could use in close quarter combat, the possibility of death or serious bodily injury occurring was high. It was common knowledge; the use of a knife in a jailhouse assault would result in the immediate prosecution for attempted murder. Right now the situation didn't demand a severe response, in the event it did, the consequences wouldn't really matter.

It seemed like it took forever for dinner to arrive. I waited for last call before I finally emerged from my room. Unlike lunch, dinner was relatively quiet. I later learned it was the unit policy to refrain from talking during the evening news which was just beginning.

"Good evening, I'm Michelle Landry, our top story this evening details the life of a San Diego Police Officer who is in critical but stable conditions after his patrol car was forced off the highway by three armed robbery suspects. Spokesperson Mitch Walls confirmed that three armed robbery suspects were arrested after leading police on a 60-mile high speed chase that started in Riverside County and ended in the City of Escondido. Authorities believe these suspects are responsible for a series of armed robberies and carjackings that have plagued the areas in the past six months. In custody are Kenneth Latrell Banks, eighteen, Floyd Eugene Anderson, eighteen, and Eric Jacob Hodges, nineteen."

The news displayed our booking photos; followed by news footage of a flatbed tow truck towing the police vehicle from a deep bed canyon.

I turned from the TV and found the entire unit staring at me with admiration. Regardless of color or gang affiliation, one thing we all shared in common was our disdain for the police. I stepped to the food cart and was greeted with smiles from the same two dudes; that just a few hours ago stared at me with contempt. They nodded, I nodded back.

"Nigger, you think you're some big time hot shot now!"

"Roger, let the kid be," a short fat Mexican came to my defense.

"Richie since when you start babysitting Niggers?"

"Since five minutes ago, you got a problem with that?" Without waiting for an answer Richie turned towards me. "Hey kid you can eat with us."

Dinner passed peacefully. It became obvious Richie was the most powerful figure inside the unit. Shortly after dinner he whispered something in Spanish to one of his sidekicks. A few minutes later that same individual returned with a care package.

Shower shoes, soap, toothpaste, deodorant, cigarettes, and an assortment of snacks. I thanked him and promised to pay him back. He said that wouldn't be necessary. These items were a gift, his way of saying thanks for fucking up a cop.

As I proceeded to my cell I could feel Roger staring at me. He was fuming mad; bitch mother fucker allowed a short fat Mexicanto check his ass. Little did he know Richie was the least of his troubles? I made a silent promise to split his shit open the first chance I got. The tricky part about the game, the opportunity always arose when you least expected it. I wasn't going anywhere; I just got here. Even if he didn't say another word to me it really didn't matter, his mouth already wrote a check his ass couldn't get out of.

It had been over 24 hours since I had last spoken to Nicole. An avid watcher of the evening news I was more than certain she or members of her family had witnessed the news coverage. Unable to think of a justifiable lie that would explain why I was in jail I finally picked up the phone to call the mother of my seed.

"This is a Pacific Bell Operator; do you accept a collect call from Floyd?"

"Yes!" I heard a man's voice accept. "Floyd, I'm glad you called. You saved me the trip of coming down there." Robert Winters sounded like he was enjoying one of the best days of his life.

"Could you please put Nicole on the phone?"

"My daughter is not available; as a matter of fact she will never be available where you're concerned.

"Let her tell me."

"No! I'm telling you. It took a while but she finally came to her senses. She can finally see you for who you really are."

"And who might that be?"

"The criminal; You see Floyd I had a friend of mine do a background check on you, and as it turns out this is not your first brush with the law. As a matter of fact you were in and out of juvenile facilities since the age of twelve. Floyd, I believe you're a reasonable young man, and I honestly believe you really care for Nicole. As I'm sure you're aware you're facing some real serious charges, and there's a strong likelihood that you'll be going to prison for a very long time. Now you tell me, what kind of life can you offer my daughter and grandchild from a prison cell? Believe me when I say it's best for all parties involved, you leave Nicole alone and give up your parental rights, so they can have a chance at a normal life."

"That's not going to happen."

"Daddy, who are you talking to?"

"Nicole, let me handle this."

"No, Daddy hand me the phone."

"Hello." She whispered into the receiver so compassionate I felt an instant heartache.

"Hey, how are you holding up?"

"Floyd I'm scared. Why are they saying all those bad things about you?"

"Baby, they're lying, you believe me don't you."

"Yes, I believe you."

"Baby, I need to see you."

"Where are you?"

"I'm in Vista County Jail. It's up north by Oceanside."

"I know where it's at; I'll be there in an hour."

"No! No. You got to wait until Saturday. Visiting hours are between 8:00a.m. and 11:00a.m. You got to arrive at 7:30 a.m. to visit at eight. The last visit is 11:00 a.m., so regardless of whatever you got to be here at before 10:30 a.m."

"I'ma be there at 7:30 a.m. so I can see you at eight. Baby, I miss you, how long you got to stay there. Are you going to be home when our baby is born?"

"I wouldn't miss it for anything in the world. Baby, you know I love you."

"I love you, too."

"Baby, your father is going to do everything in his power to break us up. You can't allow that to happen."

"I won't." Nicole's voice and energy was so positive, slightly naïve, but just what I needed.

"You swear?"

"Yes I swear. I swear on our life, our love, our baby."

"Thank you baby, that's exactly what I needed to hear. I

gotta go right now, I love you Nicole."

"I love you, Floyd."

I hung up the phone feeling somewhat relieved to find Nicole was still in my corner. The County Jail had a way of rendering a man defenseless against verbal attacks. Robert Winters was on a serious campaign to destroy me. I was more than certain by the end of the day Nicole would be privy to all my past dirt. Dirt that I was sure would rock her world, and make her question the true nature of my character. Was I the man she fell in love with, or the gang banger and robbery that her father was so desperately trying to convince her of?

The following day we were summoned to court and officially charged. The courtroom was packed with law enforcement agents that all appeared to have a special interest in our case. It didn't dawn on me how serious this shit really was until that exact moment. I flinched at the sight of Detective Brooks pointing me out to a group of gentlemen dressed in suits. The realization that they were singling me out was quite disturbing. It was obvious from the gate this shit was about to get a lot worse before it got better.

In the process of moving from one holding cage to the next I had a chance to converse with the homies. I was surprised to learn their housing conditions were amiable. They were housed in open dorms with no racial tension. I also learned Unit 8 was the designated unit for the AB's. I was in a hostile environment that was on the verge of erupting any day. It was a volatile situation that required me to stay vigilant and keep my eyes open at all times. County officials were playing a cold game with my life. They weren't trying to scare me; they were seriously trying to get me hurt.

I was up bright and early Saturday morning, and for the exception of a few other prisoners also waiting on visits the entire unit was sound asleep. With court, transfers and many other legal obligations running rapid throughout the week, Saturday and Sunday morning was the most peaceful part of the day in the county jail. I emerged from my room at the announcement of the 8 am visitors and never heard my name called. Somewhat disappointed I returned to my room to await the next round of visitors.

At the announcement of the 10:00 a.m. and 11:00 a.m. visitors all hopes of seeing Nicole had sizzled away. Dear old dad must have gotten to her. I thought about calling her and quickly decided against it. If she didn't want to see me the odds of her wanting to talk to me were more than likely. Just as I lied down to catch a little rest before lunch I heard my name echo over the intercom. I rose to my feet and reported to the front of the unit.

"Anderson you have a visit." The deputy informed me.

"I thought visiting hours were between eight and eleven," I asked somewhat confused.

"They are, you were authorized a special visit."

I stepped into the visiting room not knowing what or who to expect. My heart swelled with joy at the sight of Nicole sitting on the opposite side of the glass window looking as lovely as ever. As a showing of affection I kissed two fingers and pressed them against the glass. She did the same.

"Baby, what happened?"

"I been here since 7:15, they said I couldn't see you until I talked to a man named Detective Brooks, and he didn't show up until nine. I didn't mind waiting they were awfully nice.

At the mention of Detective Brooks I felt a chill run up and down my spine. My mind was racing a hundred miles an hour. I should have anticipated his next move, but I didn't. He caught me slipping. I was almost afraid to ask what he wanted, but I had to.

"What did he want?" I asked, trying hard to hide my fears.

"He said they were considering releasing you on your recognizance, and they needed to verify a little background information."

"What type of information?" I asked, hanging on her every word.

"He wanted to know how long I've known you, where we live, where you work, and things like that."

"That's it?"

"Yes, pretty much."

"Did he ask you about anybody else?"

"He asked me about Lil Bull and Salt-Rock, and wanted to

know if I knew them. I told him I did; they were childhood friends of yours."

I quietly stared at Nicole as I contemplated this serious error. I should have anticipated Brook's next move. I didn't have anyone to blame but myself; my baby didn't know better, and I hated myself for putting her in this position. "What's wrong?" She asked, bringing me back to the reality of the moment.

"Everything is fine love." I said, hoping to ease her concern.

Baby, Detective Brooks seemed very nice; he was the one that told them to give us an hour visit because I had to wait so long."

"Yes, that was real nice of him, that's enough about him, let's talk about you. How are you feeling?"

"I missed you," she said as a single tear fell from her eyes.

"I missed you, too. Baby, you got to stay strong. Believe me when I say we will make it past this."

I had no one to blame but myself. I should have known the authorities would try to establish a connection between Lil Bull, Salt-Rock and myself. By tying me to the homies, Detective Brooks effectively tied me to the carjacking, which in turned tied me to the assault on a police officer. My whole defense was discredited just that quickly. In the past week I made one bad call after another. I was now beginning to wonder if I was capable of matching wits with an overzealous detective dead set on sending me to prison.

I returned from my visit and discovered I had a cellmate. Charles Russell was a nineteen-year-old Crip from Oceanside, California. At six foot three, and a solid two hundred and twenty pounds he was a very intimidating figure. This wasn't his first trip inside Vista County Jail, nor was it his first trip inside Unit 8.

Although the AB's had us outnumbered twenty-three to two, they did everything in their power to avoid a confrontation with young Charles, who seemed to be egging them on every opportunity he got. Charles didn't give a fuck, it was like he was looking for a confrontation, and I knew it was just a matter of time before he found one.

The following weekend we were sitting in the day room watching Soul Train when Roger returned from a visit.

"We don't watch that shit in here!" Roger said and reached up and turned the channel. Without saying a word, Charles stepped to him and hit him with a two-piece that was so quick and powerful, Roger stumbled backward and hit the ground. Struggling to find his balance, Roger remained down on one knee desperately trying to clear his head.

"Get your punk ass up white boy!" Charles shouted, trying to give him a fair fight. Down on one knee, Roger was unresponsive with a slight glaze in his eyes.

"That's what I thought. Get your bitch ass out my face before I mop this day room with your ass."

Believing Roger wanted no parts of him, and forgetting a fundamental rule in engagement, Charles turned his back to place the TV back on Soul Train. Seizing the opportunity, Roger lowers his head and rushes Charles from behind and driving him to the ground. With a thirty-pound weight advantage, Roger managed to overpower him and get him in a headlock.

As Charles struggled to free himself, I grabbed a metal napkin holder off the table and busted Roger in the back of the head, slitting his head wide open. An agonizing scream filled the unit and blood poured from his head like a spilled cup of tomato juice.

At the sound of Roger's desperate scream the entire unit emerged from their rooms and found Roger laid out bleeding profusely from the back of his head. In the midst of all the confusion Charles and I managed to escape to our room before anyone found out what happened. The emergency alarmed was triggered and everyone was ordered back to their rooms. With a bloody towel wrapped around his head, Roger staggered into the care of two deputies and was rushed to the hospital.

Even in Victory, There's Defeat
−Chapter 5−

Charles and I gathered our property and waited for the inevitable, a one way ticket to the hole. My only regret was we didn't dispense a more severe ass whipping on Roger. An hour later I was surprised to see the food cart being pushed inside the unit. A few minutes later chow was announced and the remote control locks were released. I looked out into the day room and observed several white boys emerging from the utility closet with broomsticks and mop handles.

"Cuz I think they're waiting on us to serve lunch."

"What are they having, I'm hungry as a horse."

"Two roasted Niggers if we take our black asses out there." I watched the lynch mob gather inside the day room.

"Let me see," Charles replied. "Damn, Cuz they look mad as a motherfucker. I guess lunch is out the question, huh?"

"Most definitely Cuz, it'll be suicide to go out there right now."

Pop! The first blow cracked the window. Pop! Pop!

The second and third blow shattered it. Charles jumped back to avoid getting hit by the glass. As he did, a long white arm appeared through the window slot and attempted to locate the button that would open our door. Charles reacted quickly by grabbing the arm, and placing his feet against the door for support. Using his full strength, Charles tried to pull the white boy's entire body through the small window slot. Sheer pain could be heard in the white boy's voice as he begged Charles to release him. The unit alarm sounded, and once again everyone was instructed to return to their rooms, this time no one obeyed.

It took over twenty deputies and two high power water hoses to squash the disturbance. Dressed in riot gear with batons and shields they came in kicking asses and taking names. After all was settled and everyone was securely back in their rooms, Charles and I were handcuffed and escorted from the unit and placed in separate holding cages.

"Anderson 70554 front and center," Sgt. Billings announced from the doorway.

"Yes,." I answered.

"Captain Willis would like to see you. Once inside his office take the first seat to your right, and remain seated until instructed otherwise."

Captain Willis was a heavy set man, in his early 50's. This was the fat mother fucker that initiated the cross. It was on his authority that I was placed in Unit 8. He looked up from a file and stared at me briefly. I met his glaze which seemed to irritate him.

"I don't like that look on your face," he said, closing the file.

"And what look is that?" I retorted, having nothing to lose.

"What look is that, Sir?" he repeated with emphasis.

"I don't call my dad sir, so why should I have to call you sir?"

"Because you're in my house, and as long as you remain in my house, you will respect me."

"Respect goes both ways."

"I see you're a smart ass, let's see if a week in the hole will teach you some manners. Get him out of here!"

I was taken to the hole where I remained every bit of three hours. As powerful as Captain Willis was, he did not have the authority to revise the rules and regulations of Vista County jail, and there was no rule that said I had to address him as sir. Unable to charge me with a violation, I was escorted back to Unit 8 to retrieve my property. As I walked in the unit I studied the faces of every white boy standing at his window for future recognition. I had no doubt some of us would meet again.

Although I wasn't particularly fond of dorm living I enjoyed the racial mixture of Unit 3, which was predominantly illegal immigrants, a few blacks, and a few white dudes that weren't affiliated with any group. Unlike the Southern California Mexicans, the Border Brothers appeared to have a genuine affection for blacks.

Lil Bull was in Unit 2 and Salt-Rock was in Unit 4, which allowed us the opportunity to converse daily. We had a preliminary hearing scheduled for the following week. Lil Bull had retained a lawyer who informed him no fingerprints were found inside the Camaro, and the man we carjacked couldn't positively identify anyone. We all shared a glimmer of hope.

The transition from freedom to incarceration was a gradual adjustment that got easier by the day. I adjusted to the change like it was second nature. I understood it was an uphill fight from the moment they read you your rights. I also understood in order to fight you had to have someone to fight for you. I had given Nicole the names of several good attorneys to contact on my behalf, and I really couldn't understand why she had not done so. I left her with close to seventy-five thousand dollars, more than enough to pay a lawyer and have plenty to spare. I could no longer deny Nicole had been acting kind of strange, quiet and distant. At first I contributed her strange behavior to the pregnancy, now I wasn't sure.

I knew Robert Winters was working diligently to separate Nicole and I and I also knew he wouldn't stop until he did. The end came without warning, and Nicole faded from my life without as much as a goodbye. She turned her back when I needed her the most, and to me that was the ultimate act of betrayal. As much as it hurt, I couldn't afford to dwell, I was fighting for life; and my survival was dependent on a sharp intellect, and a focused mind.

Unlike Nicole, Lil Bull's girl Renee stood up like the Statue of Liberty, and ran like a two-2 headed horse. Every visit, every court appearance she was there front and center. In spite of her parents' disapproval, she and Lil Bull got married inside the jail Chapel, which was evident she was in it for the long haul.

Never in my life had I ever felt more alone, everyday Nicole failed to answer my call or come and visit me was like a knife digging deeper and deeper inside my chest. Eventually the pain subsided, and was replaced by hatred I never known exist. "Fuck that Bitch" I told myself, and shook her like a bad dream.

Richard Healy made his first appearance on the eve of my preliminary hearing. I was well aware of the attitude most court appointed lawyers had when dealing with unpaid clients. I was mad as a motherfucker this trick waited until the last possible moment to pay me a visit. The preliminary hearing was an important stage in court proceedings, one that required the prosecutor to offer enough evidence to have you bond over for trial. Based on Lil Bull's lawyer they had nothing on us, but then again he wasn't representing us, he was representing Lil Bull. Everything that applied to Lil Bull didn't necessary apply to Salt-Rock and I.

Richard Healy was dressed in an expensive dark blue pinstripe suit with his tie loose around the collar. He rose to his feet and extended his hand as I entered the room.

"Mr. Anderson, I'm Richard Healy, I was appointed by the court to represent you. Sorry I haven't been over to see you. I was occupied with a trial that concluded yesterday afternoon."

"Did you win?" I asked.

"In law, winning is based on client satisfaction. In the case in which I'm speaking on the case was declared a hung jury. Prior to trial my client was facing first degree murder with a mandatory life sentence if convicted. The prosecutor offered him a flat twenty-five years if he plea out. He refused. As a result of the hung jury, the prosecutor amended his position and offered my client seven years for involuntary manslaughter, which he happily accepted. So yes, I would consider that a win."

"I would also consider that a win, especially if you're guilty of said charge."

"Guilty or innocent is not a factor when it comes to the application of law. It is my job to represent you to the best of my ability. Based on the evidence or lack of I will make a legal finding and recommendation how we should proceed. As your attorney I work for you, therefore the ultimate decision whether we go to trial or not will always rest in your hands. Speaking of decisions you have a preliminary hearing scheduled for tomorrow at 9:00 a.m. The State of California has charged you with four felony counts; which consist of two counts of armed robbery; one count of carjacking; and one count of assault with a deadly weapon on a police officer. Based on the evidence there is a 99.9 percent chance you will be bonded over to stand trial on these charges."

"Evidence, what evidence?" I shouted.

"Let's start with count one and two. On February 28, 1981 James Moore claimed two black males in their mid to late teens robbed him at gunpoint. Items taken were his cash, jewelry, and his vehicle, which was a 1981 yellow Z28 Camaro, license number 199SLH. Count two; on February 29th Jose Luis Gomez claimed two black males in their late teens robbed him at gunpoint of $1845.00, which was the bank depository of El Paso's Mexican Restaurant. Also Gomez claimed the two suspects fled in a yellow Camaro with partial plate numbers 199. And count three; assault with a deadly weapon on a police officer. Yellow paint fragments were lifted from the side of Officer Larry Fulton's police vehicle, which was a positive match from the paint taken off the Camaro. The prosecutor also claims one of the twenties you allegedly gave the cab driver had a long distance phone number written on it which was traced to a customer that attended the El Paso Mexican Restaurant that evening. Bear in mind, it's all circumstantial, but it's enough to have you bonded over for trial."

"It appears you have given this case considerably though, how should I proceed?"

"In light of everything I propose we waive the preliminary hearing. Reason being, I don't want to expose you to the victims. James Moore and Jose Luis Gomez were shown a photo line-up and failed to identify your photographs. Just because they didn't pick you out does not bar them from later identifying you at a later date. Sometime prior to trial I will request a line-up, which will include you and five other individuals that resemble you in age, height, and weight. I would prefer our next encounter with the victims be at a place and time of our choosing, rather than a court setting where you'll be one of three defendants on display.

Richard Healy simplified what would have normally been a complicated issue. Growing up in the hood I learned to be suspicious at an early age. I also learned that sincerity was hard to fake, the eyes never lie. After a two hour interview I came to the conclusion Richard Healy was acting in my best interests.

****

The following morning I awoke feeling fresh, and looking forward to the opportunity to see the homies face to face. The cat was out of the bag, there was no need playing like we didn't know each other. I stepped into the hallway at the sound of my name being announced for court call. Lil Bull was four people in front of me, while Salt-Rock was five people behind me. It wasn't until we got to the holding cage we had a chance to talk.

"Cuz by this time tomorrow we should be waking up in our own bed. I can't wait to get the fuck out of here," Lil Bull said as if it was already a done deal.

"Me neither!" Salt-Rock added. "The first thing I'm going to do is roll me a fat ass joint, and call Sally. You know baby girl got the best head in the city, she'll suck the life out of you."

"I heard baby girl suck a mean dick," I said with slight humor.

"Cuz you act like you don't know, I seen your car parked over there on more than a few occasions," he responded and we all started laughing.

"Pretty Boy what are you going to do when you first get home?" Lil Bull asked.

"Cuz I hate to be the bearer of bad news but this shit is a little more complicated than you think." I pulled Lil Bull and Salt-Rock to the back of the holding cage, and explained in great detail what my lawyer said, and what he recommended.

"Cuz them mother fuckers are lying, I'll bet my life on it. A phone number on a twenty, how crazy is that? That bitch ass lawyer you got wants us to waive our preliminary hearing because he knows they don't have a fucking thing on us. Pretty Boy I don't believe you fell for that weak ass shit Cuz." Lil Bull spoke his peace and walked away.

It was obvious Cuz was disappointed, but my mind was made up. Regardless how the homies felt I had to go with my instincts.

The County Court House was a residence of despair. In the halls of justice very seldom do you hear a laugh or observe a smile. It was a serious atmosphere where tension was always at its highest, and the sharpest legal minds battled over a man's fate. The justice system was a business that dealt in human cattle, the more heads they had the more money they made. There was never a shortage of criminals to shut the system down. Just as quick as one left three came.

Lil Bull and Salt-Rock returned from court looking distraught, as if they didn't believe what had taken place. The individual that they robbed at the Mexican restaurant positively identified them. Trapped in their own anguish I stood to the side as the homies struggled to cope with this latest turn in events. In the Court Of Law expectations and wishful thinking often resulted in mind crushing defeats. The number one rule, hope for the best and prepare for the worst.

It had been nearly three weeks since I spoke to Richard Healy. I was hoping no news meant good news. From day one we had an agreement I was to be kept abreast of all new developments. It was a little after 10:00 p.m. when I was summoned to the visiting room for a lawyer visit. I felt a weary feeling in the pit of my stomach. This was uncommonly late for an attorney visit. I could only speculate what was so important it couldn't wait until tomorrow.

Richard was accompanied by Matt Wilson, his lead investigator. I had met Matt on several occasions, and just like Richard he appeared to be a straight up individual. Both men stood and extended their hand as I entered the room.

"Floyd today the State of California filed a superseding indictment against you, Banks, and Hodges; charging you with a twenty-two count indictment. The latest of these charges includes the auto thief of a 1980 Monte Carlo, which was stolen from the Paradise Hill Recreational Center. Two volunteers at the center identified your photographs as individuals they saw hanging around the center the afternoon the car was stolen. The following day that same vehicle was used in a supermarket robbery, where a palm print was lifted from the safe. The palm print has been identified as belonging to Kenneth Banks. The prosecutor also discovered in 1974 you and Banks attended the same High School, and also played on the same basketball team. The coach of the team remembered you and Banks as being close friends. He also established in 1978 you and Banks both housed at El Paso De Robles, California Youth Authority. Youth Authority records confirmed you and Banks were both listed as members of the Eastside Rollin 40's Crips Gang, and on one occasion both placed in Administrative Segregation for assaulting another inmate."

I held up my hand for him to stop. I needed a moment to think. There was no need to question the information. He was hitting me with one fact after another. The situation was rapidly deteriorating, and I was powerless to stop it.

"In terms of years, what's the worst possible case scenario?" I asked after a long moment of silence.

"Providing you went to trial and found guilty on all charges you'll be looking at thirty years."

"How much on a plea bargain?"

"It's been my experience when dealing with Assistant District Attorney John Rice he's less inclined to negotiate when a police officer has been injured."

"How can they hold us accountable for injuries he suffered as a result of his own reckless driving? It was him, not us that was driving in the wrong lane."

After describing the sequence of events that lead to the crash, Richard searched his folder for the accident report. Finding none, he turned towards Matt with a smile.

"I think we may have something here. If we discover the prosecutor is withholding favorable evidence that can help the defense, we'll have a strong bargaining tool. Matt, find out what you can about the crash, but be discreet. The longer they hold these reports the more damaging it'll be."

The prosecutor's case was gaining momentum going into the final week of trial. From the way things were looking we were

most definitely on our way to prison, the only thing left unanswered was for how long.

Since the birth of our child, Nicole moved back to her parents who forbid me from calling. It was only through a mutual
friend I learned she gave birth to a seven pound, two ounce baby
boy. After all we had been through it was still hard to accept she
gave up on us so easy. I couldn't entirely blame her father; Nicole
was a strong young woman that did exactly as she wanted. I knew
her better than she knew herself. Something was going on in her
life that was so serious, so hurtful she couldn't even face me.

Even in her absence I managed to keep hope alive. It
wasn't until my birthday came and went without as much as a
birthday card I accepted the realization it was over, she was gone. I
guess it was all for the best, because where I was headed love and
imprisonment did not mix. It was an ugly combination that made a
man's time ten times harder than it had to be.

The day prior to trial we learned the prosecutor was offering us a package deal for fifteen years. A deal that required we all
plead to the indictment. His position, if he had to take one of us to
trial he'll take all three of us to trial. Lil Bull and Salt-Rock re-
jected the proposal without a moments thought. Dead set on their
position, they refused to consider the evidence against us.

Unlike them I understood the risk and the consequences involved if we lost. What was at stake was an additional fifteen if we
lost. Instead of coming home at the age of twenty-eight, we'll be
coming home at the age of thirty-eight. Why Lil Bull and salt-Rock
couldn't see that was beyond my comprehension.

The Day of Judgment came with the weight of the world
resting on my shoulders. The mere thought of going to trial was the
most challenging endeavor I ever had to contemplate. It was imperative I figure out a way to get through to the homies. It was essential they understood the next fifteen to thirty years of our lives
rested solely in their hands. The hardest part of doing time was accepting it, after that it got easier by the day.

I was happy to find the homies in a more peaceful and sus-
ceptible mood when we arrived at the courthouse. I knew from past
experience it was an uphill battle trying to convince a hothead to

do something they was deadest against. Lil Bull was my dude; I couldn't recall one incident where we were at odds with each other. We were grown man now, and facing the same fate a grown man would face under the same situation. This wasn't a situation one could stay silent. If nothing else you had to speak your peace regardless who didn't like it.

"Pretty Boy I can see what you're saying, but Cuz fifteen years is a long fucking time, but thirty years is a lifetime."

"Cuz on fifteen all we got to do is ten. On thirty we got to bring twenty. If I thought for second we had a half ass chance of winning I'll be the first to suit up; but Cuz they got too much shit on us."

"Half the shit they charged us with we didn't do," Lil Bull stated as he thought about all the charges they hit us with.

"Yeah I know," I quietly whispered trying not to encourage a revolt. It was common practice whenever you got hit with a crime spree the authorities cleared their books. We were no exception. True enough we had nothing to do with half the charges they gave us, but the evidence on the other half was more than substantial.

"Cuz I think we should hold out until they come down some. I can live with ten years, but fifteen is too fucking long. I got to think about this shit," Salt-Rock said and turned towards Lil Bull for support. Lil Bull didn't bite.

I wasn't worry about Salt-Rock he was just talking shit. I knew when the time came he would follow the lead.

"Anderson!" a deputy shouted from the doorway, "You have a legal visit."

I arrived in the attorney room and found Richard flipping through some paper. "I have some good news; at least I hope it's good. Everything you said about the accident checked out. The Accident Reconstruction Team confirmed Officer Fulton's vehicle was traveling in the westbound lane at the moment of impact. The prosecutor acknowledged that the report is correct, and it was merely an oversight that we didn't receive it. To make a long story short he amended his position of fifteen years, and is now offering a package deal of eight years, providing that you, Banks, and

Hodges entered a change of pleads today. What do you think?"

"I think that's the best news I heard all year. Thank you Richard."

"You're quite welcome."

We accepted the deal, waived the traditional waiting period and were scheduled to be sentenced the following week. I returned to my unit in extremely high spirits considering I just signed my name on a deal that guaranteed I'd be a hostage of the State of California for a minimum of five years and a maximum of eight years.

I believed the only way a man could appreciate ten years was if he was looking at twenty. The only way he could appreciate twenty years was if he was looking at thirty. The only way he can appreciate thirty years if he was looking at a life sentence. And the only way he can appreciate a life sentence if he was looking at the death penalty. The hardest part of doing time was accepting it. Once you accepted it, there was nothing to it but to do it.

As I approached the row of telephones to contact my family and share the good news, I stopped in my tracks and was startled when a tall slim Mexican on the first phone called me by my street name. I stopped and turned in his direction to make sure I heard him correctly.

"Is your name Pretty Boy?" he asked in broken English.

"Yeah I'm Pretty Boy," I shot back like he just challenged me.

"Hey amigo my friend wants to talk to you," he said, extending the phone.

"Hello," I said into the receiver as I kept my eye on the Mexican that handed me the phone.

"You know you're a dead man?" the familiar voice of Doc came over the line.

"Hey Doc I been trying to get in contact with you. How have you been?" I asked with a huge smile on my face.

"You know you'll never make it home alive?"

"No, I haven't talk to him in a while. If I see him I'll tell him you said hi."

"I got to give it to you; you're real calm for a man that don't have long to live."

"Yeah it was nice talking to you too. Tell your family I said hi. Here's your friend."

Unlike the Mexican I didn't extend the phone all the way. I waited for him to get close enough before I struck him as hard as I could with the receiver, shattering his nose and swelling both eyes with one single blow. I quickly followed up with a barrage of blows that sent him sailing to the floor. From there all he felt were feet and concrete. Unconscious and bleeding profusely I slid out of the day room as though nothing had happened.

I quickly rushed to the living quarters to inform the blacks what had transpired. The look of sheer fright in their eyes pretty much told me I was on my own. Out of seven blacks I figured I could count on two. I was more than certain I could count on Robert Russell, Charles' older brother; being that he was aware I came to his brother aid in a time of need. I was wrong on both counts.

It didn't take long for the Mexicans to mobilize and come after me. Trapped at the back of the dorm with nowhere to go they came charging. All the blacks jumped on the top racks and got out of the line of fire. The last thought I had before they reached me, "I hope they don't kill me."

With my back against the wall I fought for dear life. Had it not been for the narrow walkway and their inability to get to me they probably would have inflicted great body injury. Finally one of them caught me in the head with a hard object that sent me to the floor. I was hurt but not serious. I folded up and took their fists and kicks like a small child getting spanked. Fully aware of my surroundings I heard the unit alarm sound, meaning help was on the way.

Surprisingly, as soon as the deputies ordered them to stop they did. When the smoke cleared I stood up and stared at the coward ass Niggas that were still posted on the tops racks with the fear of God in their eyes. I would deal with them accordingly, just a matter of when.

After being examined and cleared by the nurse I was handcuffed and escorted to Captain Willis' office. No sooner than I sat down he looked up and appeared to receive enormous satisfaction to find me battered and bruised.

"I heard you received a pretty good thumping, would you care to tell me what happened?" he asked with a smirk on his face that suggested he was enjoying every second.

"By the smile on your face it appears as though you're having a wonderful day Captain."

"I must say I am, but by the looks of you it appears you have had a pretty rough day."

"I won't go as far as to say it was rough, me against twenty Mexicans I think I came out on top."

"You think you're a real tough ass don't you?" he asked as his attitude quickly shifted.

"Nah, I don't think I'm a tough ass, but I'm tougher than you." I said and stared at him. No sooner than the words left my lips Sgt. Holland snatched me up and quickly released me when Captain Willis waved him off.

"If I didn't have this uniform on I'd kick your black ass up and down this hallway until you begged me to stop," he shot back and stared at me like I was the most disgusting creature he ever laid eyes on.

"If you didn't have that uniform on I'd knock your fat ass out and fuck you up, you punk ass faggot." Unable to contain his rage, Captain Willis dove across his desk and tackled me. As he cocked his arm to deliver what more than likely would have been a painful blow to my face, Sgt. Holland grabbed him. Had it not been for the thick cushion chair, surrounded by a hard wooden frame his weight alone probably would have crushed me.

"It takes a real coward to attack a man while he's handcuffed, take these cuffs off and let's see how tough your faggot ass really is," I responded in hopes of inflaming the situation even farther. A severe beat down by the hands of Captain Willis, while handcuffed was a lawsuit, and a guaranteed ticket to shave a few more years off my sentence.

"That's enough Anderson!" Sgt. Holland shouted as he restrained the Captain and helped him back to his feet.

"Get this piece of shit out my office!" Captain Willis yelled and quickly regained his composure.

"You're a real live bitch fat ass punk. I knew you had a pussy in your pants!" I shouted the moment Sgt. Holland lifted me to my feet.

"That's enough Anderson, and I mean it," Sgt. Holland said and rushed me out of the office.

I wasn't surprised when I was taken to the hole, I expected it. What did surprise me was the reason why. I was cited for inciting a riot with no mention of Captain Willis or the incident that had taken place inside his office. I couldn't catch a break.

The following morning Lil Bull and Salt-Rock took off on two Border Brothers in their units, sending them straight to the hole; where we remained until we were sentenced and transferred to the California Department of Corrections two weeks later.

The Cross
– Chapter 6 –

Regardless of your crime or sentence, for the exception of Death Row prisoners, I was told that every prisoner in Southern California had to stop at Chino Receptions Center where they underwent a battery of test that would later be compiled and analyzed by criminologist, philologist, psychologist, and other fields of study that would give man a better understanding how the criminal mind operated. Chino was also known as a place where you ran into present, past, and future enemies. It was also the first of many stops in my journey to hell that would test the content of your character. A stone cold killer on the street didn't necessarily translate to a stone cold guerilla behind the walls. Just like the streets measured the heart of a gangster by his heart to pull the trigger, in prison your heart was measured by hand to hand combat, and your willingness to do battle under the watchful eyes of two armed guards with instructions to shoot at the first sign of provocation. In prison, I learned over time, the weapon of choice was a knife, or any hard object that will turn a man's lights out. Whatever the weapon of choice, it still required a man to get up close and personal with his target. That was the beauty of hand-to-hand combat; and sometimes the aggressor became the victim.

Chino presented many unknown challenges, which was evident by the amount of violence taking place every yard period. The manner in which these disturbances were brought to an end only revealed how little the Department of Corrections thought of a prisoner's life. A simple fist fight was enough to get you shot dead in the chest by a Mini-14 Assault Rifle, which in all likelihood was an instant heart stopper. The method of violence they employed to squash the smallest disturbance did little to stop the violence. Although the majority of prisoners avoided the yard at all cost, it was mandatory for every gangster to make an appearance; not to do so was a sign of fear and a label that was sure to follow you whatever you transfer to in the system.

Concern or fear were two emotions a prisoner could never displayed regardless how distraught they were. In the face of uncertainty it was best to watch, listen, learn, and develop a trained eye that would recognize tension at first glance. It didn't take long for Lil Bull, Salt-Rock, and I to witness our first jailhouse murder, which took place on the recreational yard, shortly after breakfast. Three Mexicans on one; the assault was quick, brutal, and without mercy, or fear of being apprehended. It had all the markings of a contract killing.

Chino was designated as an administrative level reception center which allowed the institutions to house prisoners with crimes ranging from Grand Larceny to Murder. It was also known as a prison where the strong preyed heavily on the weak. A reputation of being weak or a coward was a stain that was hard to wash off, and one that would follow a prisoner wherever he went. Unlike the streets where a man's heart was measured by simply fighting back, regardless if he won or loss, in prison a loss was unacceptable, and demanded a quick and immediate response; which more time than not lead to murder or serious bodily injury.

We all know, the United States of America was separated by class, and comprised of many hidden societies; the crime family just being one. I, like most youngsters roaming the halls of Chino grew up in the crime game. For most, our journey started in juvenile hall; from there to a Boy's Home, better known as a 24 school. From there to juvenile camp, and ultimately to the California Youth Authority, which was the juvenile version of State prison.

It was only fitting, and by design, most, if not all would eventually land in the California department of Corrections, if by chance they lived that long. At eighteen what appeared to be an acceptable fate, would eventually become a rude awakening, a disturbing trend, one in which the United States Congress would implement laws, and aid and assist in the annihilation of a whole generation of young Black men.

In 1997 the U.S. Government implemented the new sentencing guidelines, which enhanced penalties for felons in possession of a firearm or over five grams of crack. Depending upon your past criminal history, you could render a sentence of fifteen years to life for mere possession of a firearm, or simply possession of a hundred dollars worth of crack. It was obvious by the amount of young blacks that fell victim to this scheme, it was race-based with the purpose of ridding society of a whole generation of young black men.

After thirty days of being examined like a lab monkey we all looked forward to leaving CRC. We were told the designation list would be posted immediately after lunch. Lil Bull, Salt-Rock and I made our way down the long hallway to find out our fate. There were nearly fifty people in line, but the line moved quickly. Lil Bull was the first to find his name. He turned from the bulletin board with a disappointing look on his face.

"Damn, Cuz they got me going to Tracy," he said obviously disappointed that he wasn't going to Soledad which was a lot closer to home." The Dual Vocational Institution was better known as Tracy, The Gladiator School, because there were so many youngsters there with a shit load of time, and didn't have anything to lose but their lives. It was not the type of spot you wanted to go if you were trying to reprogram and make it back to the streets.

Salt-Rock was next in line, after finding his name we learned he was also going to Tracy. I stepped to the bulletin board in deep anticipation, finding my name I took my finger tip and traced it to my destination. *This couldn't be right* I thought as I repeated the process. Certain that I read it right this time I turned from the bulletin board feeling somewhat dazed by the obvious cross.

"Pretty Boy what's the verdict?" Lil Bull asked, sensing something was wrong.

"San Quentin Cuz," I muttered. "These mother fuckers got me going to San Quentin."

"If you don't mind me asking youngster, how old are you?" An elder black man asked that was next in line.

"Eighteen."

"How much time do you have?" he continued.

"Eight years Sir," I replied.

"Be careful youngster, their sending you there to die. The State of California wants you dead, or in prison for the rest of your natural life."

Later that evening I laid awake and pondered over this latest revelation. Although I never met or seen this old man a day in my life, his face and message would remain with me until the end of time. Unbeknownst to him I conquered the fear of dying at the age ten when I became a certified member of the Eastside Rollin 40's Crip Gang. As far as I was concerned, life was overrated, and Hell for the Black Man was here on Earth. I never met anyone who died and came back and wrote a book about it. No one; and I mean no one knew what awaited the soul when you closed your eyes for the final time. I wasn't living the American dream; I was trapped in the American nightmare, the latest version. Like most young black men born in the 60's, growing up in the 70's, and coming to age in the 80's I was Cursed from Birth.

Welcome to the Big House
– Chapter 7 –

I arrived at San Quentin two days after turning 19 years old. From the moment I stepped off the bus I shook the streets and everything and everyone that reminded me of freedom. San Quentin State Prison was a maximum-security prison where the State of California housed its most notorious criminals and violent gang members in the system. The state made a fair and accurate assessment sending me there. It was only fitting a youngster of my caliber joined its ranks.

Governed by some of the most violent gang members to ever walk the face of the earth, murder, robbery, and rape was a way of life. Kill or be killed, fight, get fucked, or spend your entire sentence in Protective Custody was the law of the land.

San Quentin was a place where the strong preyed on the weak, and the weak committed suicide, I quickly learned. Regardless of your charge or past reputation eventually everyone was put to the test. It was how you responded to this test that determined how your fellow prisoners perceived you.

Upon my arrival, I noticed San Quentin was a city within a city, a death zone that consisted of four separated blocks, and the Adjustment Center. South Block was the most diverse block which consisted of four different units. A-Section was a mixture of orientation and general population. B-Section was PC, protective custody. C-Section was SHU, a security housing unit, and D-Section was MCU, a management control unit.

Upon arrival everyone started off in South Block unless

you had a death sentence; in which you received a personal escort to North Block, better known as the house of death.

East Block was the most populate block which consisted of two sides, Bayside which was facing the San Francisco's Bay and Yard-side which was facing the interior structure of the prison. Each side consisted of five tiers, with fifty (two men) cells on each tier.

West Block was an honor unit that consisted of Smacks and Mack's. A Smack was an ass-kisser, a do-boy, a motherfucker that did whatever the guards told him to do. A Mack on the other hand was an old timer; someone that's been there so long they could find their way around the prison blindfolded.

The Adjustment Center famously known for the 1971 prison uprising that left three guards, and two prisoners dead, George Jackson included. AC was designed as a maximum security unit where San Quentin housed its most dangerous prisoners. A jail-house murder, or a violent assault on a prison guard were two of a very few infractions that would guarantees you an indefinite stay in AC.

By all standards, San Quentin was an enormous prison with thousands of complex personalities housed within its walls. I adapted to life inside prison in the same manner a soldier would adapt to the battlefield. Observe, listen, and learn. Three weeks after my arrival I was housed in East Block Bayside, and assigned to the Furniture Factory, a legalized sweat factory paying slave wages. It was beyond my understanding how one could work for ten cent an hour, but refuse to work for five dollars an hour as a free man.

Just like money determined how one lived in the free world, it also determined how one lived in prison. I didn't come to prison to find a job, and I damn sure wasn't going to allow the administration to work me like a dog for a little or nothing. Finally after two weeks of poor job performance, and a number of lectures on how to do the job properly, I was fired and reassigned to the recreation department.

The recreation yard was the job in prison, especially in the summertime. It was a hustler's paradise with three poker games, and two dice games going non-stop. A certified hustler, I learned to master the art of pad-rolling in the youth authority. In the past month I had been eyeing the dice game inside the gym and waiting for the right moment to make my move. With fifty ducats to my name I realized there was no room for error. One ducat was equivalent to one U.S. dollar, and could be used to purchase weed, wine, or commissary items at the prison store. It was money in your hand, which was better than money on your books. Each prisoner was allowed to have a maximum twenty ducats at one time, which in actuality was a joke because you had some prisoners that had hundreds, if not thousands of ducats to do their bidding.

After studying each player's technique I was more than confident in my ability to win if I got on the dice first. Out of the regular players, Maze was the only one that concerned me. Maze was an old hustler with a long perm, and the mannerisms of a pimp. A well-known figure out of Los Angeles, he was serving a life sentence for killing a man he caught cheating him in a dice game. Maze was good to hit between ten-fifteen licks before he fell off. As long as I avoided him I knew I'd be alright.

"Say young blood I see you been watching the game, do you know how to pad-roll?" Stevie, an old school player out of Fresno asked.

"Yeah, I can shoot a little," I said and met his stare.

"We could use another player if you'd like to get in?"

"I'll play if I could shoot first," I responded with an air of innocence in my voice.

"I'm sure we can arrange that," he said and they all nodded in agreement.

"What's the most I can bet at one time?"

"You can bet it all if you like," Maze said, joining in on the conversation for the first time.

"Bet a quarter." I counted out twenty-five ducats

"Fade the young brother Stevie," Maze said.

"Shit Black, that's right up my alley; this is my type of gambling."

"Bet another twenty-five, I hit," I said to Maze.

"That's a bet young blood."

"I recognize you cats don't mean any disrespect, but I prefer you call me Pretty Boy Floyd."

"Pretty Boy Floyd it is," Stevie said and slid me the dice.

"Pretty Boy Floyd like Floyd Patterson the boxer?" Maze asked.

"No. Pretty Boy Floyd like Charles Arthur Floyd the gangster," I said, massaging the dice.

Although I saw them locking and shooting from the pawn, I grabbed the dice with my fingertips, stroked them on the pad four times, and sent them marching side by side, stopping on a four-tray.

"That was real pretty youngster, but from now on you got to shoot from the pawn," Maze said, somewhat mad Stevie didn't catch the dice.

"Cool," I said. "Bet the fifty."

Maze looked at Stevie, and Stevie looked at Maze.

"Fuck it, I got you," Maze replied and laid down fifty ducats.

"Bet a quarter on the side," I said to Stevie.

"Bet the quarter!" Stevie yelled as if it was a personal challenge.

By the time they called lunch I had three hundred and fifty ducats, plus the fifty I came with. Maze was the first to congratulate me; I hit a nice lick, more than enough to buy a color TV and a radio.

Later that evening I decided to treat myself to a cup of jailhouse wine and a cap of weed; which all together cost ten dollars. My cellmate was a certified smack on the waiting list to go to the honor unit. A so-called born again Christian he claimed that he didn't smoke, drink, or engage in illicit conversation about street game. From my standpoint we didn't have a damn thing in common. I fired up a joint and blew the smoke in his direction. After frowning up for a few seconds, he lay down and pulled the covers over his head.

"Little homie that smell like some good shit."

I turned around and found my OG homie Papa C standing at my cell door. Papa C was a street legend, and perhaps the most well-known and respected figure out of San Diego. Serving a life sentence for copping to a murder his younger brother committed I had nothing but love for him. Eight years my elder he looked much older, which was contributed to his huge Moses like bread that covered his entire face.

"What's up Big Homie?" I asked and extended the joint his way.

After taking a few hits, he passed it back. "I heard you knocked 'em off pretty good today," he stated with a hint of pride in his voice.

"That I did," I said and removed three large stacks from under my mattress.

"Damn, that's a nice knot, how much did you hit them for?"

"I tagged them for three hundred and fifty ducats to be exact."

"Damn, let your Big Homie borrow a hundred, if you could stand it." He asked studying my reaction.

"Stand it, Cuz I feel like Nelson Rockefeller. The question is; is a hundred all you need?" I questioned and extended a stack his way.

"Nah Lil Homie I'm cool, I just wanted to see where your heart was at."

"Check homie, Cuz I got straight love for you, you been like a big brother to me. I'll never forget the love you extended my way when I first got here, when I didn't have a pot to piss in or a window to throw it out. Whatever I got, you're good to get, all you gotta do is ask."

"I appreciate it Lil Homie."

"Check it out Big Homie; do you know anyone selling a good TV and a radio?"

"Yeah, I could get you a good thirteen inch color TV and 8 track player for about one hundred and twenty dollars. Check with me after lunch, they're about to have count, I'm going to get you in the morning."

Although the Black Market was the quickest way to acquire a TV and a radio, the appliance didn't come with a warranty, nor was it on your books, meaning the guards could come take it anytime. With Nicole missing in action, and my refusal to accept any help from my family, I was determined to live off the land. I turned away from the bars to find my nosey ass cellmate all in my business.

"Man, did you really win all that gambling?" he asked, and initiated the first conversation we had since my arrival.

"Yes," I said and flashed my huge jailhouse bank roll on him.

"Man you must be pretty good, I wish I knew how to play."

"It's not hard," I said still playing alone.

"Hey Floyd do you think I could borrow ten dollars?"

"Ten dollars, shit that's all you need?" I asked baiting him even farther.

"Well, since you asked I could really use about twenty-five ducats if that's cool with you?"

"Nah Nigga that isn't cool. Nigga you got your mother fucking nerve to ask me for anything. I been in this cell for a whole month and you haven't offered me anything. Now you want to borrow some money. Nigga you done lost your rabbit ass mind."

"Man you don't have to talk to me like that."

"Nigga I'll talk to you anyway I want, Punk-Ass Nigga!"

"Listen man, forget I even asked."

"Nigga it was forgotten the moment you opened your motherfucking mouth. Now shut the fuck up Nigga, you're fucking up my high." I said and took a hit off the joint and blew the smoke in his direction.

I couldn't believe I allowed this mark-ass Nigga get me all roused up. Feeling the immediate effects of the weed I turned towards the window and stared out into the San Francisco Bay. Suddenly, thoughts of Nicole swept through my mind leaving me even more frustrated.

Although I hadn't seen or heard from her in over six months, not a day had passed that I hadn't thought about her. Even now it was still hard for me to believe she played me the way she did. Not only did she leave me for dead, she robbed me of my son and my money, my two most prized possessions. She and her punk-ass daddy acted like I was going away for life. I wondered if they knew in five short years I'd be back on the scene a hundred times worse than I'd ever been.

Getting Used To It
–Chapter 8–

The following morning I awoke with a slight hangover. I decided to skip breakfast so I could have an extra hour to myself before I went to work. The dice game didn't start until nine and didn't stop until three. After stashing the money I needed for a TV and radio I headed to the recreation yard hoping today was just as productive as yesterday.

"Excuse me young brother, if you're not in a hurry I would like to have a word with you," an older black man in his late 40's approached me the moment I exited my cell.

"What can I do for you Sir?" I asked, somewhat curious by this exchange.

"Well my brother you know these cells don't have walls and a man's voice can travel from one end of the tier to the other with the greatest of ease. Last night I couldn't help but catch a bar of your conversation, and what disturbed me more than anything was your frequent use of the N-word. Now I understand you're fresh off the streets, and old habits die hard, but out respect for yourself, and our people, I would appreciate if you would exercise some restraint. That word is vile, repugnant and was created to rob us of our true worth as a people. We're not Niggers we're Africans!"

"When you put it like that I can't help but respect it. Rest assured, in the future I will work extremely hard to erase that word from my vocabulary."

"Thanks a lot my brother, I would really appreciate that. By the way my name is Brother Kalif," he said and extended his hand.

"Pretty Boy Floyd." I happily shook his hand, which in turn would become the beginning of a long and rewarding friendship.

Immediately thereafter, I found myself spending a great deal of time around Brother Kalif. Not only was he extremely intelligent, he was an expert in Black History, the type of history that wasn't taught in public school, but was equally as important to the black man's movement and his desperate attempt to understand his identity in this foreign land we call America.

A scholar and a teacher, Brother Kalif was knowledgeable in all aspects of African American history, especially the Civil Rights movement in which he spoke so passionately about. It was through his teachings I learned about George and Jonathan Jackson, William Christmas, James McClain, and Ruchell Cinque Magee, who happened to be the only surviving member of the August 7, 1970 Marin County Court Takeover in which young seventeen year old Jonathan Jackson stormed inside the courthouse fully armed and took the judge, district attorney, and several members of the jury hostage, before fleeing with McClain, Christmas, and Magee, all of whom were San Quentin prisoners scheduled for trial that day.

Unbeknownst to young Jonathan, San Quentin's guards were not bound by the same rules of engagement that government and local officials were. As Jonathan and his posse proceeded to the local radio station, San Quentin's guards opened fire killing the judge, Jonathan, William Christmas, and James McClain. Miraculously, the jury emerged relatively unscathed, while the DA ended up permanently paralyzed, and Cinque, although seriously wounded survived the ordeal only to be charged with kidnap, murder, and conspiracy charges.

Although scheduled for court that day, George Jackson was not on the list. Convicted of simple burglary, it was in prison that George discovered his true calling and became the most celebrated black figure in the history of the California's Department of

Corrections. After reading George Jackson's the *Soledad Brothers*, and *Blood in my Eyes*, I became fascinated by the unwavering dedication, courage, and sacrifices made by these remarkable brothers. Through Brother Kalif, I learned about Nat Turner, Marcus Garvey, and Medgar Evers. It was also through his teachings I gained a deep sense of humanity and compassion towards my fellow brothers. Although I still maintained a gangster's mentality, I knew my days of gang banging was a thing of the past.

      Brother Kalif was more than a father figure, he was by far the most honorable man I ever met. I understood and supported the struggles but I was far from pledging my allegiance to another cause. My loyalty was, and still remained to the organize advancement of the Crips. Nevertheless, I continued to drain Brother Kalif for his immense knowledge and shared his teachings with my fellow Crips, all of whom seemed to be searching for something new.

      June 1982 was the first I heard of Juneteenth. In an effort to acquire a much deeper understanding of it's actual meaning I turned to Brother Kalif. I always relied on Brother Kalif to teach me something that no one else knew. It was during this discussion I discovered Abraham Lincoln's wartime proclamation, which took effect January 1, 1863 freed slaves in parts of the south that he had no control over, and left slaves in slavery in parts of the country that he presided over. Learning more from Kalif each day, he taught me the Emancipation Proclamation freed few slaves. Slavery officially came to an end on December 6, 1865 when Congress passed a constitutional amendment that outlawed slavery. Over a hundred and forty years later, out of ignorance or indifference many blacks continued in their efforts to make June 19th a national holiday, and bestow Abraham Lincoln as the Great White Savior that freed the slaves.

      Brother Kalif had always warned me to be extremely careful when reading about Black History, which in a sense was written by Europeans. For many Blacks, Black history was a cross between urban legend and popular beliefs. Most Blacks would rather live a lie than unseal the cold vicious truth about our ancestry, which can be found in the skeleton remains buried in every city, town, and state in this land we call America.

In an effort to share my findings, I composed a four-page essay and circulated it amongst my homies. A few days later my essay appeared in the San Quentin newspaper, along with my name and photograph. I later learned Brother Kalif was so impressed he submitted the essay and requested they publish it. They readily agreed. I was surprised by the overwhelming responses. My popularity soared, and at the age of nineteen I was on the fast track of becoming one of several young leaders that were handpicked to take the Crips to the next level.

On the eve of June 19th Brother Kalif asked if I minded reciting my essay and sharing a few thoughts with my fellow convicts which were closer to my age than any of the other scheduled speakers. I happily agreed. Although my essay illustrated the significance of June 19th, I looked forward to sharing the science behind my thinking. Right or wrong, correct or incorrect, I accepted whatever Brother Kalif said as the final word, a word that I never questioned.

The festivities were scheduled to commence immediately after breakfast. The upper yard was jammed pack, with Blacks on one side and Whites and Mexicans on the other. It was a pure joy to witness so many brothers laughing and joking with one and another. In prison there wasn't a lot to look forward to, therefore when such an occasion did arise prisoners seemed to take full advantage of it, it was a beautiful day.

I lost count of how many brothers approached me and praised me for the essay I put forth. I accepted their kind words with a handshake and recorded this moment as one of the finest moments of my life. Never in my life did the thoughts and opinions of my peers have such a profound effect on me.

I maneuvered my way through the crowd at the sight of Brother Kalif approaching. Yes indeed I thought, this was most definitely a special occasion, because this was the first time I had ever seen Brother Kalif with smile on his face. Just as I reached him his smile quickly shifted to a look of grave concern. Before I had a chance to grasp the situation, Brother Kalif yanked me by the shirt just as a Mexican swung his knife at the back of my head barely grazing my scalp. I quickly regained my composure; only to

I find I was in the midst of a full-scale race riot unfolding right before my eyes.

In the heat of battle, most blacks ran like a stampede of wild horses, while those that stayed were quickly butchered by a crowd of charging Mexicans. Prison officials quickly brought the disturbance under control by delivering multiple shotgun rounds into the crowd. As I scanned the crowd in search of Brother Kalif, I spotted him battling one Mexican while another was coming up behind him. Without a moment's hesitation, I rushed to his defense and was quickly blindsided by a rubber bullet before I could reach him. The next thing I knew I was laid out face down on the ground struggling to clear my head. Unable to gain enough strength to get back on my feet, I could hear the guards ordering everyone to remain face down on the ground. The shooting came to a stop and the Goon Squad quickly moved in with batons and shields. The riot was over.

The Mexicans struck first, catching the Blacks totally by surprise and vulnerable to a well-orchestrated attack. I felt a deep sense of anger and loss when I learned three blacks were killed, forty-nine injured, with twenty-three in serious condition. Brother Kalif was stabbed six times and was admitted to the prison hospital. One by one, each prisoner was escorted back to their respective cells. It was there I learned my square-ass cellmate was sent to an outside hospital in serious condition. Knowing his bitch-ass, he was probably talking to a couple of white boys in his bible study class when he got his issue.

Later that evening, I laid awake trying to make sense of the day's events; I wasn't mad but I was disappointed at the realization that so many Blacks ran. Growing up in the hood I was taught no matter what, a man didn't run. Win, lose, or draw you had to fight. I could understand a man running at the sight of a gun, but a knife required hand-to-hand combat.

The prison was placed on total lockdown and for the next three weeks all activities were suspended and we were confined to our cells and given a hot meal and a shower every three days. The prolonged confinement was designed to weaken a man's aggression. It was a proven fact that time healed all wounds, and mended bruised egos. That would whole true in most cases but not this one. There was no way possible a real gangster could allow what the Mexicans did to go unpunished. It was on us to rewrite the wrong, and I was determined to play my part. They made their move, now it was time for us to make ours.

Twenty-two days following the riot we were escorted to the chow hall one unit at a time. Control feeding was the first step in a phase-out program designed to return the facility back to normal operations.

Willie Payne was an old school soldier out of Oakland, and one of Brother Kalif's closest associates. An elder statesman and one of the most recognizable and respected figures in San Quentin. It was only fitting that he took the lead in organizing our response. I sat quietly at the chow hall table and listened as a number of suggestions passed back and forth. It was a meeting of old minds, a process that was designed to create the best possible plan of attack. I couldn't do anything but respect and trust those in charge to lead us to victory.

"I say the best time to strike would be immediately after lunch. Pretty Boy, we need you to skip lunch and post up in your cell. On our way to lunch, each of us will slide you our knife. As soon as lunch is over we got to be the first ones back to the unit. While the guards are busy patting everyone down, leaving the chow hall will give us the perfect opportunity to secure our weapons and position ourselves for attack. Once they open the grill gate that'll be the signal to take off. Take off on the closest Mexican to you, hit him quick, hit him hard, then retreat back to your cell."

"Check it out OG, that sounds like a winning strategy, but Cuz I'm not trying to sit in the cell and pass out knives, I'm a Crip. I got to be on the front line. I think it'll be better suited if Smooth stayed behind." Smooth's eyes lit up like that was the best news he heard in years.

"How you feel about that Smooth?" Willie asked as he acknowledged Smooth for the first time.

"Yeah I could handle that," Smooth said and breathed a sigh of relief.

"Okay that's a done deal."

The plan was finalized, there was nothing else to talk about. On our way back to our cell, Smooth pulled up on me.

"Pretty Boy, I really appreciate that. Man I'ma tell you I didn't know how I was going to get out of this one. I owe you big time. Man I'm a pimp, I'm not a gangster."

"Don't worry about it homie, you don't have to explain. Look at it like we helped each other." I knew fear when I saw it, and Smooth was most definitely scared to death. I liked Smooth and I was glad I was able to give him a way out. Everybody wasn't born to fight, and I understood the difference between being scared and being a coward. A scared man under the right circumstances would eventually overcome his fears, but a coward would sacrifice his mother, wife, and kids to save his own ass.

For a youngster that was about to embark on my first mission I slept relatively easy. I had already selected my target, and I couldn't wait to serve his ass. Puppet carried himself like he was the hardest motherfucker on the planet. Bald head and tattooed from his neck to his feet, he looked the part, but the million dollar question was could he play the part. With my height and weight I knew I couldn't afford to come at him half-stepping. My first blow had to disable him, and my second blow had to lay him out. Anything less might come with severe consequences.

In the event things didn't go as planned, I packed all my property. What concerned me the most were the two trigger happy armed guards posted inside the unit with orders to shoot at the first sign of a disturbance. Operating inside the unit always came with greater risk. I was standing at my cell door when the locks were released for chow. I stepped on the tier and came face to face with my target. I smiled and nodded which seemed to take him totally by surprise. He nodded back but maintained his cold deadly look. Just as planned, Smooth was waiting inside his cell, I slid him my knife and proceeded to the chow hall.

Considering what was about to take place, the chow hall was free of the tension that usually accompanied a plan of this magnitude. I guess you could say it was the calm before the storm. Immediately after devouring my lunch, I said a quick prayer asking

God to watch over me as I set out to inflict serious bodily harm on another human. At the announcement chow was over, I rose to my feet and headed to the exit. After undergoing a thorough pat-down I proceeded back to the unit where I found Smooth standing nervously at his cell door.

"You be careful Pretty Boy," Smooth said and handed me my knife.

I was surprised to see he had little stickers on the knives to assure everyone got what they came with. I placed the shank inside my waistline and proceeded to my cell where I posted up and waited.

Prisoners were slowly returning from the chow hall in a gradual attempt to steal as much time out of their cells as they possibly could. Although solitary confinement didn't bother me, I knew from past cellmates it weighed extremely heavy on some. I kept my eyes on the grill gate waiting for Billy Bad Ass to hit the tier.

My heart pounded with anticipation when I finally spotted him. I couldn't believe the nerve this dude had as he walked pass a group of blacks like he was invincible. His bold behavior only increased my desire to inflict serious harm upon him. I waited until he got to his cell before I slid my hand under my shirt and gripped the handle of my seven-inch shank. Keeping a close eye on the two-armed guards I waited patiently for the grill gate to close.

Click! the sound of the grill gate closing, follow by another click that allowed the cell doors to open resonated down the tier like the opening bell at a championship fight. At that very moment the 4th tier of East Block Bayside erupted in an uproar that even caught me by surprise. By the time I pulled out my knife, my intended target had his hands full fending off a brutal attack from James X, an old school member of the Nation of Islam. Seizing the opportunity, I came up behind Puppet and drove my knife so hard in the back of his neck I could feel his spine shatter under my force. If he wasn't dead, he was most certainly paralyzed from the neck down. As Puppet hit the ground I slung my knife over the tier and retreated back to my cell while James X smiled and stared at me in amazement.

From start to finish, the brutal assault lasted no more than a minute before the two armed guards squashed the disturbance with multiple shotgun rounds. The smell of heavy gun-smoke and an air of silence lingered inside the unit. I stood at my cell door and watched as they carried the wounded away. I couldn't believe the amount of damage we inflicted in such a short period of time. This was a constant reminder that one must remain vigilant at all times. Relaxing for even a second could be detrimental.

Willie Banks and James X were among ten blacks that were immediately taken to the hole. Control feeding was suspended and we were officially placed back on full lock-down status once again. Just as I prepared to turn in for the night two guards appeared at my cell.

"Anderson, cuff it up."

I could tell by the expression on their faces this was anything but a routine cell search. I was handcuffed and escorted downstairs to a holding cage no bigger than a phone booth. One guard stood watch while the other returned to my cell. Ten minutes later he returned carrying what appeared to be a nine-inch shank.

There was no need to speak on the obvious; the set up was clear from the gate. In accordance to prison policy, I was transported to a D-Section, the Management Control Unit to await a disciplinary hearing.

From the moment the security door closed I felt an air of evilness, an unholy force looming inside the building. This was most definitely the devil's house. As I was escorted to my cell, I could feel the hardcore stares from the Mexican population. In their eyes in order for me to be placed in the hole during an institutional lock-down meant only one thing, I must have participated in the afternoon melee that left three of their homies dead, and several injured. No sooner than I stepped inside my cell I heard a low pitch whistle, a coded call used among Crips. I whistled back.

"Say homie I got a line coming your way," an unknown voice called out.

A few minutes later a fish line with a note attached to it appeared in front of my cell. It was an introduction from Askari, a Rollin 60's Crip. Cuz gave me the location of enemy fractions, which to my surprise didn't consist of Mexicans, but another group of Blacks that called themselves the Vanguards.

With the migration of Crips and Bloods coming to age and entering the California Department of Corrections in mass numbers every major prison in the system rushed to create an organized movement to compete and challenge the existing powers that be. At California State Prisons San Quentin and Folsom you had an organized body of Crips from every hood known as the C-Machine. At Soledad there was an organized body of Crips known as Blue Magic, and at Traci there was an organized body of Crips and Bloods known as the Vanguards. As brilliant as that ideology appeared on the surface, their leadership lacked the vision or intellect to see it through. Imagine a world where Crips and Bloods were united under one front, that's a frightening look.

Immediately after arriving at San Quentin, following a riot at Tracy, the majority of Crips in the Vanguards begin to defect to the C-Machine. The Vanguards responded by declaring war on the C-Machine which eventually lead to their demise. Unable to hit the compound or any other unit at San Quentin the surviving members were placed in D-section; which eventually became their stronghold. Askari informed me we were scheduled for recreation at nine in the morning, and there was a strong likelihood they didn't know me.

In the event I made it to the yard before him, I was to take off on the first dude that tried to question my affiliation. Every gang had a security team whose job it was to check the status of all new arrivals to determine if they were friend or foe. Regardless of the odds against you, when questioned, a true gangsta must claim his affiliation. Not to do so was the act of a coward that came with severe repercussions. Thirty minutes later he sent me a Speed Stick deodorant, a book of matches, a half of bottle of baby oil and a step by step manual how to make a knife.

I followed his instruction to the letter and felt like a proud student that got an A in chemistry. Less than twenty-four hours after putting in work on the Mexicans, I was about to embark on another mission, this time it was against a faceless enemy who skin was the same color as mine. Against a crew I never saw a day in my life. The first time I ever heard of Vanguards was when Lil Bull wrote and informed me that Salt-Rock had joined forces with them.

It didn't matter what the beef was about, or who the fuck you were, if you had a problem with a Crip you had a problem with me. The following morning I was up bright and early. For some strange reason I felt uplifted. Unbeknownst to me at that time I had developed an appetite for putting in work. Askari and I were the only Crips in the unit. Depending on which end of the tier they started on, would decide which one of us hit the yard first.

As fate would have it, Askari won the luck of the draw. I was standing at my cell door when they escorted him to the yard. We acknowledged each other with a smile and a nod. Not only was I surprised to find he was way smaller than I, he was smiling and joking with the guard as if he was on his way to play handball or some other type of recreational activities.

No sooner than Cuz hit the yard shots rang out. My chest swelled with pride. Cuz went out there and took care of his business. It was nothing short of an honor meeting him. In all my years of banging I never met a scared Crip.

Later that afternoon, I was transferred to C-Section, a Security Housing Unit, which also had a sense of evilness lurking inside its wall. Unlike D-section there was no introduction. Not only did the Mexicans and Whites eye me suspiciously, so did the Blacks.

A Born Soldier

– Chapter 9 –

The following morning, immediately after breakfast, the blacks were allowed to go the recreation yard, which consisted of an enclosed concrete and steel structure and supervised by two armed guards. Prior to hitting the yard, each prisoner was stripped searched and had to spread the crack of their ass to make sure they didn't have any weapons hidden in their rectum. This was the most humiliating act a man could ever experience; it was also one you never got use to no matter how many times you had to go through it.

I approached the main entrance of the yard and did a quick visual scan. As I waited for the guards to remove my handcuffs I noticed a group of blacks watching me from afar. By the expression on their faces it was hard to tell if they were friendly or foe.

I stepped on the yard and spotted Willie Banks, James X, and Papa C sitting at a table engaged in a conversation with several other brothers. As I proceeded in their direction I heard an old familiar voice call out my name. I turned around and a smile instantly appeared on my face.

"Slow Drag," I said and embraced my old school partner.

Slow Drag and I first met when we were twelve, serving our first term at California Youth Authority, Fred C. Nellis. Although we never kicked it on the streets, every time I served time he was there. For the exception of our height we could have passed for brothers. Dark skin and handsome by all measures, we used to bet on who could knock the prettiest girl at our unit dances.

"Pretty Boy, what's up Cuz?" he asked.

"Same shit, different location. What's up with you?"

"Shit you know me, a little bit of everything. Cuz you haven't changed a bit. I heard about your work. Willie Banks and James X said he tried to sideline you, but you weren't having it. Cuz said you told him you got to be on the front line."

"Yeah, Cuz was tripping. I guess he felt I was too young to be on the battlefield. He wanted me to wait in the cell and pass out knives; you know I wasn't going for that."

"You know if anybody knows; I know. Come on Cuz the big homies want to meet you."

As we approached the trio that had been scrutinizing my every move just a few moments ago I immediately felt an overwhelming sense of superiority. The poise and confidence each man exhibited was much like Willie Banks and James X. The only difference was these men were Crips. The fact that Slow Drag, a leader in his own right, paid homage to these individuals only clarified what I already believed.

"Cuz this is Pretty Boy Floyd, East Side Neighborhood Rollin 40's Crip Gang," Slow Drag announced and added. "Pretty Boy this is Tabari, Askari, and Suma."

I acknowledged the big homies with a handshake and a nod. I took an instant liking to Tabari and Askari whose handshakes were just as affectionate as their smiles. Suma, on the other hand was a mystery, quiet and serious with a handshake so firm for a brief second I wondered was he trying to test my strength.

"We heard you put down a cold demonstration yesterday," Tabari said like a proud father. "We appreciate the way you represented Crip. As a Crip, regardless what city or set you represent, the actions of one will always reflect on Crips as a whole. Just like we smash those that disgrace us, in the same light we must complement those whose actions are worthy of our praise. You did your thing little homie."

With a simple nod Tabari surrendered the floor.

"Lil-Homie you took it upon yourself to handle what needed to be handled. If more homies would have taken the same initiative, the Mexican Mafia would think a thousand times before they try that shit again. The only thing they understand and respect is power. Mark my word, this is only the beginning, and I guarantee you before it's all said and done Crips will be running this shit. It's crucial that we come together in the name of Crips and establish a force so powerful that anyone in their right mind would think twice about challenging us."

He scratched his chin and continued, "It's obvious by your willingness to stand up without being called, and your intellectual mindset, speaking on your published piece on June 19 that you embody everything Crips stand for. Cuz, it's neither our aim nor our desire to force our thoughts and beliefs upon you. It is out of love for Crips that prompt us to share with you what others have shared with us. Under your pillow you will find some literature. Read it, study it, and if you're interested we'll go more into detail next yard. If not, we do understand everything is not for everybody."

"Alright Little Cuz, we'll see you next yard," Suma concluded and smiled for the first time. I walked away overwhelmed with a deep sense of pride.

Tabari, Askari, and Suma were Crip legends. Their names echoed in every hood, their representation of Crips was noted and reported in every prison, Youth Authority, and neighborhood in the State of California. They were the brain behind the Crip movement that was sweeping through the state like an organized wildfire. I was touched by their presence and honored by their words.

I returned to my cell and immediately retrieved the literature that was titled: *The Clandestine Revolutionary International Party Structure*; which turned out to be a ten page thirty-eight article constitution. My immediate impression was one of confusion. With words like revolutionary, comrade, the party, the people, the government, I felt like I was reading a manifesto straight from Black Panther Party. I was dumbfounded; this was most definitely not what I expected. I wasn't a freedom fighter, nor did I give a fuck about the people. I was a Crip, a criminal, a gangster with an undying thirst to get rich. I was about organizing crime, the creation of the first Black Mafia.

Unable to make sense out of any of this, I shot Slow Drag a kite expressing my concerns. Cuz responded immediately. Cuz claimed the revolutionary aspect of The Party was necessary to turn young gang bangers into warriors, and indoctrinate them with a greater purpose. Although the language, in many ways was similar to the Black Panther Party and Black Guerrilla Family the purpose was entirely different. The greatest threat to Crips was the Crips itself, which was evident by Crip on Crip violence that was plaguing the streets. The party purpose was to recruit the brightest minds out of every hood, and establish a force so powerful that every Crip in the nation would be held accountable for their actions.

Slow Drag made a convincing argument, and the following yard period I became the youngest member of the Clandestine Revolutionary International Party Structure. When a leader becomes a follower, the teacher becomes the student. And I was willing.

During the next six months I became a dedicated pupil with a dying thirst for knowledge. Through Tabari, I learned the art of diplomacy; sometimes it's not what you say but how you say it. Charismatic with a gift for gab, Tabari taught me under the right guidance you could turn a scared man into a stone cold killer. Through Askari I learned to be decisive and never waiver. A stone cold disciplinarian, Askari followed the rules and regulations set forth to the letter and held everyone accountable that didn't. Through Suma, I learned to lead by example and never order a man to do something I wouldn't do myself. The most respected and feared member of The Party, Suma, was a General that led his troops from the front line. At the end of my orientation, I was given the Swahili name Jabari, which meant fearless, and Slow Drag was given the name Kujua, which meant knowing of all things.

The Party was a secret society within the C-Machine, which was governed by the Central Committee which consisted of Tabari, Askari, and Suma. Although each man had his own unique style of leading, their ideology and objective was the same. By the end of 1982 the C-Machine was over three hundred strong and steady growing.

C-Section was the central headquarters where all major decisions were made. The recreation yard resembled a military style boot camp where each member was required to participate in an hour long exercise regimen, followed by an hour long class in Swahili, and a verbal lesson in how to make knives, zip-guns, and crossbows. It was amazing how many weapons a man could make out of common goods such as magazines, baby oil, and speed stick deodorant.

With the turn of the New Year, 1983 would mark one of the most violent years in San Quentin history. The war between the Blacks and Mexicans would escalate to new heights and eventually spill over into the SHU. The Mexican Mafia closed the year by carrying out three planned attacks against the Black Guerilla Family, prompting the C-Machine to intervene by issuing a warning stating 'the next time they laid a finger on any Black inside the unit we would perceive that as a declaration of war'. The Mexican Mafia responded the next day by stabbing Jahi, a top ranking BGF in the eye causing him to lose his sight.

It became evident when Kujua and I were invited to sit in a Central Committee meeting, as they planned our responses, we were being groomed for a higher calling. It was during this session I received an in depth look at the inner working of the committee, and the Raw Intellect each man brought to the table. Not only was I impressed, I was extremely proud to be a part of this group. I quietly listened as strategies were kicked back and forth, once a plan of action was decided, it became Askari's duty to see that it was carried out. Askari instructed me to select ten hitters, two on each tier, ready to go on a moment notice. He also instructed Kujua to examine the daily security reports and search for the best targets to hit.

Although the Security Housing Unit was one of the most secured buildings in the prison, it was also the most dangerous. Reason being, the entire population was there for disciplinary sanctions. The number one objective in any assault was to inflict as much damage as possible, regardless of the consequences. Unlike general population where you could kill a man and get away, in the SHU whatever you did was done with the understanding you would get caught.

C-Section had five tiers, with fifty cells with open bars on each tier. Going back and forth to the recreation yard, or back and forth to the shower was like a game of chance. Walking too slow or too close to the cell bars was enough to get your whole head knocked off. Taking a page out of the Mexican Mafia playbook we allowed a whole month to pass before we launched a full-scale assault on the entire Mexican population as they returned from the recreation yard. Handcuffed and defenseless, they were like ducks on the pond. . In a Security Housing Unit, prisoners were allowed to go the recreational yard three times a week. On days the Blacks went to yard, the Mexicans and Whites remained in the unit to take showers, and attend sick-call, vice-versa. When they went to the yard we remained in the unit.

As a security measure each yard period a designated Black was instructed to stay inside the unit and keep an eye and ear on the Mexicans to see what they were up to. Going and coming from the yard was a game of chance that required each prisoner to travel down a narrow walkway, pass countless enemies, each or anyone bearing a spear, zip-gun, or weapon designed to cause great bodily injury.

Nearly a month had passed since the Mexicans stabbe Jahi in the eye. Satisfied, the Mexicans were relaxed and with their guards down CCO ordered a full-fledged assault. With attacks being launched from every Black cell, the administration ceased all movement and lined the gun rails with extra armed guards, and escorted the remainder of the Mexicans back to their cells under the protection of full body shields. All and all it was deemed a success, a well-coordinated strike carried out by the C-Machine, the BGF, and the UBN, the United Blood Nation. The Mexican Mafia had forced past rivals to become future alliances. It was a beautiful day to be Black. The following day was our turn to step in the line of fire. After undergoing a strip search and having my hands cuffed behind my back I exited my cell fully aware of the six enemy factions that were posted up like landmines in my path to the recreation yard. Relying on instincts and my ability to react quickly to danger I proceeded to the center stairs that lead to the yard.

Much to my surprise and relief, we received a pass to and

from the yard. While the Mexicans showed great restraint, the C-machine, BGF, UBN continued to launch a full-scale attack on selected targets. The longer the Mexicans went without answering, the more concerned the homies became. It was obvious to all they were up to something, exactly what, no one knew.

The Mexican Mafia were the architects of some of the most elaborate killings noted in the California Department of Corrections. They were by far the most violent and most powerful organization in California's prisons, and on the streets. Anyone that said different was in denial.

The day we all dread came twenty-seven days later during yard recall. No sooner than the guards escorted the first group of blacks to their cells the unit alarm sounded, followed by a succession of shotgun blast. We soon learned Ghost from Venice Shoreline Crips was the victim of a vicious attack. As it turned out, a Mexican was hiding under Ghost's bed when he returned from the yard. Before the guards had a chance to remove his handcuffs, the Mexican rolled from under the bed and stabbed Ghost twenty-six times before a black female guard stormed inside the cell and stopped the Mexican from killing him. Miraculously, Ghost survived the attack; but the cold part about it, it could have been prevented had Ghost rolled up his mattress before going to the yard; which was something we all did as a security measure to prevent this sort of thing from happening. The Mexicans recognized a flaw in Cuz' security and capitalized on it. Lucky for him it didn't cause him his life.

In response to Ghost's assault, the C-Machine shifted its attacks from the Mexicans to the guards. No one was spared, not even the black officers whom we had a cordial understanding with. Every guard that came on the tier, regardless of rank or color got his issue. The administration responded by calling for a sit down between the Blacks, Mexicans and prison officials.

Slow Drag (Kujua) was delegated to speak for all Blacks. One of C-Machine's main grievances was the fact that a vast number of Blacks were being held in the hole even though their SHU program had expired. The situation with the Mexicans was an entirely different matter. Too much blood had been spilled to enter into a peace agreement. The homies only did so after the administration had agreed to all our terms.

Staying true to their word, the following week Tabari, Suma, and fourteen other blacks were release to general population. Gradually, C-Section returned to normal operations. Under Askari's leadership, the C-Machine took on a more serious vibe. With Askari, everything was black and white, there was no in between, and there were no justifiable excuses. Rules were made to follow, if you violated you got dealt with accordingly.

Ten days later, Ghost returned from the hospital in bandages, bruised and in obvious pain. There wasn't a single homie that didn't feel his pain. Out of twenty-six stab wounds, five were to his face, and two to his neck. The mere sight of Cuz had induced a renewed call for vengeance, which Askari not only welcomed, but encouraged.

The following yard period, Slow Drag (Kujua) and I pulled Askari to the side in a last ditch effort to convince him it wasn't in the C-machine's best interest to violate the peace agreement. It was our position that our word as an organization was more important than the bruised egos of a few radicals. As far as we were concerned breaking our word would not only kill our credibility, but would also destroy any chances we may have in the future of negotiating other matters that we deemed important.

After saying our peace, Askari informed us C-Machine never had any intentions of honoring a truce with the Mexicans. It was obvious from past dealings that the Mexicans couldn't be trusted, and in Guerilla Warfare trickery was a tool commonly used to mislead your enemies into lowering their guards.

Askari closed by saying, "Peace with the Beast was not an option, the Party's main objective was the total annihilation of the Mexican Mafia and its supporters."

I took Askari's words to heart and returned to my cell with a deeper understanding of the state of affairs between the Blacks and Mexicans. The more I learned the more I realized things were far beyond repair. The hatred between the Blacks and Mexicans was fueled by a fire that had been burning far beyond my years on earth. True peace was nowhere in sight; only time would determine the winner.

While some believed an organization was only as strong as its members, it was my belief an organization was only as strong as its leaders. The C-Machine was blessed with some of the sharpest minds Crips had to offer. After spending a year under the likes of Tabari, Askari, and Suma I had no doubt whatsoever in the homies' ability to formulate a winning strategy that would lead us to victory.

Little did I know I was engaged in a war that started way past the beginning of my time, and more than likely would still be relevant years after I was dead and gone. As days turned into weeks, and weeks turned into months, and months turned into years I begin to take a long deep look at the events that led to this moment. I was twenty-one years old, but I felt like forty, and for the first time I couldn't say for certain how things were going to turn out. I was all in, and determined to make a serious impact. In order to do that I had to stay focused, and abandon all thoughts about the streets and my past life. C-Section was my home, built of concrete and steel. Hot in the summer and cold in the winter.

Due to the overcrowding in North Block, death row inmates were being transferred to the fifth tier in C-Section. In an effort to ease the overcrowding, and establish a new front for the growing number of Death Row prisoners, I along with fifteen other Crips were transferred to East Block Bayside, a newly formed SHU unit.

It was there I met Bam, aka Nassar, Rollin 60's Crip. From the moment I introduced myself I got a funny vibe from Cuz, as if he didn't respect a Crip representing San Diego. Being that Cuz was the chairman of the subcommittee in East Block, and therefore the highest-ranking member in the unit I kept my tongue in check. But I vowed if Cuz ever tried to disrespect me I would deal with him in the same manner I would deal with anyone else that disrespected me, regardless of the consequences.

In an effort to contain us, the administration cleared out the fifth tier in East Block Bayside and made it a designated Crip tier. It seemed like every week Crips were rolling in by the numbers. Most of whom I knew from my three tours in the California Youth

Authority.

One thing good I could say about Nassar, Cuz was an exercise fanatic, which was evident by his massive structure. For a big man he moved fast. There were more times than not when the machine was forced to exercise the entire yard period. At first it appeared excessive; those that originally frowned down on this vigorous routine quickly accepted it when their strength and endurance grew. Just as I started to take a liking to Cuz' style of teaching, BJ, Freddie Mingo, and a group of Crips known as Blue Magic arrived from Soledad following a race riot.

Blue Magic hit our yard and refused to follow our program, which was mandatory for every Crip to follow regardless if you was a part of the C-Machine or not. Nassar's inactivity made a few of us question his leadership. Little did he know, while he was in peaceful negotiations with BJ and his crew, which wasn't getting him anywhere; myself, Mumbles from Rollin 60's, and Devil from Shotgun Crips were plotting to blast them all, Nassar included.

Following protocol, I shot a kite to the mainline requesting permission to take off. Tabari and Suma responded by attending our next yard period from general population. It was clear to all we had reached a point of no return.

I stood at security with a twelve-inch steel knife while Tabari, Suma, BJ, and Freddie Mingo met for three consecutive yard periods. I would have given my right arm to be a part of those meetings. The tension was so strong I could feel the adrenaline running from the top of my head to the bottom of my feet. In the event things took a turn for the worse, I was instructed to take off on BJ who was the bigger target in the Blue Magic crew. I knew my work and I knew it well. I never questioned, not for a second in my ability to bring this giant to his knees. It was obvious from the outside looking in things weren't going well. Whatever it was, BJ wasn't happy and Tabari and Suma weren't giving an inch.

Shortly before the meeting concluded, a small drizzle of rain was quickly followed by an outpour. While most inmates, and even the guards ran for shelter I remained at my post. Soaking wet Tabari and Suma rose from their crouched position, shook BJ's hand and patted him on the back. At first it appeared as though they had reached an agreement. Just when I began to relax, Tabari gave me the signal, and without hesitation I came from behind BJ and drove my knife through the back of his shoulder blade, and punctured his heart. I left the knife inside of him and kept moving. Death was immediate, and not even the guards knew he was hit until his huge frame stumbled forward and his lifeless body hit the ground face down.

On the fourth yard period, all the Crips were summoned to a meeting. It was there that the remainder of Blue Magic were informed at the age of nineteen BJ ratted on his fall partner. He gave a meager explanation why he did what he did, which went through one ear and out the other. Cuz disrespected the game, and as a result it cost him his life, plain and simple. Freddie Mingo stepped up to represent Blue Magic's interests and when it was all said and done Blue Magic and the C-Machine merged creating CCO, the Consolidated Crip Organization.

When Two Gangsters Collide, One Will Die
—Chapter 10—

After completing a twelve months SHU program, a straight year for a knife the guards placed in my cell I returned to general population to join Tabari, Suma, Talib, and a cast of Crips that were pushing our agenda with deadly force. It seemed like every week a busload of Crips were arriving from the county jail. Due to the lack of bed space in general population I was placed in A-Section. It was there I first met Sparks, an OG from Raymond Avenue Crips. It was also through Sparks I first learned of Blue Notes, a newly formed Crip organization that prided itself on the traditional values of Crips. The only two Crips in A-Section, Sparks and I became first friends despite our political differences. Standing a little over 6 feet 2 inches tall, with twenty-inch biceps, and a massive chest, it was obvious Sparks was capable of handling any situation that came our way. Like most Crips from Raymond Avenue Sparks was also serving a life sentence.

Upon my arrival back in general population, I was astounded to find how strong CCO had become. Under the guidance and vision of Tabari, Suma, and Talib another CCO General, CCO had risen to strengths beyond my wildest dreams. Taking a page from the past, "An enemy of my enemy is my friend," CCO joined forces with the Black Guerrilla Family and The United Blood Nation and unleashed a deadly campaign on the Mexican Mafia and its sympathizers; which so far had resulted in several killings and a grave number of assaults. The full might and resolve of a United Black front proved to be more than the Mexicans could handle.

By the summer of 1984, CCO was running general population and the flow of illegal contraband distributed on the compound. Talib, another one of CCO's Generals appointed me treasurer; which made me responsible for keeping a log of all CCO's holdings. I kept a meticulous record of every dollar made and every dollar spent. I knew how many TV's and radios we had and where they were located. Every member that made commissary was obligated to contribute five dollars, which quickly added up to hundreds every week. Every member that was short on funds was provided with a free TV and radio and a reasonable amount of commissary every week. CCO took care of its members; and in turn its members remained loyal.

CCO's presence was felt in every corner of every prison and every neighborhood in the State of California, as evidenced by the number of new arrivals and reports coming every prison and neighborhood. It was widely understood: anyone that came to prison for killing another Crip could never walk the compound. No one was exempt from getting a knife in the chest or their skull smashed. From the average Joe to a correctional guard, we didn't give a fuck, if you stepped out of line and we had something for you.

Just as CCO's strength and influence grew on the compound the Mexicans strength remain intact inside the SHU, which was particularly true in C-Section where the administration transferred over half the homies to East Block, diminishing our power significantly. Once the move was completed the administration called for another sit down between CCO and the Mexican Mafia. Against the advice of several homies, Askari sent Slow Drag to represent CCO, despite the fact we already broke our word once before.

Under heavy guard and with their hands cuffed behind their backs, Slow Drag and his Mexican counterpart were escorted downstairs to the classification room to discuss the terms of a peace treaty. Prior to entering the room, the Mexican managed to removed his handcuffs, retrieve a knife from the small of his back and stab Slow Drag twice in the chest while ten guards stood inches away. The sound of rapid gunshots being fire; followed by the sound of the unit alarm, and a still quietness that left everyone wondering what happened. Later we learned at the promising age of 21, Louis Montgomery aka Slow Drag was pronounced dead on arrival..

As in all tragedies there was a lesson to be learned. Never underestimate the will of your enemy, or the extent to which he will go to get revenge. Guard your life like a rich man guard his wealth. The Mexican Mafia had served us with a devastating blow; not only did they rob us of one of our most celebrated soldier; they stole our air of invincibility. It was a rude awakening, a valuable lesson, and one that came at a tremendous cost.

Immediately following Slow Drag's death, the California Department of Corrections implemented a statewide lockdown of all level three and four prisons. It was a predictable move, but there was nothing humanly possible they could do to stop the inevitable. It was obvious to all Slow Drag was set up, and it didn't matter if the lockdown lasted a week, a month, or a year; the administration was about to feel the full might of the Consolidated Crips Organization.

With a little less than two years left on my sentence, I accepted the cold reality I might not survive this experience. I was knee deep in the game, and freedom was secondary to surviving. Living in the lion's den, in order to survive you had to adopt the same mentality as a prisoner with a life sentence. I knew the score before the game started. The code was simple and could be answered with a few quick questions. How do you control a man that doesn't give a fuck about anything, not even life? Whose hatred runs so deep he'll kill you right in front of the police. How do you pacify a killer who seeks nothing out of life but the death and destruction of his enemies? You can't. In order to survive you must become just as cold, just as daring, and ten times as ruthless.

Following the death of Slow Drag; Tabari, Suma, Taliba and Talib were placed back in the SHU, leaving me and a hand full of CCO members on the compound. Less than forty-eight hours after general population was released off lock down, a Mexican was found dead in his cell with his skull crushed in. I was on the lower yard engaged in a conversation with Corrections Officer Williams, my work supervisor when the alarm sounded, and all prisoners were ordered back to their cells. As I approached my unit I noticed two members of the Goon Squad, which was equivalent to a Special Force Team, standing at the entrance searching the faces of everyone that went inside. No sooner than I made eye contact with one, I knew their search was over.

"Anderson follow us, the lieutenant would like to see you."

This was an order not a request. Once we hit the upper yard, out of the presence of other prisoners they stopped and placed me in handcuffs, which was a clear indication I wasn't returning back to my unit. Just as I was being led into the lieutenant's office, Sparks was being led out. I acknowledged his presence with a simple nod and took the first available seat inside the office.

"Anderson my name is Lt. Ryan. I'm here to inform you of your rights. You have a right to remain silent, anything you say can and will be used against you in a court of law. You have a right to legal representation, if you can't afford a lawyer one will be appointed for you. Do you understand these rights?"

"Yes," I respond.

"Due to the seriousness of these charges I would advise you to exercise your right to remain silent."

"If you don't mind me asking could you please tell me what is this about?"

"It's about the murder of inmate Victor Morales."

Unbeknownst to the administration Victor was a sleeper cell for the Mexican Mafia, and a important member in their organization. One of three workers in the prison commissary, Victor's sole duty was filling SHU's commissary orders where he smuggled drugs, hacksaw blades, handcuff keys, and classified communications going inside the hole. He had to be stopped!

After a formal reading charges there was nothing else to discuss, shortly thereafter, Sparks and I were escorted to the Adjustment Center, a maximum security housing unit, designed for prisoners charged with staff assaults and jail house murders. The Adjustment Center was the most secure unit in the state, but in actuality it was the Mexican Mafia stronghold, their headquarters where they governed not only every prison in the state, but every Mexican Gang on the streets of Southern California.

The following morning, I discovered not only was I the only black on the back of the first tier, I was two cells down from the Mexican that killed Slow Drag. On my way to the recreational yard, I passed his cell and made eye contact for the first time. He met my stare and held it for a moment. There was no need to speak; only cowards talked shit behind locked doors. He knew, just as I knew if the opportunity ever presented itself the odds of one of us surviving were slim to none.

Unlike C-section, the Adjustment Center recreational yards were much smaller and absent of any recreational equipment. Sparks was waiting at the gate when I hit the yard. After embracing five members of CCO, all of whom were in AC for stabbing a guard following Slow Drag's murder Sparks and I found a corner we could talk privately.

"What's up Cuz?" he asked.

"Cuz to be honest I don't have a clue."

"Yeah me neither. I think the only reason they grabbed us is because we were the only Crips in A-section."

"You know these pigs don't need a reason to do what they do. All they got to do is think a motherfucker did something to jack his ass up. I'm not tripping, fuck 'em and feed 'em fish. What cell they got you in?"

"I'm in 3AC 15, right next door to Bankhead. All the homies is on the third floor. What cell they got you in?"

"Cuz I'm in `1AC10, two cells down from the Mexican that killed Slow Drag."

"Cuz I know it's hard as a motherfucker seeing dude and you can't get at him."

"Cuz I'll risk my life to get at his ass."

"I know you would."

"Excuse me brothers," a black man in his early 50's with a salt and pepper beard, whom I recognized as a member of the Black Guerilla Family interrupted our conversation.

We acknowledged his presence and nodded for him to

speak his peace.

"I was told by the other brothers to speak to you about an issue that has been brewing for quite some time. As you can see this is a relatively small yard, and your numbers has been growing significantly in the past few weeks. We believe it would best serve all our interests if we have a sit down with the LT and secure your own yard, if that's cool with y'all?"

"That's fine with us," I said, feeling somewhat disturbed by his non-personal approach.

The brother didn't even feel the need to introduce himself, or greet us in the same manner of a soldier that was engaged in the same war. It became quite obvious the BGFs only desire was to get us off their yard, which we were more than glad to accommodate them.

After speaking with the other homies I learned they already had several fall outs with BGF that nearly resulted in knife play. Based on the relationship CCO had with the BGFs on the compound a physical confrontation was not in the best interest of either party. CCO's agenda was quite clear and regardless of my personal views it was my duty to enforce it.

I returned to my cell and had a better opportunity to check out my surroundings. At second glance it became obvious the administration had placed me behind enemy lines. Out of eighteen cells on the first tier, the Mexican Mafia occupied eleven cells. The remaining seven consisted of five Aryan Brotherhood, which in a sense were strong Mexican supporters, and one BGF, and I. There was something most certainly fishy about my placement.

Later that afternoon I received an incident report stating:

On July 14, 1984 at approximately 7:45 a.m., inmate D'Andre Anderson C-36222 and inmate Marcus Player D-75542 were observed by a reliable informant exiting the cell of Victor Morales B-74552. Shortly thereafter, inmate Anderson was observed placing a large object inside the fourth tier waste basket. A search of this area uncovered a 32 inch long steel pipe covered with a red substance.

At 8:05 a.m. I discovered the body of Victor Morales stuffed under his bed. A preliminary examination revealed inmate Morales

*was no longer breathing. I immediately activated the emergency
alarm, secured the area and contacted Sgt. Steve Kelly.*

I pled not guilty and requested a staff investigator. Using
their timeline there was no way possible I could be in two places at
the same time. San Quentin as most prisons in the California Department of Corrections operated on a control movement schedule.
On the morning of July 14, 1984 control movement started at 7:25
a.m. and ended at 7:35 a.m.. By 7:40 a.m. the prison was secure
and all movement was over. There was no way possible Sparks and
I could have made it from A-section to the lower yard during a
close movement without anyone seeing us. I was confident state
officials lacked the necessary evidence they needed to convict us.

On the day of my 22nd birthday I received a letter from the
Marin County District Attorney's Office stating:

*In the matter of Floyd Anderson and Marcus Player; Case
number: CA7466310, violation of penal code 187 is hereby dismissed due to insufficient evidence.*

I read the letter three times and kissed it. "Thank you God,"
I whispered and felt a huge sigh of relief.

"I take it you just received a bit of good news." Officer
Wilson startled me. Officer Wilson was my work supervisor and
alibi witness I used to verify my whereabouts at the time on
Morales murder.

"Yes, I did, and I guess I got you to thank. You're a long
way from the recreation yard, what brings you to AC?"

"I came to see you," he said, looking somewhat apprehen-
sive.

"What's on your mind?"

"I know you used me. I don't know how you got from A-
section to the lower yard during a close movement, but you can bet
your last dollar I won't rest until I find out."

"Get your bitch ass away from my cell before I spit on
you."

"Do it you little punk, come on do it, I dare you."

"Bitch ass boy, you're talking plenty of shit right now. I'm
ma see how tough your bitch ass is when I hit general population.
You see this letter right here, yeah bitch that's my ticket out of

here. And as soon as I hit the yard I'm not going to be there long because I'm ma come and find your bitch ass; and slap the fuck out you, you coward ass, uncle Tom ass Nigga."

"Let me let you in on a little secret, that letter don't mean squat. Mark my word, you will never be allowed in general population ever again. Now sleep on that."

The following week, just as CO Wilson predicted, prison officials found Sparks and I guilty of the institution version of murder and sentenced to an indefinite SHU program, which meant it was highly unlikely I would ever see general population again. Shit I wasn't tripping, the SHU was just a prison within a prison. I was built for this shit, like a lion was built for the jungle.

After a number of failed attempts to get a cell change it became obvious CCO lacked the necessary influence to get the smallest task completed. My first order of business was to establish a strong foundation. The administration only respected those that would resort to violence to get their point across, and violence was the threshold CCO was built upon. We were seven deep, and it was on us to pave the way so future Crips wouldn't have to go through the same shit we were going through.

From day one it was clear the Mexican Mafia was the most dominant force inside AC. In light of their superiority I was surprised they hadn't made one aggressive move against us. To the contrary some of their members were overly friendly with a few of the homies going as far as exchanging magazines and books with one and another. I'd been in the game long enough to recognize deception when I saw it. The Mexican Mafia was the best in the business when it came to trickery.

The Adjustment Center was so isolated only certain guards were allowed to work there. Unable to establish a secure line of communication to the mainline we were basically operating in the blind. It wasn't until I received a visit, and Compound Officer Nate Johnson came to escort me that I received the first warning that all was not what it appeared to be. Nate Johnson was a short fat black guard fascinated by CCO and what we represented. Little did he know he was just a tool to be used. It was obvious by his reluctance to bring in contraband that he wasn't as fascinated as some claimed. Nevertheless, his willingness to pass messages was suffi-cient for now.

"Pretty Boy, I been trying to get over here to see you for the past week, but these officials in AC are real strict on who comes in and out the building. Tabari said to tell you to watch your back. They received word someone on the streets put a contract on your head and the Mexican Mafia accepted it."

"Good looking Nate," I said, pondering over this latest rev-elation.

The first thought that came to my mind was Doc. Doc not only had the resources, he had the connections. The threat in itself really didn't bother me because I was a viable target for the Mexi-can Mafia anyway. Not only was I the highest-ranking member of CCO in AC, I was accused of killing one of their own. What trou-bled me was my vulnerability, and AC guard's notoriety for open-ing the wrong cell while a prisoner was handcuffed and en route to the shower or the yard. There was simply no defense against it; and more times than not the administration would declare the incident excusable based on human error.

I immediately felt the cold winter chill when we exited the building. In the three years I'd been at San Quentin I had only one visitor; my step-father who made it a practice to fly from New Or-leans and come see me four times a years, at my mother's egging. Although I enjoyed seeing him, I'd rather he didn't come at all; be-cause it was four times a year I was forced to think about my loved ones.

I returned from my visit more vigilant than ever, searching for the slightest sign that would substantiate or dispel any threat against me. Seeing nothing out of the ordinary, I came to the con-clusion it was time to tighten up my security, and pay more atten-tion to my surroundings.

My second warning came when Babaru, the shot caller for the BGF spoke out. A native of San Diego, Babaru and I went way back to our juvenile hall days. In the six years since I last seen him it didn't look like he'd aged a day. Half black, half white with a face filled with freckles, and a light brownish afro, growing up he had to travel an extra mile to prove his blackness. There was no one in our group who knew more about Black History than Babaru, that's why it didn't surprise me when I later learned he joined forces with the Black Guerrilla Family. The following yard period he pulled me to the side and informed me the Mexicans on the first floor had been putting in a lot of work on the back bar. From the sound of things it appeared as though someone was doing a lot of cutting, and using their radios to drown out the sound. Steel cutting steel had a distinct sound that could easily be detected by a trained ear. He also informed me that most of the cutting was being done while we were on the recreation yard; and being that there were only two blacks on my floor, a BGF and I he was wondering would I mind staying inside every other yard period until we had a better handle on what was going on. I readily agreed.

"Pretty Boy, I'm glad we're on the same page," he said with a sign of sincerity. "As you can see by our numbers we're at a huge disadvantage in AC, we simply don't have the manpower to cover all the area that needs to be covered. I'm confident if we put our minds together we can greatly increase our Intel."

After promising to pursue a better relation between our groups we parted company.

"What did Cuz want?" Sparks asked as I joined the homies.

"He'd like to establish a better relationship with us by coordinating a security watch that will better enable us to keep a closer eye on the Mexicans."

"Why the change of heart, last yard he didn't say two words to us?"

"I think someone on the compound pulled rank."

"Cuz I say fuck them, we don't need them. What we need is to figure out a way to make the administration move us all on the same floor so we can watch each other's back," Black added.

Bald headed and blacker than an eight ball, the name Black fitted him to a tee. Just as I, Black was also serving an indefinite SHU program for stabbing a guard seven times before the tip of his knife broke in the guard's skull.

"Yeah, Cuz I got to agree with Black, we been over here damn near a year and they haven't extended one helping hand. Sound like they need us more than we need them. I say we get at

Lt. Baker one more time, if he refuses to move you I say we start blasting these racist ass guards every time they come on the tier."

Everyone nodded in agreement.

Lt. Baker was a stone cold redneck that appeared to have a personal grudge against Crips. Every request we made he denied; now it was time to show him. Although we were only seven deep, each and everyone of us had a reputation for putting in work. Violence was the only thing the administration respected, and violence they shall have.

"Yard recall in five minutes," the announcement came over the intercom.

After embracing each of the homies I made my way to the main exit where I was handcuffed and escorted to my cell by prison guards O'Neil and Wiley. The third and final warning came when I approached the grill gate leading to my module and noticed the floor was covered with water and debris. There was a cloud of smoke clearly visible and a strong odor of burnt newspapers lingering in the air. The scene resembled the aftermath of a major disturbance. I paused at the gate and quickly scanned the entire floor. As I proceeded to my cell on full alert I found it odd no one was standing at their cell doors. The unit was so quiet you could hear a pin drop.

"Open 1AC10!" O'Neil shouted.

The electronic door slid open and I stepped inside and waited for O'Neil to issue the order to close 1AC10 so he could remove my handcuffs. Instead, I heard the sound of feet running. I turned around and found no signs of O'Neil or Wiley.

Just as I was about to step out of my cell and see where they went I was confronted by Night Owl, a soldier for the Mexican Mafia coming at me with a knife in his hand. With nowhere to turn I quickly retreated to the back of cell and tried to time his approach. Just as he lunged forward my right foot shot up striking him dead in the center of his chest. He stumbled backward giving me a renewed sense of hope.

Without hesitation I rushed him like a mad man kicking wildly, hoping to deliver a crippling blow that would disable him. Just when I thought I had him he caught my foot in midair and overturned my legs sending my body face down on the ground. Trapped between the concrete bed frame and the cell bars I turned my body inwards to protect my left side where all the main arteries are located. Unable to free my hands I could feel his knife tearing into my skin.

"Doc said goodbye," he said then continued to stab me.

With no other recourse, in a desperate attempt to save my life I played dead. All of a sudden the pain subsided and I could no longer feel him stabbing me. After what seemed like an eternity, and believing I was dead he stopped and surrendered. The ordeal was over.

Once Night Owl was handcuffed and in custody several guards rushed to my cell expecting to find a dead man, instead they found a determined young rider very much alive. I couldn't believe my good fortunes. I stared death in the eyes and survived. I was so happy I felt like I was high. The guards lifted me upright and tried to place me on the gurney, I refused. I wasn't about to give the Mexicans the satisfaction of seeing me carried out. Although the pain had returned and I was bleeding from 33 stab wounds, I was well aware of everything around me. With my hands still cuffed behind my back I walked out of my cell and received an enormous amount of satisfaction as my enemies stared in disbelief. Stopping at cell 1AC3 I looked Fat Tony in the eyes. Fat Tony was one of several shot callers for the Mexican Mafia, and more than likely the one issued the order.

"Never send a bitch to do a man's job you fat mother fucker!"

Never Send a Bitch To Do a Man's Job

–Chapter 11–

Barely sedated, I laid in agony as two prison doctors worked diligently to stitch me back together. I was hit thirty-three times, including four stab wounds to my neck. The pain, although excruciating was a blessing in disguise. It was a constant reminder of how lucky I was to be alive. Night Owl had every opportunity to kill me, why he didn't only he could say.

Later that evening I laid awake staring at the ceiling, reflecting over the past week that led to my assault. The warning signs were clear, why I failed to acknowledge the severity of the threat and implement better safeguards to protect myself was beyond my understanding. I wasn't the type of man that left things up for chance, or underestimate a threat. I took nothing for granted, and relied heavily on my senses to avoid dangerous situations. The realization that my instincts failed me troubled me dearly.

In a feeble attempt to minimize their role in my assault, San Quentin officials instructed the hospital staff to treat me as a victim rather than a maximum security prisoner. The following morning shortly after breakfast I received the first in a long list of visitors.

"Floyd did I wake you?" an elder black man along with two female companions entered my room.

"No," I replied then sat in an upright position.

"I'm Pastor Bernard Wilkins and this is my lovely wife Linda, and our beautiful daughter Trisha."

"Sir, in all due respect I'm really not interested in hearing a church sermon. I think your time would be better spent tending to needs of other prisoners."

"Son, we're not here to hurt you. If allowed we'd like to help you. I believe through spiritual counseling you can learn the true power of love and forgiveness. Considering everything you have been through I understand why you may be reluctant to talk about love and forgiveness at this time, but believe me son you'll be amazed how peaceful you'll feel discovering the true essence of love and forgiveness."

"Sir I appreciate your concerns, and I thank you for coming, but I must ask you to leave. It's nothing personal; it's just the way things are."

"I must say in the twenty-five years I have been in ministry I can't recall one time where I was asked to leave. Are you an atheist? Do you believe in God?"

"No, I'm not an atheist, and yes I believe in God." I replied, giving the man the answers he wanted.

"Well, than what's the problem?" He held out his hands in question.

"Under different circumstances I would love nothing more than to sit here and talk to you and your family. But being that things are what they are I'm afraid I can't. The last things I need right now is for people to think I'm seeking spiritual salvation. A lot of people are watching and wondering how I'm going to emerge from this ordeal. I know my enemies are hoping they broke my spirits, and your presence here would seem to suggest that. I'm a gangster, and the last thing on my mind is forgiveness. Now, if you'd really like to help me you would leave."

Exasperated by my answers, he spoke, "Floyd, what else does it have to take to make you realize there is no future in the life you have chosen. If you continue down this path more than likely you will end up dying or spending the rest of your life in prison. Is that what you want?"

"What I want is for you to leave." Doing my best to hide

my anger and sweat beading up, "There's nothing you can say that will change how I feel. What part of this you don't understand?"

"Very well, I will respect your wishes. But before we leave I ask only that we join hands in prayer. Please allow us to pray for your fast and speedy recovery."

Before I had a chance to decline, Trisha stepped around her father and took my hand. Her small delicate fingers quickly slid between mine and she stared in my eyes with compassion so powerful it sent a rippling sensation inside my heart. With a tender smile and slight squeeze of her hand, she managed to dismantle my defense. I bowed my head and allowed her father to lead us into prayer. *The warm feeling surrounding me was her, not the love of God*, I told myself.

Long after they left Trisha remained a part of my thoughts. It was amazing how the mere presence of a simple church girl could have such a profound effect upon me. Trisha wasn't the prettiest girl in the world, but she had an inner beauty and a gracefulness that was just as appealing. At five feet six inches and a little over a hundred and thirty pounds she was a petite figure with an ebony complexion and tender brown eyes that appeared to be very observant. Although I realized the odds of me ever seeing her again was slim to none, nevertheless I enjoyed the momentary pleasure I received from a few pleasant thoughts.

The reality of my present situation hit me like a ton of bricks as I struggled to get out of bed for the first time since being held in the prison infirmary. With no nurse around to help, I stood up and felt my legs wobble beneath me. It had been 72-hours since I last showered and I felt a desperate need to cleanse myself. The simple task of going to the bathroom was proving more difficult than I had anticipated. I slowly proceeded to the shower taking a step at a time. I felt vulnerable; injured in a way I couldn't even protect myself. I paused at the bathroom door and was surprised to find it had all the accommodations of home. It had been years since I last took a bath, or sat on a shitter with a toilet sit. It was funny how the little small things a man took for granted in the free world held so much value in prison.

After two weeks of lounging in San Quentin's finest living

quarters I was informed that I was scheduled to be discharged the following morning. I received the news with mixed emotions. While one side looked forward to getting back in the lion's den, the other side enjoyed the solitude of being housed in a peaceful environment. Even the hardest gangster needed a break from the game every now and then; I just didn't need one at the expense of being stabbed thirty-three times.

Although I paid little if no attention to what was going on in the free world, I knew everything in prison someway, somehow became local news on the streets, which was evident by the over pouring of letters and get well soon cards I received. With nothing but time on my hands I read each and everyone of them. I couldn't deny it felt good to discover so many cared; but what I found so troubling, and even heart shattering there wasn't a single letter from Nicole, or a picture of my son. Little did she know her disengagement was a fire that inflamed a hatred that was going growing stronger by the day. I felt played.

I was standing at the window watching a flock of birds fly freely over the San Francisco Bay when I heard a knock on the door. I turned around and felt an instant joy.

"Trisha what a pleasant surprise, what brings you by?"

"I'm surprised you remember my name. My father is here visiting another inmate, so I decided to stop by to see how you were doing."

"As you can see I'm doing quite well considering how I was doing the last time I saw you. And how can I forget your name, it's not every day I find myself in the presence of such an extraordinary woman."

"What makes me extraordinary, if you don't me asking?" she blushed while asking.

"Many things; I always pride myself on being an excellent judge of character. When I look at you I see a tenderness and warmth so refreshing I find myself relax and at ease in your company. I'm not the type that trusts easily, but my senses tell me I'm in very good company."

"Thank you for such a lovely compliment. Well another reason I stopped by I brought you a gift," she said, extending a

Bible.

"The King James version," I muttered and ran my hand over the soft black leather with the gold encrust lettering.

"I wrote down a few passages so I hope you read them."

"For a woman I barely know you sure are asking a lot."

"Am I?" Hands on her hips, she got a little sassy.

"Yes, you are."

"So, is that a yes?" she asked with a glimmer of hope.

"How can I deny you? The least I can do, considering you went out of your way to come check on me. Thank you for caring."

"You're welcome." Sitting down in the chair beside my bed, she remained her perfect posture

"Trisha may I ask you a question?"

"You certainly may."

"Why do you care so much?"

"Because I believe you are a very special young man, and I also believe if I can help you, you in turn can help others. Is that a good enough reason?"

"Yes, it is; but is that the only reason?"

"What are you implying?"

"I'm not implying anything, I was just wondering."

"Wondering about what?"

"About us, me and you, and this strong sensation I feel brewing between us. I like you, and I sense the feelings are mutual. Am I wrong?"

"Floyd you can't talk like that."

"Why not, am I wrong?" I asked and closed the distance between us.

"Because we can get in trouble," she replied and stared at the door.

"Baby, the last thing I want is to compromise you in any way, but I fear if I don't speak my mind right here, right now I may never get this opportunity again. From the very moment I held your hand and looked into your eyes I felt an overwhelming attraction to you. Can you stand here, look in my eyes and tell me you don't feel the same way?"

"Floyd I can't answer that." She stood and took a step

backward.

"Why not, what's so hard about speaking what's inside your heart?"

"Because it's too soon; things are happening too fast. I think I better go."

"Baby, one thing I've learned about life is that tomorrow is not promised. I live in the moment; and from the looks of things more than likely this will be the last time I will see you. Baby, all I asked is that you confirm or dispel my suspicion. If I'm reading this wrong please tell me, it's the not knowing that's killing me inside."

I reached out took her hands and drew her body into mines, knowing my words were having the most profound impact on her.

"Floyd we can't do this," she said with the least amount of resistant.

"Yes, we can," I whispered and pressed my lips gently against hers.

Feeling no resistance I slid my tongue inside her mouth and drew her into a long passionate kiss. Never in my life had I experienced a kiss more satisfying. I slid my hands down her waist and could feel her body relax. *Damn, she felt so good and it had been too long since I'd had a woman's touch.*

"I hope I answered your question?" she said with an affection that was so compelling all I could do was smile.

Trisha was a twenty-three years old student at UC Berkeley majoring in Physiology. Consumed with her studies and obligations to her church she neither had the time nor the desire to pursue an intimate relationship with anyone. Never in her wildest dreams did she imagine she would fall for a prisoner, especially one that represented everything she and her family preached against. Although surprising, the prospects of being with a prisoner had rejuvenated her and added a new sense of excitement to her life. She was infatuated, but the cold thing about it, so was I.

I was up bright and early the following morning. The vacation was over, and it was time to get back to business; the business of survival. The Mexican Mafia had gone to extraordinary measures to kill me. It was my understanding Night Owl had used a hacksaw blade to cut out four bars from his cell. In the Adjustment Center the cell bars were checked at least three times a week, which only confirmed the guards played a significant role in conspiring to kill me.

Although it wasn't in my nature to attack a defenseless man I understood there were no rules of engagement when it came to Guerilla Warfare. It was a cut-throat business where the end always justified the means. I felt no ill feelings towards Night Owl; he was just a soldier following orders. It wasn't personal it was business. The bulk of my rage was directed at Officer O'Neil and Wiley, the two racist pigs that set me up.

San Quentin Prison Guards were playing a deadly game which was obvious by the growing numbers of blacks being assaulted in the Security Housing Units. It was also obvious they were operating with complete immunity. The more I thought about it the more I came to realize the Mexican Mafia was not our greatest threat, it was these crooked ass guards that were aiding and abetting our enemies.

I was told the night before to be packed and ready to leave the first thing in the morning. It was passed 11:00 a.m. and I was still waiting. The Adjustment Center had a reputation of retrieving its prisoners at the first opportune time. Just as I was about to doze off I heard the sound of steel shackles coming up the hallway, which was my calling card, and confirmation that the vacation was officially over. I looked around the room to make sure I hadn't forgot anything; satisfied everything was in order I approached the door as it was being open.

"KW what's up Cuz?" I asked; somewhat surprise to find CO Kevin Wiggins here to escort me.

Unlike Nate Johnson, KW was an actual CCO member. Born and raised in Los Angeles, KW emerged from the belly of the beast unscathed and without a criminal record. After serving four years in the armed service he applied for a job at San Quentin. It was here; unbeknownst to the administration and the majority of homies he became a CCO member.

"Pretty Boy it's good to see you back on your feet," he ordered as he searched for any visible signs of my injury.

"You know you can't send a dog to slay a lion. Don't tell me they got you working in AC now?" I said as a moment of reflection ran across my face.

"Nah, I'm still in C-section; the administration called this morning and told us to find you a cell?" he replied, surprised no one told me.

"No one told me, I thought I was going back to AC."

"Cuz you got the administration running around like a chicken with his head cut off. You got grounds for a major law suit and there's not a damn thing they can do to get out of it. If I was you I'd jump on this shit as quick as possible."

"Yeah, I think I will; I could damn sure use the money. What's up with Sparks and the rest of the homies in AC?"

"AC Officials got all the homies in dry cells. The day you got hit they took off on the guards. The administration is considering moving all of them out of AC."

"What else is going on?" I asked in hope of learning something more pleasant.

"You heard what happened to Night Owl?" he shot back with a smile and a hint of excitement.

"Nah what happened?" At the mention of Night Owl, suddenly I felt a deep sense of rage.

"He got killed two days ago." He studied me briefly, hoping this information brought me some measure of pleasure.

"Damn, I didn't know that. Who did him in?" I asked, feeling indifferent to his death. The fact that his own people killed him brought me no sense of joy. Revenge was personal, and could only be satisfied by me personally sending him to meet his maker.

"His own people; they told him if he came to the recreation yard they would kill him. He went out there, and they killed him. He knew it was coming, there was no escaping it. He had every opportunity to kill you and he didn't. That was the price he had to pay."

His eyes told me the seriousness of it all.

I arrived back in C-section and was reunited with Tabari, Askari, and Suma. I was overwhelmed by the love and support I received from the homies. It had been nearly a year since I last seen most of them; and in that time I had paid my dues in blood and sweat. I lived by the code of the double edge sword and represented CCO like a decorated soldier. As a result of my steadfast loyalty and unwavering faith I was promoted to the rank of Intelligence Officer which made me the fourth highest in rank, and answered only to the Central Committee who had veto power over any and all decisions.

The interior structure of C-section had changed drastically due to the increased numbers of death row prisoners arriving at San Quentin. The administration cleared out the 5th tier and started moving death row prisoners in by the numbers. The most notable of these prisoners was Big Tookie Williams, the founder and most celebrated Crip to ever walk the earth. Second in line was Evil, an OG Crip from Raymond Avenue, and the founder of Blue Notes. Third in line was Treach another co-founder of Blue Notes, and also a member of Raymond Avenue Crips. Blue Notes was rapidly becoming a major player in prison politics, and growing at a rate CCO could no longer ignore.

My first assignment from the Central Committee was to monitor Blue Notes activities and make a record of anyone associating with Evil or Treach for an extended amount of time. Due to my close relationship with Sparks I often found myself engaged in long conversations with Evil, who I found to be highly intelligent; and very much on top of his game. The more we talked the more I came to understand the message behind the man. Not only was Cuz in a desperate fight for his life, he was strategically laying the foundation for his legacy. Unlike Tookie Williams, his mentor, and founder of the Crips, Evil's appeal didn't transcend California's borders. In order to do so, he had to turn the Blue Notes into a force stronger than CCO.

I took an instant liken to Evil who was twelve years my senior and well-schooled in Crip History. Evil was a visionary with a unique perspective on Cripping and the direction he felt Crips should be heading in. Just as I acknowledged his strengths I also searched for signs of weakness. In our business, sometimes today friends, turned out to be tomorrow's enemies. That's why it was never wise to get close to anyone outside your crew.

As we approached the first anniversary of Slow Drag's death, there was a growing uneasiness looming in the air. Although no one spoke on the tragic death of our dear friend, it was obvious it was on everyone's mind. In an effort to commemorate his life, I suggested we take off on the guards in a way they'd never been hit before. Instead of launching a full-scale assault I felt we would be more effective if we selected our targets, strike and retreat. The Central Committee liked the idea and gave me the green light to put it in motion.

On the first day of June we paid homage to Slow Drag by sending L-Dog to the infirmary. As planned, L-Dog told the guards, while bench-pressing, the bar slipped out of his hands and landed across his chest. In a role worthy of an academy award, L-Dog exited the yard like he was in extreme pain. At 6 feet 3' and a solid 235 pounds, L-Dog didn't need a weapon to inflict great body injury. Serving two life- sentenced for a double murder, in which he killed two rival gang members with a baseball bat, Cuz was the perfect candidate for the job at hand.

Due to his size and reputation, C-section officials sent two guards to escort him to the infirmary. As anticipated, the X-ray technician instructed the guards to remove L-Dog's shackles so he could get a clear picture of his ribs. Reluctantly, they complied. Like a caged animal that tricked his prey into a trap, L-Dog savagely attacked both guards while the X-ray technician fled. By the time help arrived it was too late; both guards laid unconscious, suffering from multiple fractions, one of the two guards had a fractured skull that resulted from L-Dog's body slamming him on his head. It took two tasers and over eight guards to subdue him. On all accounts it was a successful hit.

Three days later, we sent Bullet to sick call with a knife and a handcuff key. Sick call was held Monday, Wednesday, and Friday on the 1st tier in the classification room. While waiting in the holding cage for his chance to visit the nurse on call, Bullet removed his handcuffs and waited for his number to come up. No sooner than the guard opened his holding cage Bullet sprung into action. His first blow caught the guard in the side of his face, penetrating his skin and shattering two of his teeth. His desperate cry for help could be heard all the way on the exercise yard. At the sound of the unit alarm the unit erupted into a loud chant. "CCO, CCO, CCO," followed by cell bars rattling. By the time they subdued Bullet he had stabbed his victim nine times. Two up, two down.

As prison officials scrambled to make sense of this new round of violence, CCO searched for new ways to attack. After four successful attacks, prison officials called for a sit down; CCO declined. We were not interested in peaceful negotiations, for these attacks were in retaliation for atrocities they already committed. With each one, stock rose. Praises were coming from all directions, but it meant little. My satisfaction came from bringing my enemies heartache and pain.

My experience in AC left me somewhat suspicious of the BGF and their motives. It was obvious we didn't share the same sentiments although we had shared success at one time, I simply didn't trust them. In an effort not to undermine years of hard work, I kept my misgivings to myself. I knew my every move was being scrutinized by the Central Committee to see if I had what it took to lead. Looking back I could see the change, the young boy that became a man. I was a soldier with ambitions of someday becoming a general; I wasn't interested in jailhouse politics, nor any other role that would have me negotiating with those I seek to destroy. Unlike most, I believed from the moment you picked up arms there was nothing else to talk about.

I always enjoyed the winter, the cold crisp air, and gray skies. It the perfect time to run; and run I did. I had just completed 100 laps around the small exercise yard when I stopped for a breather. After catching my breath I looked up and discovered Zaki less than three feet away. Zaki was a shot caller for the BGF's, and a highly respected head banger with two jailhouse murders under his belt. We made eye contact and he smiled and extended his hand. I returned the smile and accepted his hand.

"Pretty Boy, I'm glad to see you back in top form," he said and studied me briefly. A compliment was always accompanied by a favor.

"What can I do for you?" I asked hoping he got straight to the point.

"First of all, I'd like to compliment CCO on some very nice work, I'm impressed; you got these pigs running scared. Second, I don't know if you're aware but Sgt. Underwood has been hanging out on the 4th tier in the wee hours of the morning. We believe he's passing knives to the Aryan Brotherhood. Several nights ago we spotted him talking to White Boy Buck at three in the morning; a few minutes later we heard a heavy piece of metal hitting the ground, which only confirmed what we already suspected."

"Is that right?" I stated, already aware of these facts.

"The reason I'm mentioning it is because we were thinking about moving on him, but we didn't want to step on anyone's toes just in case CCO already had plans."

"We have no interests in Sgt. Underwood," I said and studied his reaction.

He was obviously disappointed. I had a strong sense he was looking for someone to do their dirty work. Zaki was a master manipulator; constantly plotting and scheming in search of the next battle. The BGF had a long-standing fuel with the ABs; this was one war CCO had no interest in. In the past, CCO and the BGF shared a lot of success battling the Mexican Mafia; since then a lot had changed. This was a new time, a new era, and we were fighting a new war.

On the eve of June 17 we received a courtesy notice from the BGF to get our house in order. This was a telltale sign that something serious was about to go down; an incident that more than likely would cause the entire unit to get shook down. As in all major hits, rumors and speculations gradually circulated from one ear to the next.

The most prevalent was an attack on Sgt. Underwood. I, for one, wasn't particularly fond of ordering a hit from behind cell bars; because you only got one shot, and if you missed the cell bars would prevent you from advancing on your target. To execute a successful hit from your cell would require a lot of skill and an equal amount of luck.

It was a little after midnight when Officer Boulder and Sgt. Underwood stepped on the tier to conduct the 12:00 a.m. count and retrieve outgoing mail. Sgt. Underwood made it a practice to trail behind and retrieve the mail while Officer Boulder counted without delay. At 5 feet 7 inches and pushing damn near 3 hundred pounds Sgt. Underwood provided the perfect target. But on the flip side, anything less a face shot probably would render minimum damage. Just as I turned off my light, I heard the sound of heavy feet racing down the tier followed by the frantic sound of someone fumbling with keys. Panic was in the air and there was no denying it. Suddenly it became quiet, so quiet you could hear a pin drop. In prison, this is what we called the calm after the storm. A quiet breeze that usually could be felt when the Grim Reaper came to claim a man's soul.

The news of Sgt. Underwood's death hit C-section with thundering applause. The sound of loud screams and cell bars rattling could be heard as far as the warden's office. Only in a maximum-security prison could you find grown men celebrating the death of a peace officer without the fear of reprisal. C-Section housed 250 of the most dangerous prisoners in the State of California and I was one of them. It was hard to punish a man that simply didn't give a fuck.

I later learned that Sgt. Underwood died from a single stab wound to his chest. Unable to save or help his colleague, Officer Boulder sat on the stairs behind the grill gate and wept at the sight of Underwood's lifeless body face down on the second tier.

By mid-afternoon every prisoner on the front bar of the second tier was kidnapped and taken to an unknown location. The backlash that followed Sgt. O'Neil's death would mark the beginning of the administrations fierce campaign to reclaim California's most dangerous prison. The administration started off by suspending all programs, which meant no showers, no visits, no recreation, no commissary, and for the first time no mail.

They shook down every cell and confiscated anything they believed could be converted into a weapon, which was damn near everything. With the flick of a switch San Quentin Officials went from a passive regime to a strict authoritarian force that wasn't taking any shit from anybody. By the end of the week every major shot caller from every gang was kidnapped and transferred to California State Prison at Folsom. The CCO was at a standstill.

Time Flies By
–Chapter 12 –

After thirty days of implementing new security measures we were finally allowed a breath of fresh air. I stood at the back of the recreational yard and studied the flow of new faces hitting the yard. No one was more suspicious than I to see Zaki. How he managed to dodge a major sweep of all head of states was a story only he could tell. Zaki was the highest-ranking BGF in C-section, a well-known head banger; his reputation for putting in work was legendary. In hindsight, he would have been in the top three candidates targeted for transfer. I had a great deal of respect for Zaki but I didn't trust him.

Our first day back on the yard I had four sets of eyes on him. He appeared agitated; disturbed in the way he avoided anyone that wasn't a part of his crew. After conversing with a few of his comrades, prison officials pulled him from the yard. On his way to the exit we made eye contact, a slight smirk appeared on his face as to suggest he didn't give a fuck what anyone thought, which was a common attitude most OG's displayed when they punked the game. It was at that moment I knew he sold his soul to the devil.

News of Zaki's defection spread quickly. For many it was hard to believe a man of Zaki's stature would betray the very oath he killed on several occasions to uphold. His own people refused to believe he would do such a thing; but I knew better. Officer Nate Johnson, a CCO's sympathizer, not only confirmed the rumors but informed me Zaki was transferred immediately to the Marin

County Jail for his own protection.

Even with the loss of Tabari, Askari, and Suma CCO remained structurally sound. Our first week back on the yard we reestablished rank and file. As the highest- ranking member in C-section I became the chairman, and Hoover Cal and Diablo took their respective positions as co-chair. Hoover Cal and I went way back to my Youth Authority days. He, like I came up in the ranks by putting in work. Diablo, on the other hand, earned his stripes at Soledad where he paralyzed a member of Vanguards and choked a correctional officer to sleep. Although we operated on the premise of 'majority rules' when it came to cabinet appointments, I had the power to veto all decisions.

A few days prior to my 23rd birthday, I received word Lil Bull and Salt-Rock had been released. I felt an enormous sense of joy and relief that the homies were back on the streets. Deep down inside I always felt somewhat responsible for our downfall. I understood everything in life had a starting point, and in our case it all started when I took the ring. It was funny how one small act could alter the course of so many lives.

Looking back it was hard to believe only four years had passed since I'd last seen Lil Bull or Salt-Rock. In actuality it felt like a lifetime ago. The realization that they were home and I was still in prison was a testament how different things were in a level three and four prison. I had exactly one year left and still couldn't see the end of the tunnel. The climate at San Quentin prohibited a prisoner from entertaining thoughts of freedom. Doing time required a man to maintain a battlefield mentality from sun up to sun down, every second of every day. Surviving the jungles was my number one priority, everything else was secondary.

Immediately following the killing of Sgt. Underwood the war between the Blacks and Mexicans came to an end. Although there wasn't an official declaration of peace, each organization understood it would take a concerted effort by all prisoners to regain some of the power we lost during the administrations fierce campaign to reclaim control. Everyone was feeling the heat, even the most scared guards were playing hardball. Threats of violence fell on deaf ears, and acts of violence were met with tear gas and stun guns.

Trisha was more than a pen-pal; she had become a valuable friend that had grown on me considerably. Although I was a man of many interests there was nothing I found more gratifying than exchanging meaningful literature with a female companion. As hard as I tried to dictate the course of our communication, Trisha was just as determined to talk about her faith. Eventually she won the battle. Much to my surprise I became fascinated with her Biblical tales of the past. She wrote passionately about the Old Testament and how it was filled with African History. According to her, the Holy Bible was written by Black Egyptians, and Africa was the birthplace of civilization. She went on to teach me that Abraham was half black and half white and was born in Chaldea, an Asiatic nation under African rule, and Moses was an Egyptian and his wife Zipporah was an Ethiopian. She reminded me although the Bible described Jesus as a man of color, feet the color of fine brass, and hair like wool; Europeans and Americans portray Jesus as a white man with long straight hair. They know the truth but they just hate to admit it. As time passed Trisha made a very convincing argument and succeeded in her quest to lure me inside her world of Christianity. For the first time in my life the Bible became a daily part of my studies.

In an effort to expand my knowledge and explore different ideologies on religion I turned to Brother Robert X, a dedicated servant of the Nation of Islam. An elder black man in his late 50's Brother Robert X was considered a religious scholar in Islamic and Christian affairs.

I approached Brother Robert X wide-eyed and with an open mind. Unlike the majority of those in prison that read the Bible I wasn't looking for solace or a peace of mind, I was simply searching for a deeper understanding about the Christian Faith and the Holy Bible. To clarify my concerns I sent Brother Robert X a three-page letter requesting his assistance in my efforts to distinguish truth from falsehood. I trusted Brother Robert X explicitly. An eight-year resident of C-section, he had twenty-two years in on a life-sentence for killing a man that raped his daughter. Fifty-three years old, and twice as old, and in better shape as most convicts in

C-Section Robert X was considered one, if not the best handball players at San Quentin. A smaller, slimmer version of Morgan Freeman I can't recall one time he didn't have a serious expression on his face. Had it not been for his religious and political views, he would have made parole years ago. Staying true to his convictions he vowed to die in prison before he denounced what he believed to be real and righteous inside his heart.

Brother Robert X removed his glasses and placed them in the folds of his book when I approached. "Mr. Pretty Boy Floyd, please have a seat," he said and waved to a vacant seat on the opposite side of the recreational table.

"Good morning Sir. I gather that all is well and progressing on your end."

"Well, you know, my Brother, everyday we're allowed to breathe is a blessed day, and every day we strive for knowledge is a day of tremendous growth. The more you know the farther you will go."

"True, true, I couldn't have said it any better." I nodded in agreement.

"I must say I wasn't surprised when I received your letter. I've walked past your cell on a number of occasions and noticed you were reading the King James Bible. Knowing you as well as I do, and seeing no inspirational changes in your behavior I naturally assumed something else was motivating your studies."

"How correct you are."

"Well, my friend, how can I help you?"

"What can you tell me about Christianity?"

"Plenty, but let's start with the book you're reading; The King James Bible. Although it's one of the most popular version of the Bible among Christians, it is just one of many Bibles derived from the Egyptian Book of the Dead. Back in the days, King James formed a committee to rewrite the Roman Catholic Bible, which in turn became the official King James Bible." He stopped for a moment to read my eyes, then continued. "The King James Bible became the Christian Bible of choice only after Britain used the strong arm of its military forces to influence the people under its powers to accept the King James Bible as the true and only Bible.

The Bibles you see today are nothing more than an altered text filled with half-truths and whole lies."

After listening to Brother Robert X I had more questions than answers. I walked away feeling elated that I discovered something new that could stir my interest so deeply. I was intrigued by religious studies, and found it was consuming most, if not all, of my leisure time. I accepted Brother Robert X's version of events as the truth, but not the absolute truth. I was still having a hard time believing how modern man could say with any amount of certainty what had taken place over four thousand years ago. I sensed he knew what I was thinking.

To support his claims, Brother Robert X allowed me the opportunity to examine his vast collection of religious literature. The more I read the more I begin to understand the logic behind his reasoning. Gradually, I began to challenge Trisha on her religious beliefs by posing questions to her that Brother Robert X had posed to me. At first she accepted the challenge and tried to answer the questions as best as she could. Every question she failed to answer I provided her with the correct answer and challenged her to prove me wrong; which she never did. The strain that resulted from months of religious indifferences proved more than our relationship could handle. Eventually Trisha stopped writing, and after two unanswered letters so did I.

The eve of my release I awoke to find a sealed envelope on my cell floor. I quickly retrieved it and immediately recognized Tabari's handwriting. Inside were a set of new codes and contact numbers of the people I needed to contact upon my release. After storing the information inside my memory, I lit the envelope on fire and flushed the ashes down the toilet. A light smile ran across my face as I realized by this time tomorrow I would be a free man.

The Nightmare Is Finally Over

–Chapter 13 –

After five years and six months the nightmare was finally over. San Quentin had been an eye-opening experience. One that provided me with the necessary skills needed to survive in the darkest corners of America. The transition from prison to a free society would require a more serious mindset, which was evident by the untimely death of several CCO members that occurred within the first year of their release. Unlike those before me, I understood the streets were far more dangerous than prison. It was one thing being confronted by a knife, but an entirely different story staring at the barrel of an AK-47 which now was the weapon of choice on the Cali streets.

The metallic sound of steel clashing with steel froze inside my mind as the huge metal gate closed behind me. Although it was considered bad luck to look back, I stopped, turned around and paused for a moment to study the huge massive structure that had been my home for the last five years. From the outside looking in, San Quentin showed no visible signs of the violence lurking inside its walls. To the contrary, on all accounts it gave the appearance of a research institute of some sort, an elusive disguise designed to conceal the barbaric conditions that was forced upon its population.

"A penny for your thoughts," a soft gentle voice came from behind. I turned around and a smile instantly appeared on my face. Trisha was twice as beautiful as I last remembered her.

"Trisha, you forever seem to surprise me." I smiled like I hadn't smiled in years.

"I hope it's a pleasant surprise?" she asked and paused for a moment to study me.

"Most definitely, why wouldn't it be?" My shoulders shrugged in an exaggerated manner.

"I thought you would be furious with me, but I simply couldn't allow our friendship to end without at least telling you why. Can we go somewhere and talk?"

"I don't see why not."

Trisha found a small hillside deli less than ten minutes away. She selected a small table on the patio that had a perfect view of the San Francisco Bay.

"This is a beautiful setting," I said as I gradually took in the scenery.

"Yes, it is. I come here at least twice a week when I'm at the prison. Have you had lunch?"

"No, I'm not really hungry, but I could use a glass of iced tea, no sugar."

"Two iced teas coming up." Trisha stood and disappeared inside, giving me a nice view of her backside. I could tell the way her dress was gripping her hips she had a lovely body underneath. Trisha was, without a doubt a very gorgeous young lady.

"I'm glad you came," I said with sincerity.

"Are you?" she asked, giving me the first indication this was anything but a social gathering.

"Yes, I'm glad. You know it's been over five months since I last heard from you. You disappeared without as much as a good-bye. I was worried; I didn't know if something had happened to you and I didn't have any way to find out. I'm glad to see all is well with you."

"You know looks can be deceiving." Her eyes closed in on me.

"Is that the case here?" I asked, paying closer attention and staring directly into her beautiful brown eyes. .

"Yes, it is. My life has been a living hell and I can't seem to get it back on track."

"Why, what happened?"

"You!" she yelled. "My life was fine until I met you. In all my years on earth I have never had someone doubt or question my Christian faith. When I met you I thought you were looking for salvation, a new start, when in actuality you were just playing mind games with me."

"Do you really believe that?" I asked on the verge of becoming upset.

"Yes, no, I don't know, but what I do know I refuse to share my life with a man that does not share my Christian faith."

"I'm sorry you feel that way." Sipping my tea, I looked away.

"Is that all you have to say?" She was becoming visibly upset, a trait I hadn't witnessed in years.

"What else do you want me to say? It's obvious you've given this a great deal of thought. No matter what, it all comes back to the same. I'm not a Christian, and I have no intentions of becoming a Christian."

"What are you then, a Muslim?" She shouted back.

"No, baby girl I'm not a Muslim, I'm a Crip. If I gave you the impression that I was anything else, I apologize. It was not done intentionally. I've been accused of a lot of things, but I've never been accused of lying to someone I care about. Baby, this is not how I envisioned my first day of freedom. I think it would be best if I caught a cab from here. Believe me when I say I'm truly sorry things turned out the way they did."

At this point, I was itching to go, but had nowhere to be.

"Wait, please sit down; I'll give you a ride. Where are you going?"

"Trisha, I don't want to argue with you"

"Me neither, where are you going?"

"The closest airport. I believe it's Oakland International." The look on her face told me she didn't want me to leave but I knew what was best for me, *or did I?*

There was an awkward silence looming inside the car. It was obvious neither wanted things to end on a sour note. I adored

Trisha, but not enough to compromise my beliefs, or pretend that things were anything other than what they were. In an effort to ease the tension I turned on the radio, allowing the sensuous soulful sound of Sade to fill the atmosphere. It felt good to be going home to what I knew and the city I loved.

"Baby, I'm sorry." Trisha softly whispered, placing her hand on top of mine. "Do you forgive me?"

"Yes, I forgive you," I said, lifting her hand to my lips and softly kissed it, bringing a warm and tender smile to her face.

"Are you in a hurry?" she asked as if she had something in mind.

"No, baby, I'm completely at your whim. Whatever you like to do is fine with me?"

"Good because I have a surprise for you."

Twenty minutes later we were pulling up at a huge two-story home. I immediately recognized the address as the one I had written to on many occasions. Trisha guided her Toyota into the three-car garage and came to a stop next to a cherry red drop top 300 Mercedes.

"That's my baby right there," she said with a smile that lit up her whole face. "I fell in love with her the moment I saw her. Kind of like what I did with you."

"I'm glad I know who I have to compete with to win your heart." She nudged my shoulder.

"There is no competition; you won my heart the first time we kissed."

"This home seems awfully big for one person. Who all lives here?"

"Well there's me, my cat Sirius, and hopefully you. How does that sound?" she asked and turned her body sideways to study my reaction.

"Are you serious?" I questioned, carefully considering what she just insinuated.

"Never been more serious in my life, if you haven't noticed, I'm head over heels in love with you and I have been since the moment we met."

"Baby, the feelings are mutual. Believe me when I say it

was not my intentions to challenge your religious convictions, or make you uncomfortable even discussing it. My sole desire was to solicit your help in discovering the truth. In all the years I have researched this matter, I have discovered only one thing; there is only one power that knows the truth about all things in Heaven and on Earth, and that's God himself."

"Thank you Baby." She was on the verge of crying.

"You're quite welcome my love."

My heart swelled with joy the moment I stepped inside the lavishly decorated living room. I was astounded, totally overwhelmed by the "Welcome Home" decorations. Trisha had gone to great measures to make me feel welcome. If it was her intentions to show me how much she cared, she succeeded.

"You did all this by yourself?" I asked.

"I did," she stated proudly. "Do you like it?"

"I love it," I beamed, imagining waking up in her arms.

"I'm glad because I wanted this day to be special for you" she softly muttered, all teary eyed.

"Come here baby," I said, lifting her chin and slowly kissed her tears away.

Trisha looked so beautiful laughing and crying at the same time.

"I said I wasn't going to cry, but I get so emotional when I'm happy," she said, struggling to regain her composure.

While Trisha prepared dinner, I decided to take a tour of her spacious home. My favorite part of the house was the huge backyard with perfectly cut grass and a six-feet deep swimming pool. I quickly disrobed, and dove head first into the water. The cool water provided much relief from the August heat. Naked as the day I was born I swam several laps enjoying every minute like a seven-year-old kid swimming for the first time.

"Dinner in five minutes!" Trisha shouted from the patio door. Reluctantly I climbed from the pool, dried off and threw on the Fila outfit Lil Bull sent me to come home in.

Trisha had just lit the last of the four candles on the dining room table when I came through the patio door. The Dramatics "In the Rain" was playing in the background, which created a warm

CAREER *Criminal*   By: D. Henderson

and romantic atmosphere. I was surprised, after all we had been
through, she remembered my favorite R&B group.

Trisha prepared two T-Bone steaks, medium well, baked po-
tatoes with sour cream and butter, a chef salad and an expensive
bottle of red wine to set the tone. Several times during the course
of the meal I found her staring at me with a deep penetrating glow
sparkling from her eyes. I never had a woman look at me the way
she did, not even Nicole.

"Can I ask you a personal question?" I asked and turned to
face her.

"You can ask me anything you like."

"Baby, when I look at you, I see everything a man could
possibly want in a woman. You're intelligent, very attractive, and
very attentive to a man's needs. What I'm trying to ask you is how
did I get so lucky? What is it about me; that separates me from all
the others that have been trying to win your hand?"

"To be honest you're so different than any man I ever met,
and I don't say that in a negative way. What I admire most about
you is your strength. When we first came to visit you, we were expecting to find a distraught, traumatized young man, but instead we
found a young man that was more concerned about his image than
anything else. My mother thought you were putting up a front, but
my father thought you were a born soldier; but you were just fighting the wrong war. I happened to agree with my father. I believe
you're a very special young man; you just don't realize it. And
contrary to what you may believe, I strongly feel beneath it all
you're a good man that just needs a push in the right direction."

"Baby, that was deep; and to be honest I can feel everything
you're saying. I've often wondered what my life would be like had
I chosen a different path. Being a gangster does not afford a lot of
time to reminiscence on past mistakes or decisions. Once you in-
vest so much time in this lifestyle you find yourself so deep in it
there's is no turning back."

"Floyd, it's never too late to turn your life around. Look at
you; you'll be twenty-four in a few weeks. On all accounts, you are
still a young man, and I believe if you put your mind to it there's
nothing on God's green earth you can't accomplish if you apply

134

yourself. I believe in you; and I would love to help you if you allow me."

"That's something to consider," I said.

Deep in the back of my mind I knew she was telling the truth. For the Lord in me, I simply couldn't understand this over- whelming attraction I had for the crime game; that so far had claimed nine years of my freedom, and damn near got me killed on several occasions.

"Here, let me help you with the dishes," I said in an at- tempt to change the subject.

"Thank you but I can handle it."

"No, I insist. You wash and I'll rinse. Got to earn my keep," I playfully joked and she joined in by giggling like a school-girl.

There was a quiet intensity brewing in the air. I never imagined washing dishes could be so pleasurable. Every single act, from the slight touch of the elbows, or the glazing of our hands could be construed as a form of foreplay. The physical attraction was overpowering.

"Is that it?" I asked and rubbed some soap suds from the tip of her nose.

"Yes," she whispered softly.

"Are you sure?" I asked and slid behind her and pressed my body against hers.

The smell of her scent was like a magical potion that made me light-headed. My lion immediately responded to the softness of her posterior like it had a mind of its own. As I struggled for con- trol I slid my hands under her blouse and undid her bra. I could hear her breathing increase and could feel her body shiver as I left a trail of kisses from the bottom of her earlobe to the back of her neck.

"Oh Floyd," she moaned as I lifted her skirt and slipped my manhood between her legs.

With one hand under her blouse, I slid the other inside her panties and masterly manipulated her clit, driving her into an un- controllable frenzy. I could feel the warmth and wetness soak through her panties as I pressed my manhood harder and harder against her crotch. The mere anticipation of what was about to take place damn near drove me to the point of ejaculation. Never in my life have I ever wanted a woman as bad as I wanted Trisha. In one single move I slid her panties down to her knees. Trisha responded by taking my manhood and placing it in the folds of her love nest. Her wetness engulfed my head as I inched my way deep inside her. It took every bit of strength I could muster to maintain restraint. I was in ecstasy, experiencing the greatest pleasure I have ever known.

The deeper I pushed inside the louder her moans became. Unable to hold any longer I erupted like an angry volcano that sent a rippling sensation throughout my body; and ignited a climax inside Trisha that was so powerful she collapsed inside my arms. Completely spent; and unable to stand any longer we both rolled freely to the floor where we collected much needed relief from the cold marble surface.

"Wow that was wonderful," she whispered with a smile that spoke a thousand words.

"Yes, it was," I replied like a proud stud.

Half-clothed and rejuvenated, we made our way to the bedroom. What started in the kitchen as a spontaneous act fueled by raw passion was replaced by a more intimate touching. As she explored every inch of my body and paid particular attention to each scar with soft wet kisses, I realized how much this woman truly loved me. She was the one, the gateway to a life of love and happiness. It was at that moment I decided to hang up my flag and dedicate my life to being the best man I could be; a man that she could be proud of. With that thought in mind I took her in my arms and held her until she drifted into a quiet peaceful sleep.

It was a little past midnight when I rolled from the bed and paused for a moment to study this beautiful creature resting peacefully beneath me. Prison had a way of making a man appreciate all the true treasures in life. Less than 24-hours ago I was in a steel cage that was fitted for an animal. Now I was, free as a bird, sleeping in a king size bed with the pleasure of a gorgeous woman at my side. I wanted to pinch myself. Little did I know this was a pipe dream, a temporary fantasy of a life I could never share, regardless how pleasing it felt.

Unable to locate my boxers, I proceeded downstairs naked as the day I was born. It had been over five years since I'd last seen the sky at night or walked freely in the dark. As I sat on the patio counting the stars and thinking about my future, I figured my best move would be to go back to college and get a degree, hopefully a PHD. I'd always been fascinated with Psychology, and the study of human behavior.

One of the benefits that came from spending four out of five years in a Security Housing Unit, free from the communications and distractions of the outside world, it provided me with the opportunity to expand my studies. It was in the hole I first discovered Sigmund Freud, Wilhelm Wundt, and other great thinkers whom all contributed a new and unique approach to the evolution of psychology. In a quest to gain a better understanding of my enemies I had to first take a closer look at myself. It was during this examination I discovered all gang members, regardless of race or affiliation all shared common traits, and by the definition of Man's Law we were all Career Criminals.

The longer I sat there the more I began to realize there was nothing beyond my reach. My shortcomings in school came from a lack of interest and not my inability to learn. Any subject that fascinated me I excelled in, those that didn't I ignored. Had I known then what I know now instead of being the last to class I would have been the first; instead of sitting in the back of the classroom I would have sat in the front. It was a beautiful awakening, and one I planned to take full advantage of.

"Baby, what are doing out here?" Trisha asked from the patio entrance.

"Thinking about you and me and this beautiful future we're about to share."

"May I join you?"

"You certainly may," I said and patted my lap.

For a brief moment I lost all sense of thought as I watched as she walked gracefully towards me. At five-feet-six Trisha had the most beautiful body I'd ever seen on a woman. She was perfect in every way imaginable. She was certainly the type of woman I could love wholeheartedly. She sat on my lap and placed her arms around my neck. Her skin was so smooth and soft I couldn't stop caressing her.

"I love you," she said and placed her head on my shoulders.

"I love you, too, baby," I replied for the first time and meant every word of it.

"Does that mean you're staying?" she asked.

"That's exactly what it means; but first I must return home and file the necessary paperwork needed to have my parole transferred."

"Baby, I don't want you to leave. See if you can transfer your parole without going back. You know my father has a lot of connections with the California Department of Corrections, if we need I'm sure he'll help," she exaggerated while hugging my neck.

"You told him about us?"

"I tell my parents everything. Trust me they don't judge a person by their past. As long as you're trying to do the right thing they will support you in any way they can."

"That's good to hear. I will look into it first thing in the morning." I said as I thought about my first and only meeting with her parents. It was not my intentions to appear rude, but their presence could have created a great deal of speculation.

"Come on baby, let's go back to bed."

"Give me a minute; I got a few phone calls I need to make and I'll be right up."

The last thing I wanted was to mislead Trisha; but there were certain things about my life she could never know. True enough I wanted to be with her, but not at the cost of abandoning my dreams to one day be the Head of CCO's Street Operations and the Boss of my own Crime Family. First and foremost I was a gangster, and the only thing appealing about a square life was the front, the appearance of doing the right thing, while at the same time unleashing a virus on the underworld so deadly Al Capone would be proud.

After locating the phone, I returned to the patio to enjoy my first evening under the stars. I couldn't remember the last time I was outside at night as a free man. The sky looked so pretty, it made me wish I had a camera to take a picture of it. It was funny how prison made a man appreciate all the simple things in life, all the things the average John took for granted. Had Trisha not been waiting I would have spent the entire night looking at the constellations.

My first call was to the most important girl in my life; a woman I loved more than life; and one I would I gladly die today so she could live to see another day.

"Hey mama, what are you doing up so late?"

"Waiting for you to call, your counselor said they released you at eight this morning, what took you so long to call?"

The sound of her voice made my insides twist; suddenly I felt a stab of guilt at the realization it had been over five years since we last spoke. What was good for me didn't necessary mean it was good for others, and I now realized how selfish my actions were. Growing up, I remembered her saying, "She slept better when I was in jail; at least she knew I was in a safe environment." Little did she know, the same way a man could die in the streets, he could get his issue in prison.

"I'm sorry Mama, I got caught up. How are you?" I asked, feeling a joy so profound I fought to keep my composure.

"A lot better now that you're out of that dreadful place. When are you coming to see me?" she questioned; her voice filled with excitement.

"I'll be down there next week, but you can't let anybody know I'm coming, and I won't be able to stay long. Is Pops home?"

"No, he's at work, and he's going to be sad he missed your call."

"Don't worry about it, I will call a little later, as a matter of fact I will call everyday until I see you."

One thing I loved about my Mama, she never questioned the moves I was making. If I said I needed to do something a certain way, at a certain time, that's what it was. After spending the better part of an hour laughing, joking, and enjoying the sound of her voice we called it the night.

My next call was to my brother by another mother, my ace

boon coon, none other than Lil Bull.

"Pretty Boy Floyd, what's up Crip?" Lil Bull shouted into the receiver bringing an instant smile to my face.

"Shit you already know; what's up with you Baby Boy?"

"You know me, out here on this big money scheme, waiting for my Nigga to come home so we can take over the world. Where are you?"

"Cuz I'm in Berkeley with baby girl I told you about a few months ago." I said with a smile, happy to hear my homie's voice.

"Cuz I been looking all over for you. I called the prison three times trying to locate you. I even called your mother. For a minute I thought those tricks at the prison were lying, or something had happened to you."

"I'm good Cuz, I should've called. Shit happened so fast when I stepped out the gates I lost track of time. Sorry about that."

"Think nothing of it, when are you coming home?"

"I'll be there tomorrow. I'll call you later and give you the flight information."

"Do you need me to wire you some cash?" he asked.

"No, I'm good. I still have close to three thousand dollars from what you sent; you know in the hole you're only allowed to spend thirty-dollars a month."

"Cuz it's hard to believe you made it out that hell hole. I heard about all the shit you went through. You put San Diego on the map, every Crip I know from L.A speaks real highly of you."

"Yeah, I met a lot of good brothers up there, Crip legends from every set. Shit was real in the field; Southern California Mexicans ain't playing no games, come correct or don't come at all. Like they say; shit that can't kill you will only make you stronger. I went to hell and back; played poker with the Devil and won."

"Cuz you sound good, I can't wait to see you."

"Likewise, we got a lot of catching up to do."

"Cuz what's going on in Berkeley?"

"A special young lady name Trisha."

"Yeah, I remember you telling me about her, the church girl right?"

"Yeah, that's her."

"Sounds like shit is serious between you two?"

"It is. I think baby girl might be the one."

"I can't wait to meet her; is she coming with you?"

"Nah, the last thing I want is to expose her to this life. Baby girl is sitting up nice out here. The perfect getaway when we need a spot to chill. What's popping down there?"

"To keep it 100 I been having problems with your people."

"Talk to me," I said, already knowing the situation.

"Cuz CCO is trying to take over San Diego. A few months ago they waged war on all drug dealers. They hit four of my spots, and killed three of my workers. These niggas is coming from so many different directions I feel like I'm fighting a ghost. I don't know who's affiliated and who isn't. We got Crips on some Black Panther shit. Cuz there is too much money in the crack game for a Gangster to bow down; and as long as I got air in my lungs I'll never allow some out of town niggas to take over the hood. I need your help."

"Cuz you need not say no more, I got you."

Unbeknown to Lil Bull, or anyone else outside of the party, CCO wasn't on some Black Panther time, CCO was about Organized Crime. The revolutionary aspect was just a front. We still operated under the principles of Crips, but with different beliefs. We didn't believe in selling drugs, or committing crimes, at least not in our neighborhoods; and we were willing to use force to stop anyone that did.

Lil Bull and Salt-Rock had made it home a year before me on good behavior; and during that time they both had risen to two of the biggest drug dealers in the city. Realizing CCO was too big to wage war on, Salt-Rock packed his shit and took his operation to Seattle, while Lil Bull decided to stay and fight; and by doing so CCO had marked Lil Bull for death.

In all the years I'd known Lil Bull I'd never known him to ask for help. Cuz was a gangster of all gangsters, fearless with a heart worthy of a warrior. I regretted he was in this position, and I vowed to do everything in my powers to get him out of it. It was time to return home and do whatever was necessary to ease his concerns. I was happy Cuz survived the wrath, not many did. I couldn't protect him from prison, but I was home now; and there was no way on earth I would standby and allow harm to come his way, even if it meant going against the very oath I pledged my life to.

Can't Escape the Past
–Chapter 14–

"TWA flight 117 now boarding at gate 12," the announcement came immediately after I handed the flight attendant my ticket. I turned towards Trisha, who stood silent with a deep look of sadness in her eyes. She didn't want me to leave; and to be honest neither did I. Or did I? For a brief second I thought about taking her with me. As pleasing of a thought I knew it wasn't feasible. This wasn't a pleasure trip, a reunion of old souls; this was business; the type of business that could put her life in danger.

"Don't forget to call," she said, wrapping her arms around me and refused to let go.

"I'ma call every day and every night," I said, giving her a huge hug.

"Final call for flight 117 at gate 12." Reluctantly she released me.

"I'll call you tonight," I said, joining the rest of the passengers boarding the plane. After locating my seat, I fastened my seatbelt and closed my eyes and said a quick prayer. This was my first flight, and I must admit I was a bit nervous. What were the odds of me going through everything I'd been through only to die in a plane crash? It was too late to get off the plane; whatever life had in store for me I was going to face it like a gangster. Fuck it.

"Is this your first flight?" an elder white man asked.

"It's that obvious?" I asked, turning in his direction.

"You can say I'm an expert at spotting first time flyers.

Where are you headed?"

"San Diego."

"I'm headed to Los Angeles; I commute to the Bay area four times a week; job related. What type of business are you in?"

"I'm an urban consultant, an inner city problem solver," I answered and turned towards the window hoping to avoid any further questioning from Mr. Friendly.

"That sounds interesting, would you care to elaborate?" he continued.

"No, I would not; and if you don't mine I'm really not in the mood to socialize," I said, hoping this would bring a close to this exchange.

"Sorry, I didn't realize I was bothering you?" He stepped away sharply.

"Well, you are." Snappy was an understatement.

"Excuse me," he said and rose to his feet.

I allowed a few minutes to pass before I looked back and found Mr. Friendly sitting five rows back. We made eye contact and he quickly turned his head. Good riddance, I thought. The last thing I wanted was to be pestered by an over talkative stranger.

The solitude that came from being thirty thousand feet over the Pacific Ocean provided me with a quiet moment to ponder over my last conversation with Lil Bull. It was obvious by the fact Lil Bull waited a year to confront this problem only meant it was way bigger than he could handle alone. Lil Bull wasn't known for his patience; to the contrary he was a hot head and overly aggressive. He reminded me of Sonny in the Godfather, a stone cold gangster but easily agitated, and predictable when infuriated.

After a brief stop in Los Angeles, we arrived in San Diego twenty minutes later. No sooner than the plane hit the ground, I felt a sudden surge of excitement. San Diego was the one place in the world I truly felt at home. To most, it was known for its strong military presence and the best all year around weather in the entire USA. Home to the western fleet, miles of battle ships lined up and down the coastline. It was a beautiful sight, a wonderful display of military might.

I emerged from the plane and was immediately greeted by

Lil Bull. Had he not been standing directly in front of me I doubt very seriously I would have recognized him. Lil Bull was big as house with a massive physique worthy of professional competition. My last recollection of Lil Bull was of a kid no bigger than I; five-feet- seven and weighing no more than 150 pounds. I had heard he was hitting the weights and had gotten much bigger; but I would have never imagined him to be six-feet tall and weighing a solid two hundred and ten pounds. Suddenly I regretted not hitting the weights when I had the opportunity. While most prisoners chose to work on their bodies I selected to work on my mind; but then again you had some that did both.

"Welcome home Cuz," he said and engulfed me in a bear hug and damn near lifted me off my feet.

It was clear by the strong display of affection nothing had changed about my little brother. Besides my mother, Lil Bull was the closest person in my life. After retrieving my luggage, which consisted of a few outfits Trisha had purchased, Lil Bull lead the way to airport parking where he stopped in front of a fully-reno-vated 1966 powder-blue drop-top Cadillac Sedan DeVille.

"Cuz, I see you're rolling like Ricardo Tubbs in Miami Vice.

"You like it?" he asked studying my reaction.

"What is there not to like; it's clean as a mother fucker," I said and admired it from bumper to bumper.

"I'm glad you like it, because it's yours," he said and threw me the keys.

"Damn, Cuz, I don't know what to say."

"The expression on your face says it all. Welcome home, Cuz."

"Cuz, this is the best gift anyone has ever given me; thank you homie."

"Think nothing of it; you would have done the same for me. Have you eaten?"

"No, and I'm starving to death."

Lil Bull took me to Anthony's Fish Grotto and selected a seat in the back where we could talk in private. Right now was a time to reflect and reminisce on the good times. A time to answer long awaited questions about our sentences; and separate fact from fiction. After enjoying a satisfying meal, Lil Bull ordered a double shot of Hennessy and we stood in the lounge overlooking the ocean.

"I love it out here," Lil Bull said staring out into the Pacific. "I feel like I'm a million miles away from the hood."

"Yeah this is a beautiful sight, one I could get used to." I said and took a sip of Hennessy and allowed the smooth liquor to roll down my throat and burn my chest.

"You never could handle strong liquor," he replied with a slight laugh.

"This shit is strong, but you know I'm not a drinker I'm a weed smoker, you can't be a pot head and a drunk at the same time. How's the family?"

"Little Kenny just turned one, and I got another on the way."

"That's a good thing. You remember what Doc use to say, a family keeps a man grounded. The more you got to lose, the more cautious you become'. Speaking of Doc, have you heard anything about him?"

"I heard Doc caught a weapons trafficking case and jumped bail. The word is he shot back to Mexico, and no one has seen or heard from him in years."

"I don't like that; we both know Doc is not the type of man to forgive and forget, I don't put anything past him. If I had to bet, I'd bet my life he's somewhere plotting our demise. As long as he's alive, we got a serious problem on our hands, one we can't simply ignore or leave up for chance."

"I feel you on that, what do you suggest?"

"Trying to find Doc would be like searching for a needle in a haystack. If you can't find the one you're looking for, the next best bet is to find the one closest to him."

"Belinda?" he said and smiled.

"Exactly. Last I remembered, her mother and little sister lived on Oxford Street in Chula Vista. You remember the house Doc had us pick up Belinda when her car wouldn't start?"

"Yeah, I remember exactly where it's at."

"Good, check it out. Enough about Doc, what's going on with you?"

"Every day is filled with uncertainty. It's an ugly situation out here." He sighed, shaking his head. "The hood is in ruins. We got Main Street Crips selling crack in the hood; and they're doing it with the backing of CCO, and some OG homies that will kill you quicker than a fly on the wall."

Feeling buzzed, I stood up and began walking around the table while he continued filling me in.

"Cuz, they been trying to shut me down since I been home. They came at me a couple of times, slipping and got their issue; but a few of my workers weren't so fortunate. It's a war going on out here, on every set, in every hood. There is so much money involved in the crack game you got to be careful who you trust; it's like the Wild West out here, it's every nigga for himself. Cuz, you got to have a small army out here to survive up in these times."

"No, you don't, you just got to be smart. The more cats you got on your team the more visible you become. Two gangsters are more dangerous than fifty, because they can strike and move without leaving a trace. The number one objective is annihilating the problem. It's not about taking credit; are being recognized as the hitter."

Lil Bull cut me off, "I know, I know, Cuz."

"If you knew then you would know that one thing about all gangsters is that most have too many enemies to count. Soldiers are expendable, Generals not so much. Kill the head and the body will self-destruct. Say we take CCO out of the equation, I can squash that. Main Street that's a different story; all we gotta do is find out who's running their show and cash his check."

Shaking off my words of wisdom, Lil Bull folded his arms and spoke with concern. "The word on the streets, a cat name Lil Man is the running the show for Main Street, but he's not the problem, I could have killed Cuz a long time ago. The problem is Zuberi, his cousin, and from what I gather is the top dog for CCO. I got to give him his proper dues; Cuz is a stone cold killer. For the exception of Main Street, Cuz is taxing every crack dealer on the streets; and the ones that refuse to pay is sent the full might of CCO."

True enough, Zuberi was the head of CCO's Operation in Southern California, which was hard to imagine being that he never spent a day in jail. College educated, with a degree in business, and strong family ties to the higher ups he was hand-picked. If everything Lil Bull said held true, that meant Zuberi was down in San Diego doing his own thing, outside the watchful eyes of the homies in Los Angeles.

I patiently waited for him to finish his rant and vent about CCO, knowing he didn't have a clue about the events materializing around him.

"Cuz, on one hand, CCO advocates peace and unity, and establishing a drug free zone in the Black community; then on the other hand they're systematically erasing one drug dealer, and replacing him with one of their own. Cuz there is no way; as long as I'm alive I will allow an outside influence to dictate what's going down in the hood. I don't give a fuck who these niggas is, or who they claim to be. I'm ready to go war."

"I feel you on that. Cuz, it's hard for me to believe CCO is in the crack business. If that is the case, not saying it is, that would mean everything I value and hold true to my heart is a lie. If that's the case, I will come at them in a way they will never understand. In the event we got to come at Zuberi, it must be done in a way it can never come back on us. In the meantime, you must lay in the cut and let me figure this shit out. I don't know Zuberi, but I'm close to his brother. If we have to get at Cuz, it would be best to do it as quickly as possible. What do you know about him?"

"Cuz, you won't believe who he is married to."

"Cuz, I don't have a clue." I said, wondering who he was talking about.

"Tanya," he said, nodding like I really knew who he was speaking of.

"Tanya." I repeated after a brief moment of reflection. "Don't tell me you're talking about Tanya Roberts?"

"The one and only; and the cold thing about it, I ran into baby girl a few weeks ago and mentioned you were coming home.

She gave me her number and made me promise I'd give it to you. Cuz, baby girl still got a thing for you. I'll bet my last dollar on that."

I retrieved her business card and stuck it in my pocket. The mentioning of Tanya brought a smile to my face. I had always wondered what became of her, now I knew. It wasn't surprising to find she married the biggest gangster in the city. Her mother taught her well.

Unbeknownst to Lil Bull, Tanya was not my main concern; it was Lil Man and his ties to CCO. Although Lil Man wasn't CCO, his brother was; and just so happened to be one of the contact numbers I received when I went to LA county jail. The more I learned, the clearer the picture became. Selling crack in a black community went against everything CCO represented. I wasn't naïve to believe we could rid the Black community of all ills, but at the same time I couldn't understand how we could openly support some, and kill and tax others.

I realized the day I pledge my allegiance to CCO, I gave up all previous commitment and alliance to the Eastside Rolling 40's Crip Gang; in which I still stood by. But one thing I never abandoned was my ties and loyalty to my family; and by every sense of the word Lil Bull was family. It was clear CCO had forsaken my hood, and in doing so marked Lil Bull for death.

I shot dice with the coldest hustlers, played poker with the coldest bluffers, and won. I'd been in the business long enough to know to keep my concerns to myself, and never share my thoughts, or let even my closest homies know what I was thinking. I was more than positive the Central Committee knew Lil Bull was my fall partner, just as I was positive they gave this situation a great deal of thought. The worst thing I could do was raise an objection where Lil Bull was concerned. Not only would it raise a red flag, the Big Homies would put an extra set of eyes on me, and keep me in the blind on the moves they were making. It wasn't about the hood; it was about total dominance over the city; which was a feat I could only accomplish with the full backing of CCO and its resources. It was a tricky situation, one that would require intense thought, and careful and complete planning.

A New Beginning
–Chapter 15–

The following week I laid in the cut at the Embassy Suites enjoying all the simple things life had to offer; like hanging out on the beach, going to the movies, and spending hours on the phone discovering new and exciting things about Trisha. She was amazing, and had a wonderful sense of humor. My parole agent informed me it usually took between four to six weeks for a transfer to get approved; which in a sense gave me between three to five weeks to take care of business.

Considering everything I was about to embark upon, I felt it was in my best interest to relocate and return to my new home with Trisha. Laid the foundation for a new front in the event things didn't go as planned in San Diego. No one outside of Lil Bull knew about Trisha, and that's how I planned to keep it.

The vacation was over, money was getting short, and it was time to put in work. Besides Lil Bull, no one else knew I was home, now I was about to add one more to that list. Tanya had always been more mature than most people in our age group; and coming up in the hood she knew better than to speak on my presence, especially if I told her not to.

"Hello," a warm sensuous voice answered on the second ring.

"Hello sexy." I whispered into the receiver.

"Who is this?" she asked somewhat puzzled.

"Who would you like it to be?" I shot back.

"Floyd?"

"The one and only, how are you?"

"I'm wonderful."

"Is that right?"

"Yes that's right; where are you?"

"Why?"

"Because I'd like to see you; is something wrong with that?"

"No, baby, it's all good; I like to see you too. I'm at the Embassy Suites in La Jolla, room 323."

"I live less than ten minutes away, I'll be there shortly."

I was talking to Trisha when I heard a gentle knock on the door. *Damn, that was fast*, I thought when I hung up the phone. I opened the door and was confronted by one of the most beautiful woman I ever laid eyes on. Gorgeous was too inadequate to describe this lovely creature standing before me. There was something very different about Tanya, something I couldn't put my finger on; then suddenly it hit me, she was all grown up.

"Are you going to invite me in?" she asked and hit me with a smile that made me feel like I was ten years old.

"Excuse me," I said and stepped to the side and allowed her to come in.

"You look like you saw a ghost," she replied obviously relishing in this most awkward moment.

"Nah baby I wouldn't go that far, but I must admit you have aged exceptionally well."

"Thank you Floyd; and you don't look too bad yourself."

"May I take your coat?"

"You most certainly may," she said and removed her cashmere coat revealing a see through thigh high nightgown with a perfectly toned body underneath and the prettiest legs I ever laid eyes on.

"Wow!"

"You like?"

"You're nice; real nice," I said, unable to take my eyes off her. "You always dress like this?"

"I dress according to the occasion. May I have a hug?"

I took Tanya in my arms and instantly felt her nipples harden against my chest. The warmth and softness of her body combined with an intoxicating fragrance was more than I could bear. My lion responded like a cage animal fighting to be freed.

"What do we have here?" she asked, and forcefully squeezed and massaged my lion until it was rock hard and resting in the pawn of her hand.

"Floyd, you have grown considerably since I last saw you. Let me see if I can help you with this."

She slid down to her knees and slowly took me inside her mouth, allowing her tongue to do a seductive dance around the tip before drawing me deeper and deeper inside her mouth. I fought for restraint as the intensity grew. The pleasure was unlike anything I had ever felt before. Never in life would I have imagined a woman's mouth could deliver more pleasure than her snatch. Unable to hold back I erupted like a high power water hose; and like a professional dick sucker Tanya swallowed every last drop, and I loved her for doing so. Completely drained, I collapsed on the bed and stared at the ceiling in a semi daze.

"I'll be back around 11 am to take you shopping; please be here. There is an envelope on the dresser with a little spending money. And Pretty Boy, please don't give my dick away; you know how these bitches is when they find out a brother just got out of prison."

Too weak to move, I looked up at the sound of the door closing. My eyes shifted to the dresser, and sure enough there was an envelope on top. I closed my eyes and drifted off into a peaceful sleep.

I awoke four hours later in the same position Tanya left me in. At first I felt refreshed and completely satisfied; but the more I thought about it, the more disappointed I became. Not in Tanya, but in myself. Not only did I allow Tanya to dictate the course of our rendezvous from the moment she arrived to the moment she left, I also allowed her to established control. That was not the plan, and I felt like a complete trick by allowing it to happen. A soft laughter escaped my lips at the realization my pants were still wrapped around my ankles. After successfully freeing my legs, I headed to the shower.

There was nothing more rejuvenating than a cold shower. Back in top form, I realized I made a crucial mistake, one that might set me back. Time was of an essence, and I didn't want to be in San Diego a day longer than I had to. Realizing the error of my ways, I knew what it took to correct it. I picked up the phone and dialed her number. It was 2:45 am.

"Hello," a tired sleepy voice answered after the fourth ring.

"I need to see you."

"What's wrong?" her voice became stronger.

"I need to see you. Either you're coming or you're not." I said and hung up. It was a gamble, a power play designed to see how much control I had over her.

No sooner than I turned off the lights and climbed back in bed I heard a soft knock on the door. Deep in the back of my mind I knew she would come. I opened the door and was immediately greeted with a frown and an attitude.

"This better be important," she said and stepped inside the room.

"What do you mean this better be important?" I challenged her.

"I got a test at 8:00 a.m. and I haven't had any rest."

"I didn't realize you went to school."

"There is a whole lot about me you don't know. What's so important you got me out of bed at three in the morning?"

"I see some things never changed with you, like your smart ass mouth. You got me fucked up with one of those lame ass cats you been dealing with. As a matter of fact lock the door on your way out." I said and jumped in the bed.

"Floyd, why are you tripping, what have I done now? You called, I'm here."

"I'm tripping off your attitude. Your mouth, you better watch out how you talk to me."

"Okay, I'm sorry. Baby, I'm just so tired. Can we go to bed and talk about this in the morning." She said and removed her clothes. I lifted the covers and she wrapped her body around mine and dosed off without another word. Tanya was sound asleep when room service arrived with a strong pot of coffee. "Baby girl it's time to get up," I whispered in her ear followed by a trail of light kisses on her face.

"That smells like coffee," she said and slowly opened her eyes.

"It is, would you care for a cup?"

"I would love a cup," she sat up and wrapped herself in the sheets.

"Would you like sugar and cream?"

"I like my coffee like my men, strong and black."

"So, that's what I am, your man?"

"You will always be my man; you're the only man I ever loved. What time is it?"

"It's 6:45."

"That's wonderful, that'll give me enough time to head home, take a shower, get dressed and still have time to burn. Why don't you come to my place and hang out? I'm sure you'll be a lot more comfortable there then you would be here."

Tanya had a three-bedroom condo in walking distance from the beach. With the place all to myself I decided to take a look around in a hope of finding some useful information on Zuberi and his crew. Careful not to disturb anything, I meticulously searched every dresser, cabinet, and closet. Much to my surprise, there wasn't a single trace of Zuberi or any other man inside her home. Something was wrong, things weren't adding up. I figured the least I would find were men's clothes, a robe, house shoes, cosmetics, a toothbrush, something that would suggest Zuberi even existed. There was nothing; perhaps Lil Bull was acting on old information.

Tanya mentioned she was going to school but didn't say anything about having a job; and from the looks of her place someone with deep pockets was most definitely paying the bills. And not to mention, the thirty-five hundred she gave me and called it a little spending money.

I was sitting on the balcony watching two white girls roller skating in biker shorts when Tanya returned. I couldn't tell if they were putting on a show for me or were just overly friendly. They waved and I waved back. Although I never dated a white girl I had a few homies that did and they spoke very highly them.

"Are you enjoying the scenery?" Tanya asked as she took a seat and waved at the two girls.

"Yes, it's nice out here."

"I see you met Jane and Amy," she stated while studying my reaction.

"I wouldn't say I met them. There was no formal introduction. What are you implying?"

"I'm not implying anything; but you know how these white girls are, they love to wrap their lips around a big black dick."

"Baby, you're tripping; I know you aren't on a jealousy kick?" I turned to face her.

"No, I'm just saying, I'm not into sharing my man."

"Spoken like a true player coming from a woman that's married."

"Where did you hear that?"

"What does it matter; either you're married or you're not, which one is it?"

"Yes, I'm married, but it's not what you think."

"Why don't you explain?"

"It's complicated."

"Most relationships are; we have plenty of time, why don't you start at the beginning?"

"Have it your way; but understand this, as long as you feel you can't tell me certain things, don't ask me certain things. You know baby this shit goes both ways."

"Yes, I'm married, but Zuberi and I are married in name only. We have never lived as husband and wife. We have a unique arrangement. The type of arrangement where he pays all my bills, school tuition, and provides me with a generous allowance each month."

"You said a mouth full, but at the same time you haven't said anything." *Keep talking, baby girl.*

"Like I said it's complicated, and I'd rather not speak on it. Why must you know every small detail?"

"I don't. All I'm saying, as long as you have secrets don't question me about anything I'm doing, and as long as you're married all you could be is a side piece."

"Floyd, you haven't changed a bit; if it isn't your way it's the highway."

"I'm glad you understood that. Baby, anytime you want more than you willing to give you're bound to come up short fucking with me. When you're ready to come complete, we can sit down and talk about being exclusive. As long as you're doing you, I will do me. That's only fair. What's that white girl's name with the yellow shorts on?" She playfully smacked me.

"Alright, you made your point. What I'm about to tell you, you can never repeat, because if you do it will mess up everything for me. Zuberi is a homosexual, he doesn't like girls. As a matter of speaking, Zuberi and my brother Calvin are in love. As you're aware, Zuberi is a powerful man, with a lot of enemies. If this information ever got out, it would not only destroy him, it would also destroy me. I love our arrangement, it works for us both. Baby, you must promise you will never utter a word about this."

Everything I needed to hear and more. She fell right into the trap.

"His secret is safe with me. I feel a whole lot better knowing I didn't fall for a married woman. Despite my failings I am a man of strong principles. When I heard you were married I felt like half my heart was ripped from my chest. My immediate reaction was to confront you, which resulted in a three am phone call. In order to move forward this was a conversation we had to have, and I'm glad we did. Now that we have that out the way, woman there is nothing standing in the way of the life we always dreamed about. You remember on your 14th birthday, when we made love, and I told you I loved you for the first time, you cried so hard your mother came storming inside your room and found us naked."

"How could I forget? I was so embarrassed, I didn't know what to do."

"Not me, I jumped out the bed like Superman, dick harder

than penitentiary steel. I saw your Mama checking out my tool, and licking her lips. Shit I thought Silvia was about to rush me and take my dick. I could have been boyfriend and step daddy at the same time."

"Boy you wish," she said and we both started laughing.

"On a more serious note, what I am trying to tell you? Baby, we got history, and regardless what we've both been through can't no one take that away from us. From the very moment I first set eyes on you, I knew you were the one. I love you, woman."

"I love you, Floyd, and there hasn't been a single day I haven't thought about you, and wondered how you were doing. Baby, I wrote you at least a hundred letters, why you never wrote back?" I didn't always treat Tanya with respect and the love she showed me was undeserved.

"Baby, love and prison is like gas and water, it just doesn't mix; and as a matter of fact it makes a man's time a thousand times harder than it needs to be. In order to survive, and maintain my sanity I had to separate myself from the streets and everyone in it. Sometimes when you love somebody you have to let them go. If it was meant for us to be together our love will survive the test of time. As I sit here right now, talking to you, looking at you, I know without a doubt you love and care about me just as much as I love and care about you. Baby, you're my soul mate."

We clasped our hands together and became one at that very moment. I could not wait to tear her walls up.

"I do love you, and I never stopped. You're the only man I have ever loved. Look at me, I am about to cry," she said and the tears begin to roll from her eyes.

Just as quick as they fell I kissed them away. Time seemed to stand still as I held her body close to mine. Tanya was my girl, but I wasn't her man. I was married to the game; Power and Money, and everything that came with it. One thing prison taught me, I didn't need a woman to sustain, and after Nicole, I vowed never to love a woman more than I loved myself, and never place her needs before my own. I was a gangster, although passionate about my paper, I was power hungry, and there wasn't anything I found more appealing than being the most successful gangster that ever played the Crime Game.

      My acting was getting better each time I came in contact with these broads. Now, if I could just locate that white girl on the roller blades, I could build a crew stronger than the United Nations.

The Crack Game
–Chapter 16–

I roamed the dark streets of Southeast San Diego feeling like a foreigner in a strange land. The community I once called home was nothing more than the wasted ruins of a forsaken neighborhood. I drove past countless people searching for a familiar face but found none. Crack dealers and Crack heads ruled the nights. There was a new kind of violence plaguing the streets of southeast; crimes so chilling it made gang brutality seem like child's play. Everyone I knew was selling crack, but I wasn't about to follow suit. I couldn't, in good conscious, participate in a scheme that was victimizing so many. Every gangster had his limitations, this was my line in the sand; a line I vowed never to cross.

I returned to my hotel room and was surprised to find Tanya resting peacefully on top of the bed. It was only after closer examination I noticed a trail of dry tears running down her face. Although I was concerned about her state of mind, I was more concerned how she gained access to my room without a key. After six years of incarceration privacy was something I valued immensely. I glanced at the phone and noticed the red light blinking, indicating I had a message. As I reached to wake her I was startled by the phone. I let it ring several times before I finally picked it up hoping it wasn't Trisha.

"Hello." I quietly whispered into the receiver.

"Pretty Boy, I'm glad I caught you, what are you doing

right now?" Lil Bull asked.

"I just walked through the door. I was about order something to eat and chill. Why, what's up?"

"I need you to ride with me; meet me downstairs in forty minutes."

"How about an hour? I got a few things I need to handle."

"An hour it is. Cuz, do you want me to snatch you a burger or something?"

"Yeah grab me a Big Mac, fries, and a Strawberry shake." I hung up the phone and found Tanya staring wide-eyed at the ceiling.

"What's wrong baby?" I asked and sat on the bed beside her.

"It's Tina," she softly muttered with her voice slightly trembling. "My mother called and said Tina is HIV positive. Floyd, my little sister is dying and no one knows where she is. What am I going to do?"

The tears came quick, an uncontrollable flow of grief and despair rolling down her face with no ending in sight.

I was stunned; at a loss for words, desperately searching my mind for a remedy that would console her. Finding none, I sat there trying to make sense of this most devastating news. My heart went out to the little girl that once called me her big brother; and whose eyes always lit up every time she saw me. *Damn*, I thought, life had dealt her a cold blow; a death sentence at the tender age of eighteen.

"Do you have any idea where she might be?" I asked after a long moment of silence.

"The only time we hear from Tina is when she's in jail," she said hopelessly.

"Jail," I repeated.

"Yes, jail. Floyd, Tina is a crack addict."

The picture suddenly became clear, and everything started to make sense. Tina was out there, way out there; more than likely having sex with anybody and everybody to feed her habit. My last recollection of Tina was of a straight 'A' student with ambitions of being a veterinarian. Where she went wrong I didn't have the slightest clue.

"When was the last time you saw her?" I asked.

"I haven't seen Tina in months. A few months ago I heard she was hanging out on Groveland. I went over there but I couldn't find her."

"That's a start, don't worry baby I will find her. I got to make a quick run will you be alright?"

"Yes, I think I'm ma go home. Can you come over there when you get done, and please call me if you find her?"

"I will, and I'll see you in a few hours."

Lil Bull was just pulling up when I arrived downstairs. I motioned for him to turn down his stereo. The hotel had already complained about him blasting his music when he came to visit. It was obvious he didn't a give fuck what they were talking about. I opened the passenger door and immediately noticed the Colt 45 resting between the center console and driver side seat, which was a clear indication this was anything but a joy ride.

"Cuz I been trying to get a hold of you for the past three hours. You're the only cat in the city that doesn't have a pager," Lil Bull said, taking a break from his milkshake. I wondered where mine was.

"What I need a beeper for?"

"So, I can reach you in times like these. You got a heater on you?"

"Nah, do I need one?"

"Cuz it's real in the field, it's better to get caught with it than without it. Southeast is like a war zone. I got a 9mm and a pager in the glove box. I suggest you take both."

I snapped the pager on my belt and stuck the 9mm in the waist of my pants. Thinking twice about what laid ahead, I asked Lil Bull, "Are you happy now?"

"Very much. Cuz, I know you been gone for a minute; and it takes about an hour to relearn these streets. Shit is vicious out here. Niggas is falling at the waist side. Last night four knuckle-heads got their issue, and the night before three got killed. Cuz it's a jungle out here, and the streets isn't taking no hostages."

"I'm well aware of that, that's why I stay where I stay, on

the outskirts. The battlefield is where soldiers fight wars, the executive quarters is where generals wage war. Cuz I'm not on some street shit, I got the full might of CCO backing my play. I'm not trying to take over the hood; I'm trying to run the city. This street shit don't excite me, San Quentin gave me enough excitement to last a lifetime. Cuz, I'm not trying to keep up with the Jones', I'm not about big gold chains, and colorful outfits; shiny rims and loud music. I'm not saying it's a bad thing, it's just not for me."

"I hear you Cuz."

It was clear by his response he didn't. I had a funny feeling Lil Bull didn't understand the severity of the situation. So far he had been fortunate. He was playing a dangerous game that was turning out a thousand losers to every winner. Contrary to what he thought he was not a serious threat to CCO or the movement. Had he been they would have dealt with him a long time ago. Knowing the homies as well as I did, it was my belief they left him for me to handle.

Although my love for my brother had not weakened, I realized we were not the same two individuals we were five years ago. As fate would have it, we grew in different directions. I also understood a difference in opinion could be resolved by science, but when two people shared different values there wasn't a whole lot to talk about. Regardless of his lack of awareness, Lil Bull was too important to give up on. I didn't expect him to feel the same way I felt, due to the fact he didn't experience half the shit I'd been through. It was on me to open his eyes and expose him to the light. If by chance I couldn't, more than likely it would result in the destruction of both of us. Our ties ran too deep, and the mere thought of leaving him hanging angered me. Contemplating death was more soothing than crossing my road dog.

"Where are we headed?" I asked when he took the I-5 Interstate heading north.

"Hotel Circle."

"What's popping there?"

"I got to drop off a package."

"Cuz don't tell me you got me riding shotgun on a crack sell?" I asked and stared at him.

"I guess when you put it like that, the answers is yes," he said, feeling somewhat awkward by my questioning.

"I'm ma ride with you tonight, but Cuz we can't do this again."

"Cuz you're dead serious about this shit, huh?"

"Cuz I never been more serious about anything in my life; I understand this maybe your hustle of choice, but it will never be mine. When it comes to your business I can support you from a distance, but when it come to some gangster shit I'm right at your side. To be honest it's my intention to draw you away from this madness."

It appeared as if he was listening then his song came on the radio and he started bobbing his head to the beat. I continued, despite his indifference to the knowledge I should have been charging for.

"If it's about money, I got a plan to put us in a position to get more money than we can count. The type of money you weigh like dead bodies, and round it off at the nearest thousand. If it's not about the money with you; and you're addicted to this street shit, then that's a problem. Not for you, but for us. It's a war we can't win, and one that will eventually lead to our downfall. To continue down this path, not only are you gambling with your life, you're gambling with mines, and your wife and kids."

"I hear you Cuz; tell me what you want me to do."

"I need you to fall back, and get out the crack game."

"Cuz, I got fourteen kilos of crack, what do you expect me to do with that; take a loss?"

"I would never suggest that. How long do you think it'll take you to down the rest?"

"About two weeks at the most."

"Could you do it in a week?"

"I guess I could if I have to."

"The faster, the better, and I promise you whatever you lose, ensure I will make up for it ten times over."

Twenty minutes later we were pulling up at the Comfort Suites. After circling the parking lot three times; and seeing nothing that remotely looked suspicious we parked. I exited the car and took the 9mm off safety. I was all in, and out on the ledge on some real bullshit. We had enough crack to render a life sentence. Regardless of the threat, whether it was a robber or an undercover cop my disposition was the same; shoot first and figure this shit out later.

We made our way to the third floor and stopped at a room with the window slightly ajar. The sound of two women giggling sounded like music to my ears. Prison had a way of making a man appreciate all the simple things that came with freedom. After spending a few minutes listening to their exchange, Lil Bull finally knocked, bringing their laughter to an abrupt end.

"Who is it?" a more serious voice asked.

"Lil Bull."

"Dang Kenny, what took you so long? You said you were on your way five hours ago."

The prettiest and sexiest of the two asked. No sooner than we entered the room I reached for the curtains and closed the window.

"When have you ever known me to be on time?" Lil Bull answered and they started laughing.

"So, you must be Pretty Boy?" she asked turning her attention toward me.

"Yes I am, and who might you be?"

"I'm Felicia, and this is my girl Lori."

"It's nice to meet you, Felicia."

"It's a pleasure to finally meet you."

"The pleasure is all mine. You got a boyfriend baby?" I asked Felicia and took a few steps closer to her.

"I have a friend, but it's nothing serious. What about you, do you have a girlfriend?"

"I have a few friends, but it's nothing serious. If you don't mind me asking how old are you?"

"I'm nineteen going on thirty, is that old enough?"

"It all depends what you have in mind."

"Why don't you two go in the bathroom and fuck so we can get down to business." Lil Bull said, catching Felicia with a lustful look in her eyes.

She quickly turned her head and recaptured her composure. I liked her; she was intriguing, young, sexy, and smart. It wasn't every day you found a woman with the heart of a hustler, and the beauty of a model. At five foot eight, petite, and with a body worthy of a New York runway it was obvious baby girl was oblivious to her attributes. She was like a rare gem that needed to be molded and shaped. As I stood behind her admiring her small, well-shaped posterior, supported by a set of long beautiful legs I couldn't help but wonder if she was just as aggressive with her clothes off as she was with them on. She turned slightly and noticed my eyes traveling the length of her body. She smiled, and I smiled back.

"I see you but I don't see my money." Lil Bull injected, ready to get down to business.

"Lil Bull we got your money, but we're a little short." Felicia said as if it was no big deal.

"What the fuck you mean you're short, you still owe me five hundred from last time," Lil Bull huffed, and dumped a kilo of crack on the bed.

"I know, it isn't like a bitch forgot. We got twenty-three thousand, but I promise you we'll make everything up to you when we cop again. Is that cool?" she asked with a girlish smile like she knew they wouldn't be denied.

"I feel like you're playing games with me. As long as as you know when you open up the door for bullshit, bullshit will come back at you. Keep playing with my money."

"We hear you Lil Bull, and I promise we'll have you right next time," Felicia said, and gave Lori the eye to go get the money.

****

The following day I drove to Newport Beach to meet with Akeelah, Tabari's wife. I knew the meeting was coming, I just didn't expect it this soon. Everything about Akeelah represented her husband. She reminded me of Angela Davis, a strong, black, dedicated sister ready and willing to give her life for the cause, and advancement of CCO without a second thought. Twenty years my elder, she was old enough to be my mother, and I greeted her as such.

"How is freedom treating you my brother?" she asked with a smile that was designed to instantly put you at ease.

"I could never enjoy freedom as long as my comrades are still in captivity," I responded, knowing my every word would later be scrutinized.

Meeting with Akeelah was equivalent to having a face to face with Tabari, although she didn't sit on a committee, or possess a formal rank it was understood when she delivered an order it was coming from her husband, and was not up for discussion.

"The comrades send their love, and said to tell you they're happy you made it home safe and sound. Your arrival has been long awaited, and much to their pleasure they're extremely happy to have a soldier of your loyalty, intellect, and vision to lead CCO into this new frontier. In the past few years we have made great strides, and due to the incompetence and greed of some we have suffered some loses. The comrades are not happy with the situation out here; and as a result they feel this individual must go," she said and slid a piece of paper across the table.

I retrieved the paper and glanced at it briefly before setting it on fire. I felt a huge sigh of relief upon seeing the name of Zuberi, who was the head of street operations. The realization Lil Bull was not the target filled me with a joy that was hard to conceal. I looked up and found Akeelah staring at me.

"My brother you appear to be taken aback, as if you're happy by their selection?"

"You can say that. Upon my return I was somewhat alarmed to learn CCO had a direct or indirect stake in the crack business. The word on the streets is Zuberi was knee deep in the crack business, and was operating with the full backing of CCO; who were systematically eliminating his competition. I found this behavior, not only inappropriate, but it went against the very core of my belief, and the very foundation in which we were built upon."

"You're right on all accounts, and I'm so happy you feel that way. So many of our young brothers have entered the free world only to lose focus, which is a testament of their strength.

Money is the root of all evil, but it also a necessity one must have to compete in a capitalistic society. There is a war going on in the black community, and the Devil has recruited our own people to do his bidding. A crack dealer by all definition is a two-headed snake. Anyone that exploits his own people for his own personal gain could never be trusted, and must be dealt with accordingly. What's at stake in the future of the black community, our children, and providing them with a safe environment in which they can grow and prosper."

"When I first heard Zuberi was knee deep in the Crack Game, I couldn't say for certain he was operating on his own accord, and without the blessings of the party. I'm glad I know now, and I must say it will give me nothing more than extreme pleasure showing him the error of his ways, and turning his lights out."

At the conclusion of our meeting I'd never been more dedicated or focused; I understood the mission at hand, and vowed to implement it even if it cost me my life. The anger and disdain I felt towards drug dealers was a hate unlike anything I'd ever felt before. Anyone who sold poison to their own people didn't deserve anything less than a brutal death.

There was something about the State Parole building that gave me the creeps. It felt like I was walking inside a trap and I might not walk out. Although I'd only been home four weeks I had committed a number of felonies, not counting the ones that occurred last night. Immediately upon my arrival I was escorted to the back where I found my parole agent sitting at his desk.

"You're late," he said, looking at his watch.

I looked at him like what else was new. To verbally respond would in a sense give him the impression that I answered to him. There was nothing personal about our relationship; his sole purpose was to send me back to prison as soon as possible; and my job was to dance circles around his monkey ass as long as possible.

"Your application for transfer has been denied," he stated and allowed a second for the bad news to sink in. "Now that's resolved I expect you to find gainful employment and a permanent address. Here is a list of your parole conditions. I advise you to pay particular attention article 14 in which I took the liberty of circling;

and I'd also like to see you every Monday at 9:00 a.m. until you find a permanent address and a job; and Anderson I expect you to be on time."

The smirk on his face led me to believe he was setting me up for the cross. I waited until I got back to my car to examine my parole conditions. Article 14 stated: No parolee shall live above their means and must be able to account for all living expenses. Based on this I was already in violation. There was no way I could account for a hundred and twenty-five dollars a night hotel room, not counting room service and additional forty-fifty dollars a day on long distance calls. I was grateful for the warning; it was time to check out.

On my way back to the hotel I stopped and purchased a dozen red roses and a teddy bear. I couldn't help but notice all the admiring glances I receive as I strolled through the lobby. There was something friendly about a man carrying flowers; it made strangers nod and smile.

"Hey sexy!" I yelled down the hallway when I spotted Tanya setting the breakfast tray outside the room. I held the roses behind my back. It wasn't until I got closer I realized she looked ten times sadder than she did when I left. Something must have happened.

"Happy birthday love, I bet you thought I forgot?" I said and presented her with the flowers.

"Thank you," she said and barely glanced at the roses. "Floyd, there's someone here to see you. I'll be waiting at home if you want to talk."

"Who is it?" I asked and stepped inside the room.

"It's me Floyd," Trisha said with a look of pure disgust in her eyes. "I bet you didn't expect to see me."

"How long have you been here?"

"Long enough to have a nice chat with your girlfriend; so what do you have to say for yourself?

"What would you like to hear?"

"How about the truth, if you're capable of that."

"By the way you're carrying on it appears as though you already know the truth."

"Floyd, why are you behaving like this; like it doesn't matter how I'm feeling right now? Do I mean that little to you?"

"Believe me baby, that certainly is not the case. Right now I'm overwhelmed, I haven't slept in two days and I can't deal with this right now."

"Do you love her?"

"I got love for her."

"Do you love me?"

"I got love for you."

"What is that supposed to mean; either you love her or you love me, you can't love us both? It doesn't work like that."

"It can work any way we want it to work. What's wrong with that?" I asked as I searched for a way to keep them both in my life.

"Because it's not right, and I won't stand for it."

"Baby, what would you like me to say?" I started unloading my pockets and thought about getting undressed, just to show her I was in control and all her barking meant nothing.

"You can start by saying you love me, and me only. And you can finish by packing you're belonging and coming home with me."

"I wish I could but I can't, at least not right now."

"Well, I guess this is goodbye," she said, turning her head to conceal the flow of tears falling from her eyes.

"I guess it is," I replied not wanting to prolong the inevitable.

I stepped to the side and allowed her to pass. I studied her closely, she didn't want to go, nor did I want her to leave. I reached out and took her hand, and when she didn't resist I pulled her against me and felt her body surrender to my touch.

"Baby we can work this out," I said, and started kissing her tears away.

"Floyd, what's wrong with me? Am I not enough for you?" she asked and stared in my eyes searching for solace, and a few tender words to ease her obvious pain.

"Baby, you're perfect in every way imaginable. It's not you, it's me. You must understand prior to you I had a life. A past filled with complication. Contrary to what you may think I can't simply walk away; to do so would not only place me at great risk, but everyone I care about. What I need from you is patience, the necessary time I need to rid myself of my past. You are my future, the woman I love and want to spend the rest of my life with, but baby you must allow everything to run its natural course, until then you must trust me. Do you trust me baby?"

"Yes, I trust you Floyd, I love you."

"I love you too, baby," I said, kissing her tears.

Unbeknownst to Trisha, Tanya, or any other women unfortunate enough to fall under my spell; not only was I on mission to build a network of killers and guerrillas, I was also on a mission to build a squad of female admirers, all of whom would play a pivotal role in my climb to the top. After spending the entire day holding her, touching her, loving her, and whispering warm words of love and encouragement, I took Trisha to the airport feeling our union was stronger than it had ever been. I returned back to my hotel, packed my belongings and checked out.

One Man Show
– Chapter 17 –

After spending three weeks in a hotel it felt wonderful to wake up to the smell of a home cooked meal. One thing I always admired about Tanya was her willingness to cater to her man. I stepped in the dining room and was happy to find her bobbing her head to the latest tunes coming from the stereo.

"That smells good, smells like my favorite." I took a seat at the table.

"It's is."

"Yeah, right like you remember."

"I remember everything about you."

True to her word, Tanya remembered every small detail. My grits was made to perfection, not too hard, and not too creamy, with plenty of butter and the salt and pepper sprinkled on top. The eggs were over easy, with turkey sausage, and light toast with grape jelly.

"Sit down, baby, let's talk for a minute." Wiping the last crumbs from my mouth, I motioned for her to sit down.

"I know that look. What have I done now?" She wore the puppy dog eyes well.

"Baby, you haven't done anything; as a matter of fact you have been the perfect hostess. I want to talk to you about Zuberi. When was the last time you talked to him?"

"Yesterday, he called and said my check was going to be a

little late."

"When was the last time you saw him?"

"About a month ago, right after he got indicted. Zuberi is in serious trouble, and he sounds worried."

"I need you to call him for me."

"Why, what do you want with Zuberi?"

"That doesn't concern you," I shot back, establishing the groundwork from the beginning. For the exception of my mother, never in my life have I ever allowed any women to question me about my business.

Tanya picked up the phone and dialed a series of numbers and hung up. A few minutes later, Zuberi called back and she handed me the phone. I was still trying to figure out how my pager worked and she worked hers and his like a pro.

"Supreme greetings my brother, this is Pretty Boy."

"Cuz I'm glad you called, I really need to see you."

"When and where?"

"I can be at Tanya's in two hours."

"I'll see you when you get here."

I hung up the phone and noticed Tanya was eyeing me suspiciously. Curiosity and concern was sketched across her face. She was wondering what on earth I could possibly want with Zuberi. The most obvious would be a drug connection; and the mere thought of that was eating her alive.

"Come here, baby," I said, tapping the top of my thigh. She sat down and wrapped her arms around my neck. I could feel her body tremble under my touch.

"Relax baby, it's not what you think. One thing I can promise you I will never get involved in the crack game, and I will never divulge what you told me. I got business with Zuberi that has nothing to do with you or drugs."

"I believe you," she said with a sigh of relief.

"Zuberi will be here in a few hours and I don't want you to be here when he arrives."

Tanya was about to say something. I gave her that look and she got her sexy ass up and headed to the bedroom.

Zuberi was a tall, dark complected brother with square

features. Nothing about him suggested he was a gangster, let alone one of the leaders of the most notorious criminal organizations sweeping through the State of California. I studied him briefly searching for any signs that would confirm his sexuality. Had I not known he was a homosexual I would have never suspected it. My man was smooth, quiet, laid back, and pushing a serious disposition.

"Pretty Boy, it's a pleasure to finally meet you Cuz," he said as we shook hands and embraced.

"Likewise, I tried calling you but the number they gave me was no longer in service."

"The same week you were scheduled to come home I got indicted, and had to shut everything down. The homies told me you were on your way home and to look out for you. Since then things have deteriorated somewhat; but I did bring you a welcome home gift. I hope twenty-five thousand can help a little." He said and handed me an envelope. "With bail, and mounting legal expenses my bankroll has taken a serious hit."

"No need to explain, I appreciate the quarter." Stuffing the envelope in my pocket, he spoke in a serious tone.

"Another reason it was urgent I speak with you; I have a situation on my hands, and my brother suggested you may be able to help."

"I'm listening, shoot."

"What I'm about to share with you is for your ears and your ears only. If for any reason you can't assist me, I will understand, and we'll forget this conversation ever took place."

"What's troubling you my brother?"

"Last month I was indicted on federal drugs and weapons charges; although I never sold drugs a day in my life. I'm certain these charges resulted from my relationship with a cat name Lil Man, an OG Main Street Crip, who just happened to be my cousin. True enough, I had some personal dealings with Cuz, but nothing that would remotely justify these charges. The mere association or support of a drug dealer is far outside party lines. I need not tell you the homies up north are not happy with this situation; as a matter of speaking, they're highly upset. It's imperative I get rid of this problem as quickly as possible. I've heard a great deal about you, and unlike most top officials I'm told, you and I share a similar belief. Although I'm passionate about our people I'm a gangster, and like the average gangster I'm about the dollar. Since joining ranks with the party, I have accumulated a mass fortune, and up until now have received an overwhelming amount of praise. Due to my present situation, and my inability to trust anyone around me I need your help. Be mindful, what I'm about to ask of you is not party business, it's personal, and I'm willing to pay a nice dollar for your services."

"Please continue," I said, hanging on his every word, not giving him the slightest clue what I was thinking or where I was coming from.

"I'm sure you're aware of the party's position when dealing with drug dealers is to tax them, rob them, and eventually kill them. Following these lines we accumulated an enormous amount of wealth, and a mass supply of cocaine. It was never the party's intention to stop the sale of drugs; they just didn't want it being sold in the Black community. The majority of crack we accumulated was pushed into various cities and states; San Diego being one, which happened to be the location where my cousin set up shop, caught a case, and went to the grand jury on me and his entire crew. The ironic part, not only did he serve me up, he hit one of our safe spots, where I hear he's now working out. This isn't business, it's personal. I want him dead, and the sooner the better. I got fifty thousand for his head, thirty upfront, and twenty when the job is done. It's yours if you want it," he said and produced another envelope.

"It would be my pleasure," I said, accepting the envelope.

"Cuz, it's imperative this doesn't get back to me. If the authorities even suspect I had anything to do with his death they would revoke my bail."

"I understand what you're saying Cuz. Trust me, it will be handled in a way you will be the last man they suspect."

After discussing the details that would lead to Lil Man's demise there was one more matter I wanted to discuss with Zuberi; and that was Tanya. It was imperative Cuz didn't suspect Tanya of divulging his secret, which was the type of information a man would kill to conceal.

"Cuz, if you don't mine me asking, what's the deal with you and Tanya? She said you're married, but legally separated. How do you feel about me seeing her? One word from you I'll shake her like yesterday's news?" I lied.

"Glad to hear that; but that won't be necessary. It's over between us, and has been for quite some time. Even after things went sour I continued to support her, but that's about to stop. I got too much on my plate right now. I got everything going out and nothing coming in. It's time to make some cutbacks, and she just happens to be one."

"That's going to kill her, but I'm sure she'll manage. Once again Cuz I hope you come out of this situation on the better end. But you can rest assured, by this time next week Lil Man will be one less problem you will have to deal with."

Just as Zuberi was leaving, Tanya was returning. He gave her a hug and a kiss on the cheek and was on his way. I glanced at the Macy's shopping bags in her hands and wondered if I should let her know Zuberi was about to cut her off. It was obvious she was high maintenance and I hoped she had a bankroll stacked because I damn sure wasn't about to support her lifestyle.

Like most drug dealers, Lil Man was a creature of habit, which made it extremely easy to formulate a plan to rob and kill him. After watching Cuz for four days, I decided the best time to hit him was on the 15th when the traffic was thick and crack heads were out in droves, spending those checks. The small duplex he sold drugs out of was built like a fortress with burglar bars and heavy steel gates on each door. As sharp and security conscious as he appeared he failed to change the locks on a spot that was owned by Zuberi. I guess he figured with Zuberi and his crew either locked up or out of town he had nothing to fear.

Lil Man usually arrived at the house around 7:00 p.m., shortly before the sun went down and didn't open up until 8:00 p.m., like he was running a legitimate business. He always entered and exited through the front door, which provided a false sense of security from streetlights and the constant flow of crackheads wandering the streets. Little did he realize a crackhead couldn't see no more than five feet in front of him because his eyes were always concentrated on the ground searching for anything that remotely resembled a piece of crack. Fortified, with burglary bars on the windows and doors, and slots on the back door to transact business, Lil Man used the front door as security, and the back door to hide his misgivings.

Dressed in shabby clothes with a 9mm and a Rambo knife, I strolled up Groveland Drive like a displaced crack head searching for a hit. It was shortly after 5:00 p.m. when I entered the back door of Lil Man's spot. This was the second time I'd been inside his apartment, and just as the first it was spotless, a home worthy of living in. If everything went according to plan, he would be dead by 7:30 p.m. and I'd be gone by 8:00 p.m. I looked at the wall clock and quietly wished he would hurry up.

As I sat on the sofa for a brief moment, I wondered how I got to this place in my life. A place where I could calmly await to kill a man I never met, nor did me any wrong. How could a middle class kid with every opportunity in the world to succeed, grow up with ambitions to be a gangster, one of the hardest and most painful professions on the planet. Why? I didn't have the slightest clue.

7:00 p.m. came and went and there still wasn't any sign of Lil Man. By 7:30 p.m., I begin to grow weary and impatient. I couldn't believe this punk was late for his own murder. I decided I would give him until 10:00 p.m., if he didn't show by then I would have to catch him another time.

After thoroughly searching the house I found four kilos a crack, a Mac 10 fully automatic machine gun, an AK-47 assault rifle, three ounces of weed, and a paper bag containing twenty-eight thousand dollars. I left everything in place just in case he didn't show. At 9:45 p.m., I glanced outside and found Groveland crawling with crack heads. No matter which way I exited someone was bound to see me. That was a chance I had to take because I wasn't about to stay here another minute. Just as I turned from the window I heard a car pulling up. I jumped behind the door to avoid the headlights shining through the living room window. My heart pounded with anticipation at the sight of Lil Man's truck pulling into the driveway. I removed the 9mm from my waistline and waited for him to come through the door. Suddenly, I was elated and filled with energy. It was a feeling mere words could not capture, the type of feeling that only another gangster would understand.

"Hey, Lil Man, wait a minute," a female voice called out.

"Tee where have you been, I haven't seen you in weeks?"

"I went to L.A. to visit my daddy. I just got back today. You got something for me?"

"You know I always have something for you. The question is do you have something for me?"

"What do you want some of this tight pink pussy, or these pretty red lips around that big black dick?" These crackheads were beyond crazy!

"I want the merry go round, a little bit of both, come in." I was standing at the entrance of the hallway. I waited for Lil Man to double lock the door before I stormed inside the foyer.

Just as he and Tee got ready to make their way to the living room, I came with my rage.

"Hey man what's going on?" he shouted, while looking around.

"Nigga shut the fuck up before I blast your fat ass. Drop the bag and lay on the ground with your fingers interlocked behind your head. You too bitch, don't make me tell you twice."

"Tina lay down," He pleaded when she hesitated.

The name Tina hit me like a hard slap across my face. I stared at the young lady, who up until now I barely paid attention to. There she was in the flesh, Tanya's little sister. In her glaze I was sure she recognized me. A thousand thoughts ran through my mind as I tried to process this latest turn of events. The thought of killing her passed as quickly as it came. There was no way I could harm this girl.

"First things first, do what the fuck I tell you and no one will get hurt. Little mama, throw that bag over here."

Tina did as she was instructed. I rambled through the bag and removed the Colt 45 Zuberi told me he kept there. Just to be on the safe side, I made Lil Man strip naked and then hog tied him. I duck taped his mouth, his eyes, and stuffed his clothes inside a bag. Satisfied he was secure I retrieved the guns, four kilos, weed, and money from the bedroom. I glanced at Tina and she smiled; and it was at that moment I decided I was taking her with me.

"Get up bitch!" I yelled and threw her the bag of confiscated goods. "Crab ass Nigga, your days of selling dope in my neighborhood are over. If I catch your fat ass over here again I will kill you."

Shortly thereafter, Tina and I made a quiet exit from the premises, and drove off in Lil Man's truck.

"Where are you taking me?" she asked.

"I'm taking you to see your sister; she's worried about you."

"I don't want to go over there. Could you drop me off on 54th and University?"

"I can't make you go somewhere you don't want to go, but I think it's real important you go see her."

"Tell her I'll stop by tomorrow, because I really need to go to 54th street and pick up some money before my friend leaves."

"How much money are you talking about?"

"Two hundred dollars; and I really need it."

"Tell you what, how about I give you a thousand dollars, and two ounces of Crack to go see your sister, would that work for you?"

"Are you serious?" she asked with a smile that reminded me of the innocent little girl I used to know.

"I'm dead serious." I was happy that this small gesture was able to bring some measure of joy to her life.

En route to Tanya's, I received a page from Felicia. This past week we had been spending a great deal of time together. It was a platonic relationship based solely on good conversation, and a lot of laughs. Felicia was a nice escape from the overbearing and very needy Tanya. Everything with Tanya was so serious, it's like she forgot how to relax and have fun. We'd been together a little over a month and I felt like we were an old married couple.

I couldn't help but stare at Tina when we stepped on the

elevator. Tina looked unsettled with an air of weariness far beyond her years. The strain and exhaustion that usually came from living in the fast lane was clearly visible. What I couldn't see was any signs of HIV, and to me that was quite disturbing.

Once we stepped off the elevator, I handed her a thousand dollars and two ounces of crack. She accepted the money and crack, and gave me a big hug and squeeze. "Thank you," she whispered into my ear.

"You're welcome; tell Tanya I'll be home a little later."

"When will I see you again?"

"In the morning if you're still here." I said and smiled. No sooner than the words left my lips did I feel a strange sensation inside my chest. It was at that moment I realized there was a real possibility this may be the last time I saw her alive. In possession of a thousand dollars; and two ounces of crack I knew Tina would shake Tanya the first opportunity she got. The realization of being HIV positive wouldn't set in until she was broke and didn't have anything left to smoke.

I returned to Lil Man and found him struggling to free himself. The sound of noise coming from behind him froze him in fear. I could only imagine what he was thinking at that very moment. Despite his present situation, I was positive somewhere deep in the back of his mind he still held onto a small glimmer of hope. The killing of another human being, regardless if it was personal or business was not to be played with.

Without further thought, I removed the huge Rambo knife from my waistline and slit his throat from ear to ear. I quietly stood over him and watch as his life seeped from his body. I removed the duct tape from his mouth and eyes and dragged his fat ass to the bathtub where I filled it up with every cleaning solution he had in the house. The strong smell of bleach and Lysol was the last thing I smelled when I exited the house. From there, I drove his truck to Lincoln Park and left the keys in the ignition with the windows rolled down.

Meanwhile, Felicia was switching hotels faster than a fugitive on the run. It was rare to find a female selling crack, especially one as young as she was. The Holiday Day Inn was an upgrade from the Comfort Suites, but I always made it a practice to avoid any place I had to walk through a lobby to get to my room, especially when I was up to no good.

Felicia answered the door in a thin silk robe that seemed to cling to her body and reveal a set of hard nipples that looked like small almonds. I glanced at her briefly, admiring the contours of her small petite body. If it was her intention to get my attention she certainly succeeded.

"You're home alone?" I asked as I did a quick visual inspection.

"Yes, the dumb bitch is in jail. She got caught in a stolen car."

"I see you and your girl are on some real gangster shit. You sell dope, steal cars, do you rob people, too?"

"I do whatever a bitch got to do to get paid." Acting tough was easy for her but I could peel back the layers quickly.

"I like that, you sound dangerous. I hope you're not the type of chick that'll drug and rob me while I'm sleeping?"

"No, I would never hurt you."

"Why not, what's makes me different than the average cat?"

"Because I like you; can't you tell?"

"I like you, too," wondering what she had in store for me.

"No, I mean, I really like you. I want to be with you." She said and dropped her robe exposing a flawless body. Felicia was the true essence of a young tender, whose body was ripe and ready for the picking. I paused for a moment to absorb her sexiness. She stepped to me and proceeded to unbutton my shirt while gently kissing me from my neck and chest to my navel. By the time she unbuckled my belt I was rock hard and straining for release. She took me in her mouth and engulfed me like a popsicle on a hot summer day.

From sun up to sun down; from the bed to the shower and back to the bed we were trapped in a passion so intense, so pleasurable I lost all track of time. Any concerns I had about her age were quickly put to rest. Her appetite for sex far exceeded any woman I'd ever met. In the heat of passion a bond was forged; one that would turn mere acquaintances into special friends. With Felicia, it was understood she had a man and I had a woman, and we had each other.

Tanya was sound asleep and looking as lovely as ever. I stood at the side of the bed and couldn't help but admire her flaw-less beauty. Even in her sleep she radiated a glow. Hands down she was the most beautiful woman I ever courted. But something was missing. I didn't feel that closeness I felt with Nicole; or that spark or intellectual bond I felt with Trisha; or that raw animalistic pas-sion I just experienced with Felicia. Tanya's most admirable qual-ity was her apparent devotion to me, which was all I was looking for at that moment. I disrobed and slid in the bed next to her. With-out waking up, she took my arm and wrapped it around her mid-section and pressed her body against mine. Shortly thereafter, I drifted off into a quiet peaceful sleep.

Strictly Business
−Chapter 18−

I was home less than a month and had a robbery/murder under my belt. Upon learning of Lil Man's death, and catching no heat behind it, Zuberi was exceptionally pleased with the way I handled business. Staying true to his word, he personally delivered the rest of my money, and had another hit, which was more personal than business.

"Cuz, I really don't know how you feel about Tanya, but I assume it can't be that serious being that you just came home, and haven't seen her in over five years. She had mentioned you several times, not knowing we were comrades, and I felt no need to enlighten her. Since my indictment, I discovered Tanya and her brother Calvin, who happens to be my accountant, have been robbing me blind; and like anyone else that has crossed me I want them dead, and I'm willing to pay a sizable amount to have it done. Are you interested?"

"Most definitely; for the right price, no one, and I mean no one is exempt from getting their wig split."

"Good, good, I'm glad to hear that," he said, and eyed me briefly.

In a moment of haste I realized I may have spoken too quickly. My willingness to gun down my girl, and her brother made him wonder was anyone safe, especially himself. Anyone capable of killing at will, and with no remorse bears watching. Zuberi was cleaning house, and eliminating anyone who posed a threat. Little did he know, Tanya and Calvin were the least of his problems; his greatest threat was sitting right in front of him.

"Tanya is not a problem; I can deal with her on a moment's notice. Calvin that's a different story, I haven't seen Cuz in over ten years. Tanya never speaks about him, I don't know if I'll recognize him if I see him, and I don't have the slightest clue where I can find him."

"That's not a problem. I can put you in contact with Calvin; as a matter of fact, I have a safe house five floors down, one that Tanya knows nothing about. I can lure him there. I have a special request. I would like to be there when you kill him." He said as though he was entertaining a sick desire that brought him extreme pleasure.

"If it's cool with you, I'd like to handle this as soon as possible."

"I like the way you think, is Tuesday soon enough?"

"Tuesday is perfect." We shook on it and agreed on terms of payment.

Sunday night was reserved for dinner and dancing; and as usual Tanya looked absolutely stunning. The true essence of beauty and elegance all rolled in one. It didn't matter if she was wearing boy shorts, or a five thousand dollar gown, baby girl was a prize in any man's eyes. A treasure of pleasure most men and women enjoyed watching. On the surface she appeared perfect, and as beautiful and seductive as she appeared she had flaws; one being her misguided attraction to gangsters. Beauty and brains, Tanya possessed all the attributes to have any man of her choosing, and she chose me, the most unpredictable and dangerous of them all.

I remained at the table when Tanya hit the dance floor shaking her hips to the latest tunes. Soft laughter and conversation quickly became a low whisper as men and women admired her moves like she was paid entertainment. I wasn't surprised nor threaten when several uninvited patrons joined her on the dance floor. It wasn't until a tall, redhead snow bunny, with a body a woman would die for slid behind her, I paid attention. Although seductive, the dance was respectful; and like a true player, I sat back and enjoyed the showcase.

This was one of those occasions where the patrons received more than their money's worth. It was an evening most would never forget, and one that would be the subject of a week-long conversation. Tanya returned to our table and informed me she was ready to leave, which was fine with me. It wasn't until we retrieved our coats I realized the evening wasn't ending, it was just beginning.

"Hello handsome, my name is Rebecca," the tall redhead announced and wrapped her arm around Tanya's midsection.

I smiled. "Floyd."

This wasn't the first time Tanya invited another woman to share our bed, but it was the first time she chose a white women; and I most definitely wasn't upset by it.

Double Cross
-Chapter 19-

From the very moment Zuberi put a hit on Tanya and Calvin, He effectively started the clock that would end his own life. Never one to accept things at face value, I couldn't help but wonder why Zuberi wanted to be there when I ended Calvin's life. Zuberi was far from naïve, and known to be a master manipulator. I was certain he contemplated the severity of his fuck up. The homies up north weren't in the business of passing down pardons. Certain violations demanded immediate death, and who was better to enforce it than one he had no influence over. Just as I was plotting to kill him, there was a strong possibility he was plotting to kill me.

I realized I was at a slight disadvantage by allowing Zuberi to select the location, and be present when I killed Calvin. But like all complicated issues, I was quick to turn a negative into a positive. After careful thought it became apparent Zuberi not only presented the perfect opportunity to kill Calvin, He presented the perfect opportunity to end his life.

Regardless of his intentions, real or imagined, I had the upper hand. Moving forward I thought about bringing Lil Bull on board, and quickly decided against it. The last thing I wanted was to involve my dog in CCO business, even though the outcome would affect him more than it would affect me; and besides I prided myself on being a gangster of all gangsters. I wasn't looking for easy, I loved a challenge; and to execute Zuberi and his lover at the same time presented just that.

For a man knee deep in a murder for hire scheme, Zuberi appeared extremely happy Tuesday morning. Upon seeing him, my first impression suggested he had a change of heart. It wasn't until we were escorted to our table and the waitress handed us a menu I realized he was tipsy. Although he was cheerful, and overly talkative I could sense something was weighing on his mind. Pressure was known to bust a pipe; it was also the substance that separated the strong from the weak.

Compassion I could sympathize, weakness I could not; especially coming from one in a leadership position. I couldn't say for certain what drove Zuberi to hit the bottle at 6:45 a.m. on a day when murder was on his mind. Every gangster had a limitation; exactly how much evilness the soul could endure was entirely on the individual. Zuberi, like most ambitious street gangsters rose to the top by stepping on a mountain of dead bodies. The amount of killings he was directly or indirectly involved in; by legal standards made him a serial killer. It was one thing to kill an adversary, but it took a certain type of gangster to kill a friend or someone he cared about.

"Pretty Boy, I see great things in your future. The big homies speak highly of you, and I see why. You're a man about your business. I wish you would have come home sooner, because I damn sure needed someone with your heart and intellect rolling at my side. San Diego is wide open, and the homies have chosen you to head the reconstruction. We have enormous resources in the city. I laid the foundation; it's on you to build the structure. My days in this city are over; and more than likely after today it may be quite a while before I come back here. As I mentioned before what I requested of you is not CCO business, and the homies would not take kindly of me involving you in my personal dealings. I needed your help and you came through, and for that I will forever be grateful."

"Think nothing of it, Cuz. In this game, I'm certain a time will come when I'll need your assistance. I love and respect the big homies, and will push their agenda to the fullest; but they're not

here. There is no way possible they can fully grasp what's going on
out here. I realize they want certain things done a certain ways;
that's not realistic. It's real in the field; this is not the penitentiary,
the streets dictate how we play. Contrary to what the homies believe, one size doesn't fit all."

After the waitress took our order and returned with coffees
did I continue, "In order to bring about change and rebuild what
our generation has destroyed, not only will it take violence and
brutality, it will also take plenty of money. How we manage to ac-
cumulate this money is still up for debate. Cocaine is like sex and
alcohol; it's a billion dollar industry, and a commodity that's in
heavy demand. I'm a gangster, and I will never advocate the sales
of either; but I'm not naive to believe we can reach our financial
goals by excluding certain forms of ill gains. I don't have a problem with pimps, hustlers, or crack merchants; my problem stems
from the exploitation of the black community. It's not CCO's aim
to stop the flow of crack, but to redirect it."

My words took Zuberi back to a place and time when he,
like I, was focused and dedicated to the cause. When there was
nothing more important than the advancement of CCO, and the
welfare of our people; which was the premise and foundation CCO
was built upon. Somewhere in his travels he lost his way; instead
of becoming a part of the solution he became a part of the problem.
Regardless of his shortcomings, he was still a valued asset; and had
he not been a homosexual, I would have argued for the homies to
spare his life.

I rose from the table, shook his hand and retrieved the
small leather bag that was the purpose of our meeting. Once inside
the confines of my rented Ford Taurus I inspected the 32. Revolver, equipped with a silencer, and box of shells. Zuberi was re-
sourceful on more levels than one.

Shortly thereafter, he emerged from the restaurant and
climbed inside a new model snow-white 500SEL drop top Mercedes Benz, which made it extremely easy to follow him from a
safe distance. Forty-five minutes later, he pulled up in front of the
Amtrak station, and a black gentleman with feminine features entered the passenger side clutching an overnight bag. I recognized

Calvin immediately, who seemed ecstatic to see Zuberi. Once inside the car, Calvin leaned over and gave Zuberi a long passionate kiss. In all my years on earth, never in my life had I ever witnessed two men kissing; and the sight of it turned my stomach. There was no one I despised more than a snitch and a dick sucker; and in my books neither deserved anything less than death.

I followed Zuberi to the apartment he shared with Calvin. Satisfied he wasn't setting me up, I returned home and waited for his call. It was clear Zuberi wanted one last rendezvous before he sent Calvin on to the next life; even a man on death row was granted one last wish.

I was lounging on the couch watching the *Young and the Restless* when Tanya returned home with a smile that radiated love and happiness.

"Baby, I have some wonderful news," she said and sat on my lap, blocking the TV.

"It's obvious by your tantalizing smile something wonderful has occurred," I said, trying to move her a little to the left so I could catch the last five minutes of the episode.

"Yes, it has, it's the best news I ever received; I truly hope you share in my happiness," she said drawing my full attention.

"How could I not? There is nothing more important than your happiness. Talk to me love, the suspense is driving me crazy."

"Floyd, I'm pregnant," she blurted out and suddenly became tense and filled with uncertainty.

"Pregnant." I repeated and met her stare. "Are you sure?"

"Yes," she said and continued to stare at me as if she was trying to read my mind.

"A baby, wow!" I softly whispered. "A second chance at fatherhood has always been a dream of mine. I'm ecstatic, thank you baby," I said and wrapped my arms around her waist and laid my head on her breast.

I was taken aback, overwhelmed with a joy so profound I lost all chain of thought. Suddenly, thoughts of Nicole and a son I never met hit me with a force that angered and saddened me in one swift motion.

In my moment of weakness, thoughts of Nicole and my son

penetrated my shield like an armor piercing bullet. I quickly recovered and shook the thought like yesterday's news.

"What's wrong baby?" Tanya asked and lifted my head.

"It's all good love," I said and smiled.

"I love you, Floyd," she replied and cuffed my face.

Her tears came without warning; this was most definitely a special moment. I looked up and in a moment of euphoria, I realized I truly loved this woman. It was strange how a single act could alter or enhance one's emotions. I never thought I could love another woman as much as I loved Nicole, and I wasn't sure I had, but one thing was certain, I felt a lot closer to Tanya now than I had the day before.

"Floyd, let's go lay down," she whispered in my ear.

"Baby, I'm not tired."

"Neither am I. I'm horny," she said and led me to the bedroom.

Tanya was a skilled and demanding lover that took enormous pride in satisfying her man. I loved the way she held me and ran her fingertips down the contours of my back when I penetrated her. The look in her eyes and the sound of her moans were like an exotic melody designed to arouse and maximize the amount of pleasure. There was never a dull moment between the sheets; and I wasn't ashamed to admit when it came to the art of loving she was the teacher and I was the student.

The afternoon drifted into evening, and the evening quickly turned into nightfall. It was close to 10 pm when Tanya finally fell asleep. I quietly rose from the bed and slipped into the guest bedroom where I got dress and waited for Zuberi to page me. The longer he waited, the more I began to hope he had a change of heart.

One of my biggest flaws was my inability to stop and change course when the situation demanded it. Regardless of Calvin's sexual orientation, I had no right to kill him. I had the power to spare his life; and besides the last thing I wanted was to cause Tanya any form of heartache. She was already in the process of losing her sister, and there was no way I could say for certain could she survive the death of her brother. I realized in a moment of haste, my strong disdain for homosexuals and I marked Calvin for death. It was a move based on convenience rather than necessity. As my mind searched for a way to spare his life, my pager went off and Zuberi's code appeared on the screen. Armed with a short 9mm and a 32 revolver, I exited the apartment and headed to the stairway and climbed the five flights of stairs leading to their unit.

The night was still young but all appeared quiet when I exited the stairwell. I rolled down my ski-mask and proceeded to their unit; and just as Zuberi promised, the door was unlocked. I turned the doorknob slowly and entered the apartment catching Zuberi and Calvin fully dressed and sitting at the dining room table sharing a late dinner. I placed my finger to my lips and leveled the 32 at Calvin; at which time Zuberi rose from seat.

"Make it fast and painless," he said and slowly stepped away from the table.

"I will," I said and quickly turned on Zuberi.

My first shot caught him between the eyes dropping him flat on his back. With my eyes still trained on Calvin, I approached Zuberi's body and put a bullet in his chest. Confident Zuberi was no longer, I removed my ski-mask and turned towards Calvin, who was frozen in his seat and stricken with fear.

"Relax my brother; I'm not here to harm you, I'm here to save you," I said and lowered the gun. "Zuberi paid me to kill you." I allowed my words a moment to sink in.

"Why, what did I do? I never did anything to hurt him, I loved him," he asked, obviously sad and distraught.

"With everything going on in his life he couldn't run the risks of anyone finding out he was a homosexual. In an effort to keep his secret safe he wanted you dead," I repeated, hoping my words would provoke a sense of anger. Instead, Calvin began to weep.

"Check it out Calvin, you need to pull yourself together and listen closely, because how you respond to what I'm about to tell you will determine if you live or die." I pointed the gun at his head.

"Please Floyd don't hurt me, I swear I won't tell," he

pleaded, and suddenly became fearful for his own life.

"I really would like to believe you, but for some reason you don't sound too convincing. Being that you're my girl's brother I'm ma give you the benefit of doubt, but this is how we're going to play it. I'm ma give you this gun and you're going to shoot Zuberi in his head. That way I know you won't snitch. Afterward, I'm ma have a few of my homies come up here, clean up the place and take his body away." I removed the 9mm from the small of my back and placed the 32 on the table.

Reluctantly he picked up the gun; and as instructed approached Zuberi's lifeless body, and after a moment of hesitation shot him once in the head. Unable to handle the death of his lover, Calvin fell to his knees and wept over Zuberi's body. It was a pitiful sight, one that angered and filled me with disgust. I removed the 32 from his hand, unscrewed the silencer and shot him point blank in the side of his head. Careful not to step in blood, I placed the gun back in Calvin's hand, waited thirty minutes and made a quiet exit from the apartment.

I couldn't deny it, killing Zuberi and Calvin brought me a great deal of satisfaction. Regardless of my shortcomings, or my failure to acknowledge the beast within me; I strongly considered myself a child of God; and the Devil was still my arch enemy. I understood the difference between good and pure; and bad and evil. Zuberi and Calvin represented evil; two sick souls that were trapped in Hell on Earth and didn't even know it. As far as I was I was concerned, I did the world a great service.

An hour later, I was safe and sound, in the confines of my own home. Undressing quietly, I hoped to sneak back in the bed with my beautiful lady. Believing Tanya was still sound asleep, I was startled when I emerged from the guest bedroom and found her standing in the dining room sipping from a glass of water. She gazed at me briefly as though she was wondering what I was doing in there.

"There you are." She smiled. "You didn't hear me calling you?"

"Yes, I heard you," I lied and closed the door behind me. Changing the subject, I asked, "Would you happen to know where

I placed my small briefcase with my birth certificate in it?"

"Yes, darling, it's in the hall closet," she said, then went to retrieve it.

Based on the life of a gangster, and constantly reflecting on past crimes I realized the human mind had a photogenic memory, and was capable of recalling and analyzing past events like they occurred minutes ago. I had no doubt whatsoever, upon learning of the death of Calvin and Zuberi, Tanya would spend countless hours replaying the day's events. It was essential she believed, and without doubt, I never left our apartment. The two main ingredients in a homicide investigation were establishing motive and opportunity; and without one, probable cause simply didn't exist.

My Greatest Fears
−Chapter 20−

Zuberi and Calvin's bodies were discovered three days later after the tenants complained about a strange odor coming from their unit. Tanya didn't have a clue why news cameras and the San Diego Police Crime Scene Investigators flaunted around our apartment building. Excited and curious by all the attention, it didn't take long for her to discover there was an apparent murder-suicide a few floors above us. The average chick would have been shaken by the news; but not Tanya; the investigator in her wanted to know who they were, and if by chance she ever bumped into them. The suspense was killing her.

Two days later, all her questions were answered when homicide detectives knocked on our door.

"Ms. Roberts, I'm Detective Ross, and this is Detective Sullivan. May we have a word with you?"

"Okay, sure, please come in. I guess you are here to ask if we knew the victims. What in the world happened downstairs?" She asked, thinking it was simply a follow-up investigation.

I rose from the couch and joined Tanya's side as they entered our living quarters.

"Ms. Roberts, I'm sorry to inform you, your husband and brother were killed in an apparent suicide-homicide." Detective Ross said unsympathetically and with a bluntness that was designed to draw a reaction.

His words hit Tanya with a force so hard she stumbled

backwards and collapsed inside my arms. Unable to grasp this star-
tling news, an agonizing and hysterical scream filled the apartment. I stared at the detective like he was a piece of dog shit for
being so insensitive.

"I think you need to leave," I said, lifting Tanya from her
feet and carried her to the bedroom. I returned to the living room
and found them still here.

"What part of 'I think you need to leave' you didn't understand?"

"I'm sorry for your loss, Sir," Detective Sullivan stated. "I
realize now is not a good time, but we need to speak to Ms.
Roberts as soon as possible. Could you please give her my card
and have her contact us when she's up to it?" he said and handed
me his card.

"I most certainly will," I said and led them to the door.

Once inside the hallway, Detective Ross turned towards
me. "Once again, I'm sorry for your loss, and by the way I never
caught your name."

I smiled and shut the door in his face. I returned to the
bedroom and found Tanya gripping the pillow like it was a lifeline.
She was distraught, consumed with an imaginable pain that was
robbing her of everything except her tears. The loss of her brother
was tantamount to losing a mother or father. I lay on top of the bed
and took her in my arms.

Her body seemed to relax under my touch, but the tears
continued to flow. For a brief moment I felt a stab of guilt, and
once again I questioned my logic in killing Calvin. It was too late
to second-guess my motives, and in actuality, minus her pain I had
no regrets. In my mind I convinced myself Tanya would eventually
overcome the tragic event; but in my heart I wasn't so confident.
Some people never recovered from the loss of a loved one.

I was happy when Tanya's mother arrived and took over
the role of caretaker. Tanya was in bad shape, grief stricken, and
incapable of handling all the business that came with burying a
love one. Although I wasn't a stranger to death, and in my life had
suffered a great deal of loss, I was clueless when it came to conso-
lation. In the hood, death was accepted with a blunt and pint of

Hennessy. The following day it was back to business; the business of surviving these violent times, and implementing the necessary safeguards to make sure you weren't the next victim.

As a token of my condolences, I volunteered to cover the funeral expenses in which I immediately regretted. Had I known every homosexual in the city was going to show up, and it was going to cost close to thirty thousand dollars, I would have cremated his ass.

Even in death, Calvin's life was accepted and celebrated like he was a child of God. From the moment the funeral started, to the moment it ended I dreaded every second of it. It wasn't until we returned home I noticed the change in Tanya's spirits. It was at that time I realized everything was going to be alright.

"That was a beautiful service." She smiled. It made her happy to see her brother was loved by so many.

"Yes it was," I said and returned her smile.

"Floyd come here, hurry up!" she shouted. "The baby just kicked," she stated excitedly.

I slid up behind her and cuffed her stomach like it was a priceless piece of jewelry. No sooner than I massaged her stomach I felt a small thump against my hand. The joy I felt was unlike any happiness I ever experienced. A child was the greatest gift a woman could give a man. Time seemed to stand still as we waited for the next nudge.

"Baby, if it's a boy I'd like to name him Calvin," she whispered, catching me totally off guard and unprepared.

"That's not going to happen." I released her from my arms.

"What do you mean that's not going to happen?" she asked and turned to face me.

"Tanya, I'm not going to name my son after your brother," I said and immediately became angered by her suggestion.

"Why not, I think Calvin is a beautiful name, and what better way to pay tribute to my brother than to name our son after him?" she pleaded.

"Tanya, I'm not going to name my son after a faggot; period, case closed."

"I know you didn't. Floyd, I'm serious, you better take it back, and I mean right now."

"I'm not taking shit back, and I'm serious as a mother-fucker. If you think for a second I'm ma name my son after a known homosexual you got life and bullshit fucked up."

"Floyd, I think you need to leave," she stated with a quiet-ness that had more of an impact than a shout.

"I'm not going anywhere."

"Floyd, if you don't leave, and I mean right now, I will call the police and have them put you out."

"Typical of a hood chick; as soon as shit doesn't go your way the first thing you holler is get out, follow by threats of calling the police. I'm ma leave but not until I pack all my shit because I'm not coming back."

It was obvious this was the end; we both said the unforgiv-able. As I packed my belongings I acknowledged I could have played my hand differently, and been more sympathetic to her feel-ings; but had I done so I would have never known the drastic measures she would have resorted to in a time of crisis. There were two things I could never forgive a woman for; unfaithfulness and the threat of calling the cops. Regardless how much I loved and cared for Tanya, it was over, and I felt a deep sense of peace and freedom when I walked out of her life

From the moment I received orders to kill Zuberi, to the end of his life, I suspended all personal ties with anyone I cared about. It had been close to a month since I'd last seen Lil Bull and his family. I was happy to find him outside playing catch with his three-year-old son when I pulled up, which was a sign he had taken my advice to step back and give me the necessary time needed to figure this shit out.

"Uncle Floyd, Uncle Floyd!" Lil Kenny shouted and ran towards me. I picked him up in one single motion and gave him a hug.

"Boy you got big, what you been doing lifting weights with your daddy?"

"Ah um, feel my muscles," he said and flexed his bicep.

"Wow, that's big," I said and watched him run off.

"What's up Crip?" Lil Bull asked with a smile that suggested he was as happy to see me as I was to see him.

There was no one I enjoyed hanging out with more than Lil Bull. Although he was two weeks older than I, I was my brother's keeper, and often worried about him becoming a victim of his own aggression.

"Congratulations, I heard about your work," he beamed.

"Did you doubt me?" I asked and gave him a hug.

"Not for a second; the only thing I regret, it wasn't I that sent his monkey ass to meet his maker," he pointed to himself and looked to the clouds.

"Had it been you, there is a strong possibility we might not have survived the aftermath. Follow my lead, and I guarantee you I'll lead us to prosperity. Cuz, San Diego is wide open. With my resources, and our knowledge of the city, it's ours for the taking."

"I feel you on that, but Cuz I hope you know I will never join CCO."

"And I will never ask you. Everything isn't for everybody."

"Good, good, for a minute I thought you were leading in that direction. Have you made any plans for tonight?"

"No, not really, why, what's happening?"

"I got something I think you'll be happy to see."

"What is it?" I asked and searched his eyes for a clue.

"I'll explain after dinner, have you eaten?"

"No I haven't, and I'm famished."

After dinner, I joined Lil Bull on the patio where he had a pint of Hennessy and two glasses sitting on the table. It wasn't until I sat down and he poured two drinks I noticed a huge Manila envelope sitting on the table.

"Here's to the real, raw, and uncut," he said, handing me a glass.

"I'll toss to that," I said, turning the glass upside down. "What's that?" I asked referring to the envelope.

"That's for you," he said and pushed the envelope across the table. "When I came home I hired a private investigator to find Nicole and your son. In the envelope is his report. If you need me

I'll be in the living room."

"Thank you Cuz," I said, overwhelmed by this unexpected gesture.

I made a double shot of Hennessy and sipped on it slowly while I stared at the envelope. Although we never spoke about Nicole or my son, Lil Bull knew well enough that it was a lingering thought inside my head. There it was; the answer to some long awaited questions.

I picked up the envelope and examined the gold seal with the word CONFIDENTIAL beneath it in big bold letters. *Did I really want to know*, I asked myself as the seed of uncertainty whispered in my ear. Without further thought I ripped the envelope open and allowed the contents to slide freely across the table. The first photograph was of a small boy with a striking resemblance to me. There was no mistaking who he was; that was me nineteen years ago.

I picked up the photograph and studied every small detail and was overwhelmed with a deep sense of joy. What touched me most was his apparent happiness. He had a glow that radiated joy. I took another sip of Hennessy and picked up a photograph of Nicole. Unlike our son, she didn't appear happy. To the contrary, she appeared subdued, sad in a subtle way. It was at that moment I realized I was not the only one who had been suffering all these years. Nevertheless, I couldn't find it in my heart to forgive her. She abandoned me at a time when I needed her the most and stole what might have saved me.

I found it quite amazing how a single photograph could have such a profound effect on my life. Everything I wanted to know was sitting right in front of me; names, addresses, images. I wondered if he knew I existed. He had my first name but her husband's last name. I picked up a picture of Curtis, a military man, stationed at Nellis Air Force base in North Las Vegas. I wasn't mad at Curtis; to the contrary I had to commend him. It took a certain type of man to raise a kid that wasn't his own, and marry a woman and hope someday she would love him as he loved her.

Robert Winters had always been fond of Curtis and could never understand how his daughter could dump such a wonderful, well-rounded young man for a thug. The mere thought of Robert, the architect of this great deception still angered me in ways I couldn't understand. For years, I thought about killing him, but death was too good. I wanted his ass to suffer in the same manner I suffered. I wanted to condemn him to a lifetime of hell and rob him for everything he cherished, the same way he did me.

It wasn't until Lil Bull informed me he was about to turn in for the night, I realized how late it had become. I gathered up everything and gave the envelope back to Lil Bull for safekeeping.

"Why don't you crash here for the night?" He suggested after seeing the pint of Hennessy empty.

"I'm cool Cuz. I got a few things I need to take care of." In the eyes of the law, I was too faded to drive; but by hood standards I could have driven to L.A. and back.

"Oh yeah, Felicia said to tell you she's at the Marriott Courtyard in Hotel Circle, bungalow 135."

I had the utmost respect for Felicia; not too many women would have accepted a man telling them he had to chill for a minute to take care some business. To me that spoke volumes about her character, and it also showed me how much baby was digging me. Very seldom did you find a young hood chick playing the game the way it was supposed to be played, especially for a man she barely knew.

It was a little after 2:00 a.m. when I pulled into traffic that was slightly heavier than expected. One thing about prison was it made a man appreciate all the simple things life and freedom had to offer; like rolling with the top down and bumping your favorite tunes. I waited until I hit Imperial Ave. before I turned up the music allowing Big Daddy Kane to entertain anybody in the vicinity. I leaned back in my seat and pressed on the gas, my Caddy leaped up and accelerated like a well-tuned machine obeying my command.

Out of respect for her privacy, I stopped at the front office and called her room. Although I was digging baby and she was obviously digging me, she was not my woman and therefore entitled to the same courtesy I would have wanted had the roles been reversed.

"Hello," a young sexy voice answered on the third ring.

"Felicia?" I asked, unsure who it was.

"No, this is Lori, who is this?"

"Pretty Boy Floyd, you remember me?"

"How can I forget you; you're all she talks about."

"Is she there?"

"Yes, she's asleep, let me wake her."

"No, don't wake her, I'm in the lobby, I'll be there in a second."

Lori answered the door in a loose fitting silk blouse with a pair of silk panties with her pussy imprint so graphic I could have closed my eyes and drew a picture of it. I made no secret I was checking out her goods, and she made no secret she didn't mind.

Lori got back in her bed and pulled the covers up to her chin. It was obvious that Felicia had told her about my sexual prowess. I wasted no time stripping off my clothes. I stroked my manhood a few times until it was nice and hard. Unable to turn her head, Lori stared at my massive hard on with pure lust in her eyes. I looked at Felicia, who was sound asleep and in a daring move walked to the edge of Lori's bed and pressed my lion against her lips.

She opened her mouth and took me in like a hungry baby on a mother's nipple. Stiff as raw steel, Lori worked her mouth up and down my rod while she played with her pussy under the covers. After a series of gags and moans that were increasingly becoming louder I stepped back and brought this brief moment of pleasure to a close. The last thing I needed was for Felicia to wake up and find my dick in her best friend's mouth. That's the type of shit a young chick would never forget.

I slid between the covers and started kissing Felicia on the back of her neck while my fingers explored the inside of her panties. A soft moan escaped her lips.

"Stop," she softly whispered.

"Do you really want me to?" I whispered in her ear.

"Pretty Boy," she softly muttered and opened her eyes.

"The one and only," I answered and continued to expertly manipulate her clitoris until she begged me to enter her; which I was more than happy to oblige. I pushed the covers from the bed and climbed between Felicia's legs. Excited beyond measures, I entered Felicia while staring at Lori who continued to masturbate while I dicked her friend down. Not a word was spoken, but the implications were clear; I came for one but I had action with two.

Take No Orders
– Chapter 21 –

For the exception of a quick visit to see my parole agent, the following week was spent smoking weed, sipping on Hennessy and flip-flopping with Felicia and Lori. I had two young tenders on my line, in search of a man they could trust, respect, and feel comfortable with him taking the lead. I was that man. From day one, I recognized their potential and understood their worth. The only thing they were lacking was guidance; which was obvious by their inability to make any meaningful gains in this cold game of hustling.

Life was just too grand; for a minute it seemed like the party wasn't ever going to end; but everything in life ran its course; and the party came to an end with a page from Akeelah, Tabari's wife, and a scheduled lunch for the following day. Playing with Felicia and Lori was fun while it lasted, but it was time to get down to business, and take my rightful position as the head of CCO's street operations. My dreams and aspirations of becoming the Boss of a Criminal network were finally within my grasp.

Laced by the best, hood legends from every set, there was no one better qualify than I to lead CCO to the land of milk and money. Unlike most Bosses, I realized once you made it to the top, there was no other place to go but to the bottom. While most became victims of the penitentiary, others became residents of the cemetery. I had plans of becoming neither. Learning from the mistakes of others, I knew what it took to get to the top and stay on the top. The number one rule in winning; stay true to the game, and the game will stay true to you.

Dressed in an ankle link Dashiki gown with handmade sandals, a perfect assortment of beads and colorful stones complementing her attire, Akeelah was a sight to behold. I rose to my feet and pulled out her chair when she approached.

"Thank you Jabari," she said with a smile that made me feel like a small child that just received a praise from his mother.

Although this was only our second encounter, I had a great deal of love and respect for this woman. To me she was an extension of her husband, who was like a father figure and never gave me anything less than the utmost love and respect. Not only did CCO give me a sense of purpose, it taught me to love my brothers and sisters in the same light I loved myself.

"I'm quite sure you know the comrades are exceptionally pleased with you."

"I'm pleased to hear they're happy," I said and felt an overwhelming sense of joy.

"Happy would be saying the least; as I'm sure you're aware several have come before you, none of which have delivered or show they possess what it takes to lead the party to prominence. Jabari, you are an exceptional young man that appears to possess all the attributes of a born leader; and that's coming from a woman that has an eye for talent. The future of the party rests in your hands, and if there is anything I can do to make your transition successful and complete please don't hesitate to call on me," she said, reaching across the table and rubbed the top of my hand.

"I thank you for your vote of confidence. I hope I don't disappoint you." I said and pulled my hand back, uncomfortable by the feel of her skin touching mine.

"I don't think you will," she said, looking in my eyes with a deep penetrating glance. For the first time in my life I bowed my head, unable to look in her eyes, I reached for menu.

"I'm starving, have you eaten?" I asked.

"Jabari you have the menu upside down," she pointed out and giggled.

Her laughter sounded like the sweetest melody I ever

heard. I joined her in laughter and looked up and felt like I was seeing her for the first time. Damn she was gorgeous I thought; the true essence of a beautiful black woman, strong, intelligent, and confident.

"Do I make you nervous?" she asked with her eyes still trained on mine.

"I won't say you make me nervous, to be honest I felt a little awkward by the way you caressed my hand. Perhaps, I read things all wrong, if so I do apologize."

"You're very perceptive, and no, you didn't read things wrong. I think you're a very handsome man, and I'm physically attracted to you."

"I'm flattered, but not only are you're married, you're married to a man I love like a brother."

"I'm quite aware of that, and I love my husband with all my heart; but being that the situation is what it is, meaning he's serving a life sentence and unable to fulfill some of my basic needs; well you understand what I'm saying."

"It's not a question if *I* understand; it's a question would *he* understand?"

"Now that you ask, yes he would. Tabari and I have no secrets, we talk about everything, and we have even discussed you at lengths. It is with his knowledge and blessing that makes this conversation possible. If you need to hear it from the horse's mouth that can be arranged."

"That's won't be necessary, and once again I'm flattered you see me as a man worthy of your comforts, but with or without his blessings I could never sex a married woman, matrimony is a union I vowed never to violate. What, why are you smiling like that?" I asked, extremely happy she didn't take my rejection the wrong way.

"Because it's not often you find a man in our business with such high moral standards and strong convictions. Tabari said you won't yield to temptation, although disappointed, I respect you for that."

"Thank you for understanding; I'm glad we had this conversation. I think communication is the greatest tool in establishing a complete understanding. I also believe this conversation has made our union stronger."

"It has, and I really enjoyed our conversation, and I must give it to you, you're a real smooth brother with a unique way with words. If by chance you ever change your position the invitation is always open."

"Thank you, I'll keep that in mind."

"Before I go, there is one more issue we need to address," she said, sliding a piece of paper across the table. "Unlike the others, the comrades would like a strong message sent, one that will serve as a warning to anyone that kills one of our comrades and thinks severe consequences won't follow. If there's nothing else I believe

"No, we pretty much covered everything," I said in hopes of bringing this meeting to an end.

After barely touching her coffee and pastry, she stood up and paused. "Well, my brother it was nice seeing you again. By the way I'm going to visit Tabari this weekend, is there anything you like to relay?"

"Extend my love to him and the comrades."

"That goes without saying. If there's anything you need, please don't hesitate to call, you have my number."

"I most certainly will," I said, cuffing the paper.

I patiently waited for Akeelah to exit the restaurant before I unfolded the paper and stared at it in disbelief. My immediate reaction was one of panic, followed by fear, and eventually anger. After a moment of reflection, I couldn't say I was surprised. From day one, I knew the comrades wanted Lil Bull dead, especially after he killed Chagina, one of CCO's prized soldiers. The killing was in self-defense, therefore it was my hope I could convince the comrades a pass was in order. To order a hit on Lil Bull was protocol, but to order a hit on his wife and three year old son was barbaric, evil by all means, and made me question those I pledged my allegiance to.

The order was issued, and there was nothing left to discuss. Had the comrades known me as well as they thought, they would have known this was one order I could not, would not follow. Their power was in prison, and mine was on the streets. I had a small window to mount a defense, and in a situation such as this, the best defense was offense, a pre-empt strike on those that presented the greatest threat. With the demise of Zuberi, and the indictments of his top lieutenants Abasi and Jahi, CCO was lacking the necessary leadership to wage and win a war. In anticipation of war, I realized my first order of business was to kill all outside lines of communication. As I sat there long after Akeelah left, I composed a hit list and acknowledged she posed the greatest threat, and therefore would be the first to go. She wanted to play, and play we shall; a good fucking, follow by a bullet in her head, and two in her heart.

Moving On
-Chapter 22-

Never in my life had I ever felt more vulnerable, as I did at the state parole building; and the feeling only seemed to intensify with every visit. Unlike my previous visit the waiting time was exceptionally long. Just as I thought about leaving, my parole agent emerged from the back and motioned for me to follow him. There were no handshakes or personal greetings. It was obvious he thought just as little of me as I of him. Regardless of how I felt about him, the fact of the matter was he held all the cards and the keys to my freedom.

"Based on the information you provided you appear to be in compliance with all your conditions, has anything changed since your last visit?"

"The information is the same," I said without giving much thought.

"That's not what I heard from Ms. Roberts. She stated you moved out and you two are no longer an item."

"I wouldn't go as far as to say that. We had an argument, like most couples often do. We're working on it; I should be back home in the next day or so." I countered and met his stare, thinking how badly I wanted to put my hands on Tanya.

"If not, I expect a change of address by the end of this week."

"Fair enough, is that it?"

"No it's not, there are a couple of gentlemen here that

would like to speak to you," he said, picking up the phone. A few seconds later Detective Ross and Sullivan appeared.

"Floyd, we meet again," Detective Sullivan said. "We'd like to ask you a few questions, if you don't mine?"

"What seems to be on your mind?"

"How well did you know Calvin Roberts, and Martin Griffin?"

"I have known Calvin my entire life, and I don't know anyone by the name of Martin Griffin."

"Ms. Roberts informed us you and Mr. Griffin met on several occasions."

"Like I said, I know no one that goes by the name of Martin Griffin."

"What about the name Zuberi?" Detective Ross interrupted.

"Why are you asking, am I being accused of something?"

"No you're not. We're just following up on a homicide investigation."

"Anderson, you can answer their questions here, or you can answer them downtown." My parole agent injected.

"I know my rights; I don't have to answer shit. As a matter of fact I'd like to speak to my lawyer. If I'm under arrest, arrest me, if not, I'd like to leave."

After a brief moment of silence, Detective Ross rose from his seat and motioned for Detective Sullivan and my parole agent to follow him. They returned shortly after and told me I was free to leave.

The anger I felt towards Tanya was enough to make me put a bullet in her head. Contrary to popular belief, a hood bitch was the quickest bitch to cooperate with the police. Mad as a motherfucker, I emerged from the State Parole Building with one destination in mind. It was obvious the police suspected more than a murder/suicide and I needed to know exactly what Tanya told them; but before doing so my first order of business was to calm the fuck down. Tanya wasn't the type of woman you could approach aggressively; she was known to match energy with energy, just enough to make me choke her ass out.

As I sat in the parking lot regretting the day I met her, I

thought about all the dumb shit I did that lead to this moment. I was a master at disguising my feelings, thoughts, and intentions when dealing with an adversary, but I was equally careless when dealing with someone in my inner circle. My inability to control my reaction when someone I cared about did or said something reckless was the root of my problems. It was a flaw I had to correct.

Gradually my anger subsided and my composure returned. In order to solicit the information I needed, I had to be on top of my game; which I realized was easier said than done. Tanya had a way of pushing my buttons and bringing out the beast within. It was a dangerous game she happened to play and get away with. Little did she know I wasn't one to discriminate, Gangstas and Bitches caught it the same; and had she not been pregnant I would have seriously considered feeding her to the fish.

I knocked softly at first, waited a few moments and knocked a little louder. It was obvious when she answered I had awakened her. In all the years I'd known Tanya, I'd never seen her look so distraught. For a brief moment, I felt sad for her. She was going through it, and had no one to hold her down.

"What do you want Floyd?" she asked and made no gesture to invite me in. No sooner than I felt a moment of compassion it disappeared. Fuck this bitch, I thought, and forced a smile.

"I stop by to check on you, and apologize."

"You did?" she asked looked in my eyes.

"Yes, baby, I'm so sorry. I shouldn't have said what I said. Regardless of Calvin's sexual orientation he's always been good to me, and treated me like family. If we have a son and you'd like to name him after Calvin I'm all for it; and if we have a daughter we can name her Tina. There hasn't been a day that passed I haven't thought about you, and wondered how you were doing. Woman, I love you, and I miss you so much."

"Oh baby I miss you, too," she whispered and a flood of tears rolled from her eyes.

I knew Tanya only too well. At first sight she expected a confrontation, one that would have led to a fury of verbal exchanges, with neither one of us backing down. *Why pour fuel on the fire, when I most definitely had far more to lose than she?* I studied women in the same manner I studied men. But unlike women, men were more predictable, because most reacted out a sense of survival, while most women didn't give a damn about personal survival as long as they destroyed you in the process. Tanya was a woman, like most women, who governed her life by her emotions. I had her heart in a way no man has ever been able to conquer, but it was obvious by our latest spat there were certain people in her life I couldn't challenge, and her family just happened to be that. I took her hand and led her to the shower, and washed her from head to toe, enlightening her in a way that enhanced her spirits. After drying her off, I led her to bedroom and held her until she fell asleep.

Even in her sleep she radiated a beauty that few women could match. As beautiful as she was on the outside, she was a live wire underneath, and if I wasn't careful I was sure she would cost me irreparable damage. My best bet was to play her from a distance, keep her close, but not to close. I had to find something to keep her occupied; something she would truly enjoy, and most definitely something she could do without my assistance.

Never Leave an Enemy Behind

-Chapter 22-

Over six years had passed since I'd last heard from Nicole; and much to my surprise the mere thought of her no longer angered me. It took me years to realize our separation wasn't totally her fault; and me going to prison wasn't a part of the deal; or something she signed up for. Taking everything into account, and considering the bond we shared I wasn't mad she abandoned me, what infuriated me was the way she did it; robbing me of my son, money, and leaving me with nothing but a prison sentence to face alone. When she first deflected, all I wanted was an explanation of why she left, now it really didn't matter what her reason was. The only thing that mattered was my son, my blood, my only child.

Henderson, Nevada was a nice, suburban area on the outskirts of Las Vegas. A twenty minute drive from Las Vegas Boulevard, it provided the perfect distance from the bright lights, noisy crowds, and shady characters that frequented the strip every night, 365 nights a year. I wasn't surprised when I learned Nicole was the proud owner of Angel's, a highly recommended and successful day care center that operated seven days a week. She had always been fond of kids, and had a unique and special way of interacting with them. I waited until Saturday morning, when she usually arrived with my son, to make my presence known. On my drive in from San Diego, I daydreamed of little Floyd being with me and us living the life I always dreamed of.

No sooner than I stepped inside the lobby I spotted Nicole sitting in her office with her head buried in a mountain of paperwork, while little Floyd was playing shuttle hockey with another kid. It was obvious by the expression on his face he was a competitive little boy that played to win. For a brief moment I was taken aback as I stared at him proudly. This was my boy, and I couldn't wait to meet him.

"Sir, can I help you?" A pretty young lady with an Angel's t-shirt asked.

"Yes, I'd like to see Nicole," I said and turned to face her.

"Is she expecting you?"

"No, she's not. Could you please inform her Pretty Boy would like to speak to her?"

"Pretty Boy?" she repeated and continued to smile, wondering what type of person went by the name of Pretty Boy.

"Yes, Pretty Boy." I had to restrain from laughing.

From the moment she walked away my eyes trailed her. This was most definitely a Kodak moment; a moment I would have paid cash money to see; the expression on Nicole's face upon hearing of my presence for the first time in six years. I was sure it was a moment she had contemplated over a thousand times; one in which she dreaded, but knew eventually would come.

Nicole slowly raised her head when the young lady entered her office. Unable to summon any emotions, good or bad, I couldn't deny on the surface she was still an extraordinary beautiful woman with a captivating appeal. After a brief exchange, she quickly stood and scanned the recreational area. Finding little Floyd she breathed a sigh of relief and turned in my direction. I smiled and waved when we made eye contact. She acknowledged my presence with a slight nod, said a few words to her employee, and sat down and picked up the phone.

"Mrs. Rousey said she'll be with you in a moment. Would you care for something to drink?" the employee asked, unsure what, if anything was wrong.

"No, I'm fine," I answered and took a seat for the first time. I kept my eyes on her, and quietly watched as she approached little Floyd, whispered in his ear and ushered him away.

Ten minutes later, Curtis came rushing through the front entrance, like he was there to save the day. I recognized him immediately from the collage of photographs the private investigator provided. What the photographs didn't provide was an accurate height and weight. In his photograph he appeared much shorter than 6 feet 2 inches, and appeared to weigh much less than 250 pounds. Based on his appearance, I figured if push came to shove I could break his fat ass down in less than a minute. Shortly after his arrival, I was escorted to her office.

Nicole remained behind her desk, while Curtis took a seat on the edge of the desk, a few feet away from me in the event he had to intervene. What I hoped would be a civil gathering, followed by a mutual agreement had quickly turned into something far more hostile.

"What can we do for you?" Curtis asked, like he was the man in charge.

"First of all, you can't do a motherfucking thing for me, except stay the fuck out my business." I said and got right in his face. "My business here don't have a motherfucking thing to do with you bitch ass boy; this is about me, Nicole, and our son. I don't know what the fuck she called you for anyway." I barked on him, ready to take it wherever he wanted to take it.

"I'm her husband." He stuttered in a voice so low I could barely hear him. "Listen Floyd we don't want any problems. I'm sure we can work everything out." .

"I'm sure we can," I said, taking a few steps back. "We can start off by you giving me and Nicole a private moment."

"Curtis it's okay, I can handle it from here." Nicole interrupted.

"Are you sure?" Curtis asked, already heading towards the door.

"Yes." She nodded and turned towards me. "How are you Floyd?" She asked, attempting to take a more subtle approach.

"Baby, we can skip the small talk and get straight to the purpose of my visit."

"And what would that be?" She looked away, afraid I was still capable of reading her thoughts.

"My son, what else?" I said and took a seat.

"What about him?" she asked, continuing to prolong the inevitable.

"First of all, I'd like to see him, second I'd like to make arrangements to spend some time with him. It's way past time we get to know each other."

"Floyd, I don't think that'll be good idea. He doesn't know you, the only father he knows is Curtis; and that's how I'd like to keep it. If you really care about him, you'll leave us alone."

"Nicole, I'm not asking you, I'm telling you what it is. If you think for a second you're going to keep me from spending time with my son, you lost your mind. We can do this the easy way or the hard way, but I promise you this is one fight you will not win."

"We'll see what the court has to say about it. I'm sure with your criminal record they won't have a problem ruling in my favor." She threatened, growing bolder by the second.

A sick laughter escaped my lips as I rose to my feet, placed clenched fists on her desk and stared down at her.

"Bitch, don't get this shit twisted, up until now you only heard about Pretty Boy, but you never actually seen him, I protected you from him. I'm everything your daddy told you I was and a thousand times worse. I use to love you, now I don't give a fuck about you. Bitch, I could kill you quicker than a fly on the wall. There is no one on this earth more important than my son. If I got to kill you, your mama, your daddy, and your husband to see my son I will; mark my word. Here is my number. If I don't hear from you within a week I will assume your position hasn't changed. When everyone you care about comes up dead, don't say I didn't warn you. Enjoy the rest of your day."

I concluded and flipped my business card in her face. The drive back home allowed me to cool off a bit and plan my next course of action.

Tanya was waiting outside her complex when I pulled up. Despite my personal concerns about her, she was still the mother of my unborn child, and therefore entitled to the benefit of my time. Unable to love a woman I couldn't trust I kept her at a distance, as far away from my heart as possible; which was becoming increasingly harder the closer she became to childbirth. I couldn't deny, as far as my personal life there was nothing I wanted more than my own family; the wife, kids, and home filled with an abundance of laughter and love. Deep inside my heart, I desperately wanted to forgive Tanya for threatening to call the police; but for reasons only another gangsta could understand I simply couldn't do it.

"Hello beautiful," I said as I got out the car and opened the passenger side door.

"My thank you, Floyd." She smiled and gave me a peck on the lips.

"You're quite welcome love."

In spite of my inability to forgive, I was still there for her, tending to all her needs and cravings for fried bananas and split pea soup; and making every doctor's visit.

Today was the big day, the day we learned the sex of our child; it was hard to tell who was more excited, Tanya or me. Although I hoped for a son, I knew I would be equally as happy if it was a daughter. Tanya was a little over six months pregnant and just starting to show, which was a testament of her daily workout. Besides a bump in her midsection, the rest of her body appeared unfazed.

"Baby, when are you going to move back home?" she asked and took my hand inside hers and gently massaged it.

"Soon," I said. "Real soon!"

It was a beautiful warm Spring day, 75 degrees with a slight breeze, the perfect weather for a drop-top.

"Turn it up!" Tanya shouted as The Deele's "Two Occasions" came over the stereo. "That's my song!" she yelled ecstatically, and began to sing alone.

Consumed by her beautiful voice, and her tender green eyes beaming at me I felt a warm sensation inside my chest. For a brief moment time seemed to stand still as I remembered the beautiful, radiant, young woman I fell in love with. I loved the girly side of Tanya, who was a complete joy to be around.

Suddenly, her facial expression twisted from a look of pure

happiness to sheer terror. Something was terribly wrong. I turned just in time to see Doc leveling a Tech 9 out the passenger side window of a white Ford Mustang. A smile appeared on his face followed by a barrage of rapid gunfire. I ducked and pushed Tanya down, made a hard left turn into the side of the Mustang, and slammed on my brakes, creating a little distance and giving me the time I so desperately needed to retrieve my Colt 45.

As I rose, I observed Doc emerging from the passenger side firing frantically, and determined to finish what he started. The moment the shots stopped ringing I came out firing, catching Doc off guard and in the process of changing clips. He quickly retreated, and the Mustang attempted to speed off, but not before I unloaded my clip, shattering the back window and striking the driver in the back of his head. Holding an empty gun, all I could do was watch as Doc jumped out of the Mustang and fled on foot.

I paused for a second to access the damage, and realized I was the focus of a thousand eyes. I was hit, exactly how many times I didn't know. The strong scent of gunpowder and fear lingered in the air creating a trance like atmosphere. Suddenly, I became overwhelmed with a deep sense of fear. I rushed back to the car and found Tanya unconscious and bleeding profusely from her head.

"Baby! Baby!" I yelled, shaking her arm and receiving no response.

Without a second to waste, I maneuvered the caddy through the congestion of stalled traffic and onlookers and punched it to Scripps Mercy Hospital. Fully aware of the events unfolding before my very eyes I hit Interstate 5 and discarded my firearm. It wasn't until we arrived at the emergency entrance and I carried Tanya inside, I realized I was also seriously wounded. At the mere sight of my white Polo outfit soaked in blood, nurses and hospital attendants rushed to our aid.

"She's pregnant," I said as they took her from my arms and rushed her to the back.

Just as I turned to leave a nurse grabbed my arm. "Sir, where are you going, you need medical attention?" she pleaded.

"I'm fine," I said, feeling weaker by the second.

Unable to stop me, I pulled my arm away and headed for the exit. No sooner than I stepped outside my legs gave way and I collapsed. Slipping in and out of consciousness, I fought with every fiber inside me to keep my eyes open. In spite of my greatest efforts darkness fell upon me and I drifted to a place where my body was unconscious but my soul was wide awake, unrelenting, and consuming me with one nightmare after another.

****

Two days later, I regained consciousness and discovered I got hit three times; the worse being in my abdomen, which entered my stomach and exited out my lower back barely missing my spinal cord; followed by another in and out wound to my shoulder blade; and a graze to the back of my head that required eighteen stitches and three staples to close. Although none of my wounds were life threatening, I lost a great deal of blood. The pain was unbearable, but it served as a constant reminder of the price one must pay for slipping. Much to my surprise I felt indifferent to the ordeal.

Unable to gather any emotions or meaningful thoughts I laid in a dire state, staring at the ceiling, wondering what I could have done differently to protect me and my girl. Thinking of Tanya, I could no longer wait another second without knowing her fate. For a brief second my heart was filled with joy as I reminisced on the moments prior to the shooting. She was happy, singing her heart out, and looking at me like I was the love of her life. Refusing to believe she was gone I summoned the nurse and said a quick prayer, hoping God protected Tanya and our child the same way he protected me.

"Mr. Anderson, I'm happy to see you're back with us," the nurse stated and started checking my vital signs.

"I'm happy to be back," I replied and attempted to smile to cover up my concerns. "The young lady that came in with me, how is she doing?" I asked, holding onto a glimmer of hope.

"I'm sorry, I'm not at liberty to say. The doctor will be with you shortly, I'm sure he'll be able to answer all your questions."

"Please," I said, reaching for her hand. "I need to know." I pleaded.

"I'm sorry, Sir." The nurse paused for a brief second and stared into my eyes. "She didn't make it." she informed, and immediately witnessed my grief.

"How about the baby?" I murmured, fearing the worse.

"We did everything humanly possible. I'm sorry, we couldn't save the baby. Sir we have a grief counselor on duty, if you like I can have him come up and speak with you."

"Thank you, that won't be necessary." I closed my eyes and turned my head slightly, desperately fighting to restrain my tears. I was no stranger to death, but this was the first time it hit me so close to home. The heartache was unlike any pain I ever felt; and all of a sudden nothing seemed important, not even life; which I would have given gladly for Tanya and my child to live another day. Being that wasn't possible, I vowed to emerge from this ordeal a thousand times worse than I'd ever been. I felt for anyone that got in my way; man, woman, or child, no one was exempt from this wrath I was about to release on society.

To Be Continued...
Part 2 Coming Soon!

@DHENDERSON.3488

PILLOW PRINCESS

By: AVERY GOODE

@THEGOODESCRIBE

HEART BREAKER
By: BRIANA COLE
@BRIANACSPICE

I SHOULDA' SEEN HIM COMING 1&2
By: DANETTE MAJETTE
@DCMAJETTE

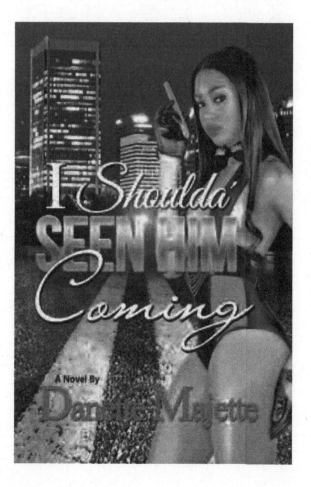

ORDER FORM

MAIL TO:
PO Box 423
Brandywine, MD 20613
301-362-6508

Ship to:	
Address:	
City & State:	Zip:

Date: _____ Phone: _____

Email: _____

Make all money orders and cashiers checks payable to: **Life Changing Books**

Qty.	ISBN	Title	Release Date	Price
	0-9741394-2-4	Bruised by Azarel	Jul-05	$ 15.00
	0-9741394-7-5	Bruised 2: The Ultimate Revenge by Azarel	Oct-06	$ 15.00
	0-9741394-3-2	Secrets of a Housewife by J. Tremble	Feb-06	$ 15.00
	0-9741394-6-7	The Millionaire Mistress by Tiphani	Nov-06	$ 15.00
	1-934230-99-5	More Secrets More Lies by J. Tremble	Feb-07	$ 15.00
	1-934230-95-2	A Private Affair by Mike Warren	May-07	$ 15.00
	1-934230-96-0	Flexin & Sexin Volume 1	Jun-07	$ 15.00
	1-934230-89-8	Still a Mistress by Tiphani	Nov-07	$ 15.00
	1-934230-91-X	Daddy's House by Azarel	Nov-07	$ 15.00
	1-934230-88-X	Naughty Little Angel by J. Tremble	Feb-08	$ 15.00
	1-934230820	Rich Girls by Kendall Banks	Oct-08	$ 15.00
	1-934230839	Expensive Taste by Tiphani	Nov-08	$ 15.00
	1-934230782	Brooklyn Brothel by C. Stecko	Jan-09	$ 15.00
	1-934230669	Good Girl Gone bad by Danette Majette	Mar-09	$ 15.00
	1-934230707	Sweet Swagger by Mike Warren	Jun-09	$ 15.00
	1-934230677	Carbon Copy by Azarel	Jul-09	$ 15.00
	1-934230723	Millionaire Mistress 3 by Tiphani	Nov-09	$ 15.00
	1-934230715	A Woman Scorned by Ericka Williams	Nov-09	$ 15.00
	1-934230685	My Man Her Son by J. Tremble	Feb-10	$ 15.00
	1-924230731	Love Heist by Jackie D.	Mar-10	$ 15.00
	1-934230812	Flexin & Sexin Volume 2	Apr-10	$ 15.00
	1-934230748	The Dirty Divorce by Miss KP	May-10	$ 15.00
	1-934230758	Chedda Boyz by CJ Hudson	Jul-10	$ 15.00
	1-934230766	Snitch by VegasClarke	Oct-10	$ 15.00
	1-934230693	Money Maker by Tonya Ridley	Oct-10	$ 15.00
	1-934230774	The Dirty Divorce Part 2 by Miss KP	Nov-10	$ 15.00
	1-934230170	The Available Wife by Carla Pennington	Jan-11	$ 15.00
	1-934230774	One Night Stand by Kendall Banks	Feb-11	$ 15.00
	1-934230278	Bitter by Danette Majette	Feb-11	$ 15.00
	1-934230299	Married to a Balla by Jackie D.	May-11	$ 15.00
	1-934230308	The Dirty Divorce Part 3 by Miss KP	Jun-11	$ 15.00
	1-934230316	Next Door Nympho By CJ Hudson	Jun-11	$ 15.00
	1-934230286	Bedroom Gangsta by J. Tremble	Sep-11	$ 15.00
	1-934230340	Another One Night Stand by Kendall Banks	Oct-11	$ 15.00
	1-934230359	The Available Wife Part 2 by Carla Pennington	Nov-11	$ 15.00
	1-934230332	Wealthy & Wicked by Chris Renee	Jan-12	$ 15.00
	1-934230375	Life After a Balla by Jackie D.	Mar-12	$ 15.00
	1-934230251	V.I.P. by Azarel	Apr-12	$ 15.00
	1-934230383	Welfare Grind by Kendall Banks	May-12	$ 15.00
	1-934230413	Still Grindin' by Kendall Banks	Sep-12	$ 15.00
	1-934230391	Paparazzi by Miss KP	Oct-13	$ 15.00
	1-93423043X	Cashin' Out by Jai Nicole	Nov-12	$ 15.00
	1-934230634	Welfare Grind Part 3 by Kendall Banks	Mar-13	$15.00
	1-934230642	Game Over by Winter Ramos	Apr-13	$15.99
	1-934230618	My Counterfeit Husband by Carla Pennington	Aug-14	$ 15.00
	1-93422060X	Mistress Loose by Kendall Banks	Oct-13	$ 15.00
	1-934230626	Dirty Divorce Part 4	Jan-14	$ 15.00
	1-934230596	Left for Dead by Ebony Canion	Feb-14	$ 15.00
	1-934230456	Charm City by C. Flores	Mar-14	$ 15.00
	1-934230499	Pillow Princess by Avery Goode	Aug-14	$ 15.00
			Total for Books	$

Shipping Charges (add $4.95 for 1-4 books")	$
Total Enclosed (add lines)	$

* Prison Orders- Please allow up to three (3) weeks for delivery.

Please Note: We are not held responsible for returned prison orders. Make sure the facility will receive books before ordering.

*Shipping and Handling of 5-10 books is $6.95, please contact us if your order is more than 10 books. (301)362-6508